THE TEACHER

Adventures of a Thoughtful Man

"All the world's a stage,
and all the men and women merely players."
Shakespeare

Ron Lancaster

The Teacher: Adventures of a Thoughtful Man

Copyright © 2006 Ron Lancaster. All rights reserved.
No part of this book may be reproduced or retransmitted in any form or by any means without the written permission of the publisher.

Published by Wheatmark™
610 East Delano Street, Suite 104, Tucson, Arizona 85705 U.S.A.
www.wheatmark.com

International Standard Book Number: 1-58736-576-6
Library of Congress Control Number: 2005936248

Prologue

THE FIRST THING I saw was the sun barely peeping over a mountain-top in the distance. I realized I was in a hospital bed hooked up to an array of tubes and monitoring devices. There still was very little light in the room. I was alone. It was early morning. My right shoulder and side ached.

What am I doing here? I thought. I shut my eyes and tried to reconnect with my memory. There it was; the lights and the dazzle as Liz and I followed Paul up to the stage in the stadium. The crowd was boisterous and loud. Some were chanting that Paul was the Second Coming of Christ. Others, and perhaps the majority, were screaming that he was the devil incarnate, and his powers came straight from hell. The police were trying to make a path for us, but the people were mad from either joy or hate. It was bedlam.

I opened my eyes to shut the memory out. I could hear the machines around me humming, monitoring my vital signs. Almost automatically, my eyes shut again and I could see the flash of the gun and felt its sting in my chest. I turned, as if in slow motion, to see Paul fall with a massive wound in his neck. Then nothing.

When was that? How long have I been here? It seemed a long time ago; ages. I looked out the window again at the sun rising over the mountains. How did it all happen? Less than a year ago I lived in California, had a wife and a good job. Now I am in a hospital in Tucson, Arizona with a gunshot wound from protecting a man who could work miracles. It all seemed so bizarre.

I thought about it and tried to reconstruct how it had all started. Then I remembered; it began that morning I thought was the worst day of my life. I had a lot to learn.

PART I

Chapter 1

It was the worst day of my life: November 14th of last year. At 6:30 that morning my wife of eleven years, Barbara, told me that she was leaving me for someone named Chad who worked with her at her job. "Chad, that lighting director," I asked?

Yes, that Chad. He is the most wonderful man I've ever met. We are soul mates."

I flopped back on the bed in shock. I remember Chad from a party last Christmas. He was tall and good looking, and at least ten years younger than Barb. He struck me as being vain and pompous. "How long has this been going on?" I inquired.

"Joe, you don't want to know. I knew he was the one the first time I saw him two years ago. We just decided to make it official and move in together."

The idea that they may have been sleeping together for a long time struck me in my chest like a medicine ball. I don't think I can describe how much pain I was going through at that moment. I didn't cry. I don't cry. But my chest was hurting and I felt like I was going to throw-up my breakfast, but I hadn't had my breakfast yet. There must have been something in there I could throw-up. No, nothing. I didn't feel like eating anything either. Maybe, I thought, I could throw-up tomorrow's breakfast; or maybe I could do lunch today.

She finished packing her little suitcase as I watched in disbelief. I couldn't say anything. I was remembering a time when my little New Age flower thought I was her soul mate. Finally, Barbara, my Barbara, said "Oh, Joe, I'm just too much in love with Chad to feel sorry for you." With those words she marched out of the room and down the hall. I heard the door shut.

I rolled over and got up. I made my way to the bathroom and turned on the shower. I decided while the water was cascading down my body to go into work and ask for a week off so I could get myself together. There wasn't that much going on at the plant lately with us losing that contract, so I was sure they wouldn't have any problem with my taking a vacation. I don't remember how I got to work that morning. I was probably on automatic pilot as I drove down the 405 Freeway toward El Segundo.

I went into my office and closed the door. I was just staring out my window at the parking lot when the phone rang. It was Bert, my boss. He asked me to come on down to his office. Good, I thought, I'll just go ahead and tell him I needed some time off. His secretary told me to go right in. I walked in and sat down in a chair. Bert had his back to me. He turned around. He wasn't smiling. "Joe, I've got some bad news. We've decided to give you your notice."

I made a noise that must've sounded like a moan. "I hate to do this," Bert continued, " but we lost that contract and we've got to let go of about half the work force."

"But why me, I've been here 16 years?"

"Don't ask me why, Joe. I'm telling six in this office the same thing. Hell, I'm sweating my job."

I slumped in the chair and decided not to tell him about Barbara. I didn't need his pity. "If it makes you feel any better," he said, "we are giving all the managers a special bonus. You should walk out of here with over twenty thousand dollars, plus all of your savings and retirement. That is quite a chunk of money."

I put my head in my hands. "What am I going to do, Bert?"

"Aw, don't take it so hard, guy," he replied, "It might be the best thing that could happen to you. If I wasn't so worried about my own job, I'd feel sorry for you old buddy, but I can't." He paused for a response. When none came he said, "Oh, by the way, we'd like you to clear out your desk by ten o'clock. Okay? You can pick up your checks at the front desk." He offered his hand. I took it and shook it. Bert seemed sincerely sorry. That made two of us.

I was out of the plant in fifteen minutes flat. I wasn't mad. I rarely got mad, and I couldn't now because I was doubly overwhelmed with the events of 6:30 on top of this. "Now what?" is all I could think of. I called my daughter in Georgia when I got home. I told her about Barbara. Cindi was her old caustic self, "Well, what do you expect? You burnt all your bridges with me when you left mother. It is about time you had a little of your own medicine, Dad. I don't feel sorry for you." That was a total of three people already who said they didn't feel sorry for me. I was going to have to hold up their end too. I was more than willing.

Twenty years old and Cindi was already just like her mother. We had been married for five of the worst years of my young life. Marge hollered at me non-stop during all the daylight hours, and was cold at night. Cindi learned her manner with men from an expert. Be completely disagreeable was the motto.

I put the phone down and sat in a chair staring at TV until late. I watched Barbara on the five o'clock news. She seemed so perky and bouncy delivering the weather. No wonder, she had just found Mr. Soul Mate number two. I made up my mind never to watch her again. I went to bed and stared at the ceiling. At midnight I turned 40. "New decade," I thought; "new life."

Well, at least I didn't have to get out of bed and go to work. That was definitely a plus. I worked at Big Missile for over sixteen years and I had hated it all of that time. I was a manager of accounting. What a joke. I fell into the job of accountant right after college and never had the nerve to change jobs; the money was too good, and besides, I was scared to leave. I rose in the ranks all right, but I don't know how. I certainly wasn't that good with numbers. Well, maybe being a manager wasn't that high; about the middle. I guess I sort of clawed my way to the middle with my personality. The job was paying me $1500 a week. Unemployment is going to pay me about $200, but then I didn't have to put up with Bert and his incessant demands for more and more charts and graphs. Yes, that was definitely worth $1300 a week. I bet he didn't know his absence was worth so much.

In the next month I had many moments where I was lucid. Most of the time, however, I was full of pain and self-pity. I kept visualizing Barbara and Chad locked in embrace in some secret dark bedroom. I would break in and make impassioned speeches about their sin against me; the damn best guy in the world. Or, I would hear that they broke up and I would go over and visit Barbara on the set and announce on TV what a bad woman she was and how I was so glad that Chad had hurt her. Oh, I was rolling in the self-pity all right, but I couldn't stop it. I just let the scenarios pour out in ever more ridiculous forms.

At night, I would run myself a bath full of water and pour in bubble bath soap. I would turn the tape player as loud as it would go and immerse myself in Bach, Beethoven and my bleeding heart. I would wake from my mean and doleful reveries occasionally and wonder aloud, "Now what?" I was sure that the Barbara and Chad show was going to come to a close at some point, then what was I going to do?

Once, while soaking in the tub, I had the thought to find out what Marcus Aurelius could tell me about this. I used to love philosophy and considered getting a degree in it, but was dissuaded by my first wife. I spent many hours with the ancient men of wisdom when I was in the army. They made me feel whole again. I found my volume on Marcus Aurelius and thumbed though the well-marked pages.

"The universe is change; our life is what our thoughts make it." I read it several times. Yes, I thought, and I've had a big change, but my thoughts are still back with the old, which doesn't exist anymore. Snap out of it! I demanded of myself. But after a few minutes I was back in my pitiful state.

I had considered suicide for a time as a way to show that awful woman just how bad I felt. Once, I was on the top floor of a twelve-story building visiting a friend, and I thought maybe I'd just jump out. That will show her. Then I decided maybe I'd go down to the first floor and do it. I wouldn't die, but it would give Barbara an idea of what I was thinking. Then seriously, I mulled the possibility of buying a gun and blowing my brains out. But then I thought about the two weeks waiting period I'd have to endure before I could actually get the gun. With my luck, I'd change my mind and then I'd be stuck with a gun. I might hurt myself.

I don't want a gun. God no. I killed a man in Viet Nam when I was nineteen. Oh, God, God. The memory of that swelled up like a nightmare. I thought he was Viet Cong, but afterward I wasn't so sure. He wasn't armed. Oh, God, don't think about that.

During the third week of my misery, the phone rang. I dashed into the kitchen, thinking again it might be Barbara begging me for forgiveness. I planned not to forgive her, but I wanted to get to the phone fast before she changed her mind. I had been practicing my speech for the full three weeks. It ran like this: "Well, Barbara dear, you made the biggest mistake of your life leaving me for that phony boy Chad. I am definitely not taking you back now, unless of course, you..." Then I add a number of silly conditions that would make it impossible.

It wasn't her though. "Hello, my name is McGee. I'm representing your wife in the motion for the dissolution of your marriage." He sounded like a pretty rough customer.

I was in shock. I had not thought about divorce. I guess that was the normal thing to do, but I was still not normal yet. "Yeah, Mr. McGoo, what do you want?"

"It's McGee, not McGoo, wise guy. Mrs. Peters wants this to be as painless as possible. Is that what you want Mr. Peters?"

"Well, that's what I want too. The least painful way would be for her to shoot Chad whats-his-face and come back to me," I said. "Aside from that, what is the next least painless way to do this?"

"Mr. Peters, my client is willing to settle out of court in a most equitable manner. She is offering you a flat sum of one hundred and forty-eight thousand dollars for your share of the house, the furniture, and the stocks and bonds you hold in common. You keep your car and she will keep hers. Does that sound fair?

I thought about it. That was about right, but I think our equity in the house was about $250,000, and the stocks were about $60,000. But she had a new, paid for $30,000 Lexus. Mine was a rattle-trap '82 Ford, worth about nothing. "Mr. McGee, I also want to be fair, but my idea of fair would be me getting about $175,000 cash."

"Just a moment," he said. He was obviously discussing this with Mrs. Peters. After about two minutes her lawyer came back on the line. "She is willing to go as high as $160,000, but no higher. Also, if you agree to this, you have to be out of the house by the first of the year."

"Tell Mrs. Peters that I agree to accept $160,000, but that I won't leave the house until I receive the money. He went away from the phone to discuss it.

"She said to tell you that you'd have your money the day after Christmas. She expects you to be out of the house on or before the first of January. Is that satisfactory, Mr. Peters?"

I was having a hundred different emotions, but something in me said, "Yeah, I'll be out."

"Fine, I'll have this written up and sent over to you early tomorrow for your signature. Good bye, Mr. Peters."

And that was it. Eleven years of marriage gone without even a whimper. I don't drink, but I got drunk that day and the next day. I took sloppy baths both days to the high, beautiful voice of Joan Baez. I tried to read Epictetus but couldn't make sense of any of it. I hadn't talked to Barbara since the day she left. Maybe I never would.

I felt like some mystical force was pushing or pulling me away from my old life. I am sure that I would have been intrigued if I believed in such nonsense, but I knew that it was some weird coincidence that, not only did I lose a wife, a job, and a house in something less than six weeks, but I also had more money than I had ever dreamed of having. I had approximately a quarter of a million dollars; most of it tax-free. I sent Cindi $5,000 as a Christmas present. It may have been a bit extreme, and maybe I was doing it to win her love or to soothe my conscious for leaving her mother. Anyway, I felt good being able to do it.

On Christmas Day my mom called from San Francisco. We had a good long talk; mostly about her new husband, Ernie, and her dog, Poochie. Mom was just being mom. She was not one to be throwing out sympathy to other people. Her only comment was, "Oh, this might be the best thing that ever happened to you, Joe." When I reminded her that it was not one thing but whole bunch of things that happened to me she started talking about Poochie again. I tried to call my brother in Germany but I couldn't get through.

What was strange about the whole day was that even if I didn't get any presents and no one came over, I think I actually enjoyed being alone. After talking to mom, I fixed a breakfast of fish sticks and eggs. I went for a long walk around the campus at UCLA, which was only two blocks from my house. I seemed to be free of those nasty day-dreams about Barbara and Chad. Later I read some philosophy by the pool and went to bed early. It was my best Christmas in a long time. All of my life I had had people around me. It was a relief to have no one who wanted to be with me. Strange.

What I wasn't free of were those questions about what to do now, but there was something in the back of my mind. A friend of mine, Greg in San Diego, told me about a guy who was supposed to be some kind of a great teacher. When I last talked to him a couple of years ago he was pretty sold on this fellow. I told him that he sounded like a cult leader. Greg said that wasn't this guy's bag at all. He took on one student at a time for about a year and then made that student go out into the world. They never had contact after that. I was skeptical, so I asked him what this great teacher charged for the year. Greg said that it was different with each student. The one student Greg knew, a physician, had to donate the year to the poor who couldn't afford medical care.

I had no idea what kind of a teacher this fellow was, or even his name, but I was drawn to the concept of a teacher teaching for one year and then releasing his student. Greg just said that this guy was wise and knew things nobody else knew. Greg had said he wasn't connected in any way to that silly New Age thinking, which I couldn't even bear to be around. I decided to go visit Greg and see if I could find this teacher and ask him to teach me something; whatever it was. I was in the mood to learn something. Even if that didn't work out, I figured I'd just travel around the country for a while and see what I could see. Life was beginning to smell like roses.

During this whole time, I was more emotional in a deeper way than I had ever been. It was like all of the pain opened me up. I had possibilities. I didn't know what they were, but the idea kept sweeping back and forth in my chest. Possibilities; that sounded good. Before I had none. My life was charted out for me by my circumstances. Now those circumstances had vanished. What could a man ask for that was more important than possibilities?

The day after Christmas, I traded in my old Ford and bought a 1991 Volkswagen Van with a bed in the back. It also had a little refrigerator and a fold-out table. It looked a lot better than the one I had in the Seventies and had considerably more power. I drove it home late that night and the next morning I started packing. Most of what I owned I gave to charity. I kept one suit, a few dress shirts and ties and one pair of black dress shoes. The rest of my clothes consisted of three denim shirts, two jeans, two tennis shoes and a pair of hiking boots. I loaded my few philosophy books and a Bible. Those things, along with an armful of underwear and socks, were all I took with me on my adventure.

Later, on the 28th, I went down to McGee's office and got my check. I took it down to my bank and bought a couple of CD's and put the rest, $150,000, in mutual funds. I came back home and took a nap. On the 29th, at 7:00 in the morning, I threw a six-pack of cokes, a beer, and a hunk of cheese in my little refrigerator. I locked all the doors of the house, jumped into my van and drove off. I cried for the first time since Viet Nam.

Chapter 2

I started down the 405 Freeway through the usual morning traffic. Once past El Segundo, I could go sixty or seventy miles an hour in the fast lane. I maintained this speed until I was in Orange County, then I asked myself the question: "Why am I going so fast?" I moved over into the slow lane and drove the way a Volkswagen should; about fifty-five. I decided that I didn't want to hurry anywhere from now on. As I poked along I thought about those awful days in Viet Nam.

After high school I spent a semester at Long Beach State goofing off. I mostly played pool, drank beer and tried to get laid. The next semester I decided to take off and see the country. That was a big mistake. I was drafted shortly before I was to leave for my journey. I thought about going to Canada, but my Dad convinced me to do my duty.

Six months later I landed in Viet Nam and was assigned to a rifle company north of Saigon. I was scared most of the time while I was there, even though I only went out on patrol about once a week. I made friends with a guy in my squad from Ohio named Eric. Eric had been in Nam six months, so as a veteran, he took me under his wing. Part of my training was to learn to drink and smoke weed. He was a master at both activities. So, except when we went on patrol, we were both pretty high.

After I had been there two months, we were flown by helicopter to a little village about thirty kilometers from our base. When we arrived a fire-fight had been going on for about an hour. Some other unit had been ambushed just outside the village. I think about six of their guys had been hit.

We were coming up around the other side of the village from

the north when I saw a movement in some brush. I crouched down behind a log. Eric was behind me somewhere. Just then I saw someone make a dash for a hut on the outskirts of the village. I aimed and pulled off two rounds. The body went down like a lead bag. Eric let out a hoop. I was sweating and smiling. "I got a kill," I thought with pride.

Mine were the last shots fired. Apparently, the Cong had slipped away into the jungle. I had gotten the only kill in our unit. I went over to the see the body. There, lying in a lump was my trophy; the back of his head was blown-off. I looked around. "Hey, where's his weapon?" I searched the area, looking for any kind of weapon. Nothing. It occurred to be that I had shot an innocent man. I must have looked alarmed because the Captain came over.

"Look son, these bastards are all Cong, whether they got a rifle or not. You did good, believe me." Just then a woman came out of a hut heading for the body. She was screaming in her language and pounced on the crumbled dead man, holding his head. In my life up to that time, I had never seen a more distraught person. She was covered in blood from holding the head. She was crying something to the ring of soldiers who had gathered. Someone beside the Captain was interpreting.

"She says that her son was only twelve and not a Viet Cong. He was hiding from them when they came into the village. Shit, she says we are pigs. Fucking bitch."

I went over to her and indicated that it was me who killed her son. I tried to indicate how sorry I was. The little woman jumped up and started a tirade at me. Just then a fist came from the side of me, smashing into her face. She fell dazed. The Captain pulled me to the side. "Look trooper, I don't know who you are, but get it through your thick skull that these people are the fucking enemy; all of them. They fucking lie and they will fucking kill you if they have a chance. Now get your ass back to wherever you came from. You make me sick apologizing to a gook."

To say that I was stunned was an understatement. I felt I was in an alternate universe. Eric led me back to where the rest of our unit was sitting. I don't remember much more about that day except that all I could see was the face of the boy's mother. Later, I discovered a smear of blood on my shirt. It must have come from the mother, from her dead boy.

In the helicopter, I cried; no, I wailed deep sobbing apologies to the image of that woman. Eric had his arm around me trying to console me. Someone in the copter said, "That is what we are here for buddy, to kill them fuckers."

Back at the camp, I was sent to the chaplain and then to the doctor who gave me something to make me sleep. I slept, but even that strong drug couldn't stop the dreams, the nightmares of my pulling the trigger and the hell it brought. In a few days the doctor said I was good enough to go back on patrol. I guess I looked okay, but inside I was a mess. It took everything I had to hold it together. I don't remember where we were. It was just another jungle trail, like millions of others. I was walking in the front of seven or eight guys along this slippery path. The point was about twenty yards ahead motioning us forward. As we picked up the pace, I slipped and sat on my butt. Eric, who was right behind me, stepped over me and laughed at my posture. As I struggled to get up in the mud, there was an explosion. It knocked me back on my butt. I looked up the path, and ten feet in front was Eric's leg.

Somebody was yelling "Mine, mine, a fucking mine." Eric was lying to the left side of the path without any legs. His bloody hands were holding his head. I ran over to him. He was just staring at me, his eyes full of fear. His lower body was gone, not just his legs. I knew he only had a minute or so to live. He grabbed my hand.

"Tell my mother that I love her, will you?"

"Sure Eric, I'll tell her when I get back to the world," I said.

"Shit, I treated her so bad," he continued, "at least let her know I died loving her. Will you do that, buddy, will you? The address is in my stuff by my bed."

"Yeah, friend, I'll do it. That mine was meant for me, but you took it for me."

Then the life left him. Just like that, he wasn't there. I fell back in real agony. Everybody was hollering for a medic. Then I realized it was for me. My leg was soaked with blood.

In the hospital in Saigon, I was a distaught. The doctor thought it was because of my wound, but it wasn't. I couldn't even say what it was exactly. "Hell boy, your wound isn't that bad." he said, "You are going to recover completely. You'll be running after these nurses in no time." It didn't help. While I was sleeping someone had pinned a purple heart on my chest. Big deal.

After a week, I heard that my whole division was going back to the States. I'd be joining them at Fort Ord when I got out of the hospital. Even that news didn't perk me up. I didn't care about much at that point.

I was almost off my crutches when I was discharged. My parents came to pick me up. On the way back to L.A., I tried to tell them about Viet Nam, but nothing I could say conveyed my own devastation. I was relieved that mom did most of the talking. It took the pressure off me. I noticed that every time I got emotional, mom would start up with something silly like her hair or new dress.

The next week I flew out to Cincinnati to see Eric's mother. She lived in a little house by the Ohio River. Mrs. Schuster stuck me as the ideal mom. She was short and heavy with a smiling face. When I told who I was, she broke down and began weeping. I led her into the living room and helped her lay down on the couch. After about 20 minutes she regained some of her composure and got up and fixed me a cup of tea. I told her everything I knew except the details of Eric's dying.

As I was leaving, I said that Eric was now in heaven. She seemed mollified. I wish I believed in heaven, in God. I saw too much pain and felt too much pain for a God to exist. If there was a God, he was evil to cause this much suffering in the world. As I walked down the steps toward my rental car I looked at the sky and said aloud, "You do not exist!"

I came out of my reverie and decided to pull over in San

Clemente and have some coffee. I couldn't believe that I had forgotten my java that morning. It must have been the excitement of leaving. Coffee was one of my morning necessities. Except for an occasional beer and cigar, coffee was my only vice and I wasn't about to give that one up. It gave me too much pleasure. I went into a restaurant overlooking the ocean and sat where I could watch the waves. I ordered coffee and toast. As the waitress was going away, I asked her, "Say, where is Nixon's old house?"

She turned around to face me and thought for a minute. "Sir, I don't think I was born back then. The cook may know, he's pretty old."

"Never mind."

It was kind of chilly outside, but there was a volleyball game going on below in the sand. Girls and guys were batting the ball back and forth. The females were good looking. I started thinking about them in my usual male way, when I realized that I hadn't given women a thought since this whole thing began. "Maybe I'm over women now for good," I said to myself. But then I looked back down at the prancing, bouncing girls in shorts and halters. I laughed to myself, "Not a chance."

I called the number I had for Greg in San Diego, but the number had been changed. I wrote the new one down and tried it. A woman answered. "Hello," she said. There was a baby crying in the background.

"Hello, is Greg at home?"

"Oh, no he's at work until about 5:30. Who is this?"

"My name is Joe Peters. I am an old friend from Los Angeles. I am passing through San Diego and thought I'd call and say hello. Who are you?"

"Pam. I'm almost Greg's wife, or in three weeks I will be anyway."

"Oh, well congratulations. Is it okay if I call around six?"

"Sure, I'll tell him. Your name is Peter?"

"No, Joe, Joe Peters."

"Got it. Greg always calls around noon to check on the baby. I'll tell him."

We said our good-byes and I hung up. So, old Greg is finally getting married. Heck, he's older than me. I should warn him, I thought. I figured that I might as well spend some time here in San Clemente. It was only ten o'clock. I thought I'd just walk around and see what there was to see.

It started raining about a half an hour later. I bought a magazine and sat in my van and read and napped until two o'clock. I ate lunch and then drove into San Diego. As I drove I started musing about my life again.

I went back to Long Beach State and was a real tiger this time. If I didn't get an "A" in a course I was upset. I eventually graduated with a 3.7 average, even with my disastrous first semester figured in. My mom and dad, plus my wife Marge and our three year old girl were at the graduation ceremony. I think that night was the night when I finally got over Viet Nam. I was truly happy for the first time in a long time.

I met Marge even before I re-entered LB State. I fell hard. She was so sure of herself and beautiful that I wanted to marry her right away. The only trouble was that she was two months pregnant by a former boyfriend. I was so smitten that I agreed, and in fact insisted, that I assume full responsibility and make the child mine. I was heaven sent as far as Marge was concerned. The fellow that got her pregnant had moved to another state.

She treated me pretty good for a while, at least until after Cindi was born. Then her temper grew more violent. She could go off on the slightest things. One time when we had one of our few nights out, I spilt some popcorn on her dress at the movies. She started yelling right in the middle of the show. I got up and left. She followed me outside and continued all the way home. It got worse when I entered graduate school. I finally decided that I was afraid of her. I was doing anything to avoid conflict and it was getting to me.

Right after I received my MBA, I got up the nerve and told her I was leaving. Well, that caused a lot of problems. Our parents got into it. Marge's folks had helped pay my way though school, so now they thought I should pay them back. It was a mess. From then on, Marge was my sworn enemy and she infected Cindi with the same venom.

I found a nice motel near the water and checked in. It was still only four o'clock, so I ate an early dinner in the cafe and walked around the boat dock and looked at the fancy boats. Eventually I sat and tried to think through some more of my life. I don't remember ever doing that in such an orderly manner before. I guess it was because I was starting over. God, that sounded trite. Every bookstore in the country is loaded with titles about people, mostly women, starting over. Well, maybe it wasn't trite if I really did it; really had a different life in every way. I was going to do it because I hated my old life with Barbara and Bert. There was just too much pressure on me to be at my most artificial. For Bert and the rest of the people at Big Missile, I had to pretend to like what I was doing and that it was somehow important. I really thought the whole notion of building ever bigger, more deadly weapons was some kind of a cosmic joke. But I couldn't show that, no sir. I had to fake it.

But even worse was acting like I cared about those phony show business friends of Barbara's. Whereas Big Missile people wore frowns to indicate their dedication, the show biz crowd was in high gear all the time, smiling and laughing. I don't think I met one of Barbara's colleagues who weren't boisterous and loud. It was a chore getting through a party. I think their motto en masse was "It is who you know and how much racket you can make."

When I met Barbara she was a trainer at Big Missile. I was taking a class in employee relations and she was my instructor. She was funny and sincere. I asked her out and was surprised when she said yes. Even though we dated steadily for six months, Barbara only had sex with me after I asked her to marry me. There was something in me that liked that, even if I never would have admitted it to her. God, I was a panting fool for that whole time. I was a little surprised when she told me she didn't want to have any children. She said that her career was more important than kids.

I was a slightly disappointed, but not enough to insist. I thought I could make a good father if I had half a chance. With Marge life had been so hectic that it was no wonder I was not being at my best in regards to being a good daddy to Cindi. Anyway, I'm paying now for my lack.

Barbara got the opportunity to work as a fill-in weather person on Channel 8 about five years later. She made the most of it, networking every chance she got. This meant dragging me to a function every weekend. I made like it was fun, but it was a chore. Barbara was determined to make it to the top.

Just then, as I was standing up to go look for a phone to call Greg, I had a major insight. Chad, Barbara's soul mate was also the son of the executive vice-president at the station. I hadn't remembered it until that moment. I smiled. She was going to make it to the top using Chad and Chad's daddy. For some reason I felt better. Maybe it was because I felt superior to her now. Barbara had made the ultimate show business move--sleeping with someone to get ahead. I also felt sad. My chest hurt again when I thought of it. I still loved her.

I got Greg on the phone. He said he would come to my motel and we could visit for a while. He sounded harried.

When I opened the door Greg was still in his suit but his tie was askew. We shook hands and then hugged—man style. I always liked Greg. We had been in graduate school together and had kept in contact ever since. I remember in college he used to give me the business about being married, especially to Marge. He saw how she would give me hell over the slightest things. He said she was sick. Then he changed his mind and said I was sick for sticking around. I think both were true.

"Well, old buddy, how you doing?" I asked after I gave him a beer.

"I don't know, Joe. Sometimes I think I got myself into a mess, and at other times I think I'm the luckiest guy in the world."

"Pam said you guys were getting married in a few weeks. Is that the mess you're talking about?"

He flopped back on the couch. "Well, yeah. But I'm crazy for her. She just had our baby, plus she's got two of her own little kids living in my two bedroom condo."

"Oh," I said. "How old are the kids."

"Well, my boy is three weeks. Her boys are seven and nine. I like them okay, but it is like a circus there. I'd like to have my old quiet life back, but I guess it's too late for that. I'm stuck for 18 years at least."

"Why don't you do what you always told me to do with Marge and pack your bags?"

"Joe, I was real stupid then," he answered. "I thought that leaving someone would be the easiest thing in the world to do, but I didn't realize all the bad stuff that goes with that kind of thing. No, I'm going to stick around. And besides, Pam is the greatest. I have never been treated so good."

"Well, then you're lucky. I don't think I ever had that."

Greg finished his beer in a big gulp. "So, old friend, what are you doing here anyway?"

"It's a long story, but my wife left me and I lost my job. I've decided to do something else with my life."

"Wow, that's too bad," he said, "but I think I can find you something at Big Airplane. Interested?"

"No, Greg, but thanks. What I really came for is a way I can contact that guy you were talking about a couple of years ago; the one you said that takes on a pupil for only a year. He sounded real interesting."

"Oh, you mean Paul, the philosopher." He got up and went to the refrigerator and took out another beer. He twisted the top off and drank a little.

"Yeah, that's him. Do you know where I can get a hold of him?"

"Oh jeez, let's see. I only knew him a little. I think he retired and moved to Arizona. I think he's about 80 at least."

"Do you have a phone number or address or something?"

"Jeez, you are serious." He leaned back on the couch and thought for awhile. "I don't know, but I think I know someone who might.

Can I use your phone?"

He pulled out an address book from his breast pocket and found a number. He dialed it. "Hey, this is Greg, your former drinking buddy. Yeah, I'm fine. Look, do you know where Paul moved? Tucson...Do you have an address or phone number. Oh, say what's his last name anyway? Martin. I always called him Paul the philosopher. One last question; is he still taking on students? Oh, okay, that's all I need bub. Thanks."

Greg hung the phone up and took a swig of beer. "He said that Paul moved to Tucson about a year or so ago. His last name is Martin. He doesn't have any way to contact him but he said that Paul indicated he was going to buy a little piece of land and retire."

"Tucson," I said, " I'll drive out there and see if I can find him."

"Hey, wait a minute, buddy. Do you even know what he teaches?"

"No," I answered, "but I was moved by some of the things you said about him. I don't remember exactly what you said, but it made me not forget him. What does he teach, anyway?"

"Real different stuff, but mainly he teaches methods of obtaining self-knowledge. Do you have any idea what that means?"

"Only that it was something that the Greeks wrote about. They called it knowing thy self. I could never exactly figure it out."

"If you can find him and he agrees to take you on, you will be amazed at what he knows. I used to be part of a little group that met him for coffee on Saturday mornings. I always came away thinking that I had been in the presence of a holy man, but he didn't act like it. He was just kind of matter of fact. If you find him and he accepts you, which I doubt because he's retired, your life will change if that's what you are after."

I walked over to the window and looked out. "Is he gay?"

"Definitely not. His wife of about fifty years died just before he left."

"Tucson," I said almost to myself, "I'll find him."

" I hope you do, Joe. He is something special. Every time I talked to him he had a definite positive effect on me. Sometimes, when I left him I felt like praying."

"This sounds stupid, but it is almost like I'm destined to find Paul Martin. Nothing else makes sense."

"If you find him," Greg said seriously, "he will make sense. He knows himself."

Chapter 3

As I was making my way down the freeway the next day I was having second thoughts about the whole adventure. I must be crazy, I thought. I'm going out into the desert to look for some wise man that is going to tell me about life. He is going to tell me how to know myself? That sounds like those books in the Sixties that promised so much, but in the end were hollow and stupid. Maybe the whole idea is silly, but since I'm going to be in the neighborhood anyway, I might as well see if I can find him. I wonder if I'll have to prostrate myself, or fast, or give up sex? Hell, I've already given up sex, I mean not officially, but by not getting any. Then I admitted to myself that I was a little scared, scared of finding him and being rejected, and also of not finding him. But mostly I was afraid that my life was for nothing. I was going to die someday and nothing would have come of it. I would have been another blip on the screen of eternity. Maybe that's the real reason for my sojourn into the desert—an attempt to make my life mean something.

What else do I have, I asked. The whole world has left me for dead. My mom loves Pookie, or whatever his name is, more than me. My daughter has ignored me for years and my brother is always unavailable. Maybe I don't know myself? Maybe that's the problem. What I do know is that I don't like myself very much. I don't know if it started in Viet Nam or not, but I've always taken everybody's guff and never complained. I didn't think I had the right to bitch about anything. "Easy-going Joe," people would call me. If they only knew how I was on the inside. They'd see the anger and feel the disillusionment.

After I drove down the road a bit my mood changed. I smiled

and said aloud to myself: "This trip means I am truly free. I can do what I want—if I can figure it out. Paul Martin, here I come; ready or not." I paused, "I hope you can figure what I am and what I want."

I had passed through Tucson once before, about ten years ago. I was on some business for Big Missile. It was kind of nice, I thought at the time, without all that traffic of L. A.. It hadn't changed much; still not much traffic. Of course, it was nine o'clock at night. Maybe there are more cars in the daytime. Likely.

I pulled into a motel beside the freeway and got a room. After eating a snack, I got the telephone book out and looked for Paul Martin. There were about 500 Martins, but only three Paul's and two P's. I circled them. I'll call them tomorrow. I went to bed and hardly slept. I was practicing what I was going to say to him when we met.

I must have slept some because I woke up about 6:30 raring to go. Unfortunately, no one else is raring to go at 6:30, so I had to figure out something else to do until about nine or ten. I looked out my window. There was a nice view of the freeway and a construction project. I went down to the office and looked at the brochures. I spied one for the University of Arizona. The pictures looked interesting so I asked the clerk how to get there. He waved toward the east. "Three miles, you can't miss it."

I arrived at the campus and parked. It took a few minutes to realize that they were shut down for the holidays. There were some runners and walkers with dogs, but otherwise it was deserted. I planted myself on a bench near the mall and noticed how beautiful the campus was, a lot nicer than USC or even UCLA. For the next few hours I took a stroll around and ended up having breakfast about a block away from the main campus.

Back at the motel I began calling the Martins. I was in luck because everyone answered the phone, but no one knew or ever heard of the Paul Martin I was looking for. What now? I wondered. I called the Sheriff's Department. The deputy suggested I try the

County Recorder's Office and see if a Paul Martin had bought any property in Pima County. Good idea.

I went downtown to their office. I found out that a Paul A. Martin had purchased a two-and-a-half acre parcel about fifteen miles west of Tucson a year ago. I got the address and asked for directions. I was nervous. I'm probably going to drive out there and nobody will be there or he'll chase me off the property. I went back to the motel and checked out. I then followed the directions out into the desert toward Rainbow Boulevard where the property was located.

Rainbow Boulevard was a dirt road, or dirt boulevard. I stopped at a little store on the corner of Rainbow and the main paved road and asked the owner if he knew or ever heard of Paul Martin. "Oh, sure," the man said brightly. "He lives down the road about a mile. You can't miss it because he paved the road in front of his place. Real nice man," he added. I bought a soda and sandwich for lunch and drove as I ate. My hands were shaking on the steering wheel, but I couldn't for the life of me figure out why. He is just a guy, I kept saying. Nothing worked though. Something inside of me thought this was a big deal. Maybe it was.

I noticed that the land was pretty flat and scruffy, sprinkled with low cactus and brush of some sort. My car was kicking up dust behind me. In a few minutes I could see that in front of me was a black paved stretch of road of about one hundred yards. I stopped on this part and looked to my right. About fifty yards off the road was a modest sized older house made of what looked like adobe brick. Next to it was a long carport with two trucks and a little tractor parked underneath. The road to the house was also paved with black tar. I took a deep breath and turned into the driveway. Except for the house and pavement, for miles around was a most unimpressive desert. What a place to retire, I thought.

I parked off to the side and went to the front door and took a big breath and knocked. The door opened and through the screen door I could see a figure, but the screen was too dark to tell much else. A deep voice said "Yes, can I help you?"

"I hope so, I'm looking for a Paul Martin who is a teacher; a teacher of philosophy."

He pushed the screen door open. The man was tall and thin, but not gaunt. He didn't look 80. He was smiling. "Why it looks like you've found the right place." He extended his hand and said, "I'm Paul Martin."

I took his hand and shook it. "And my name is Joe Peters. I've come from Los Angeles to talk to you."

Paul stepped back and motioned to me to enter. "Please come in. I'm always happy to see somebody from California."

As I walked through the door the first thing I noticed was the thick walls; they must have been three feet thick. "Wow, look at these walls."

"This is a 'rammed earth' house. The wide walls make it cooler in the summer and warmer in the winter. It's an old design."

He led me into the kitchen and indicated a chair for me to sit. "How about some hot tea?"

"Sure, that would be great." The house had a Southwest motif and was especially neat. There were baskets on the walls and Indian rugs on the painted cement floors. I sat down and Paul brought out two mugs and poured some hot water up to the brim. He pointed to a little basket of teas.

After we both settled down with our beverage, and after some small talk about California and Arizona, he asked, "Well Joe, what can I do for you? I presume it is important to have come all this way to see an old coot out in the desert."

I took another sip. "Well, Mr. Martin, I think it is important. You see, I heard about you a couple of years ago; the kind of work you do. I mean with students; you teach them about life. Since then, you have been in the back of my mind. So, after I got fired from my job and my wife left me, I decided to find you and see if you might take me on as a pupil."

"I am flattered. Did you know that I'm retired from that sort of teaching?"

"Yes, I heard, but I was hoping...I was hoping to see if you'd un-retire and teach me."

He chuckled. "I see, but don't you know about life? You look like you're 35 at least."

"I thought I did once," I answered, " but now I'm pretty sure I don't know shit. Excuse me. So, I've come to you hat in hand to see if you'd help me. The truth is I don't know much about you, Mr. Martin, and almost nothing about what you know or even your methods, but I've come ready for anything. You come with the highest recommendation."

"Please call me Paul." He paused for a long moment. "Let me think about this for a couple of minutes." He got up from his chair and walked out the back door. I could see him standing next to a small cactus, his hand on his chin. Then I realized who he looked like; Abe Lincoln. He wasn't quite as tall, but his face had the same structure and the eyes were kind and deep, just like Lincoln's. His hair was the same brown color speckled with grey. He walked back and forth in front of the cactus, deep in thought. Finally, after about five minutes, he turned and came back into the house with a smile on his face.

"Son, what can you pay me for my services?"

"Money?" I asked, " I can pay you almost whatever you want; I guess."

"No, not money. I don't need money. But what I do need is help around here. I'm preparing to make this property into a garden, mostly roses, but other things too. The land came with its own well, so there is plenty of water to do what I want. Would you be willing to help me make this place into a small paradise?"

I took a gulp. "Yes of course. I'll do whatever you want."

Paul poured some more water for both of us. "All right, here is what I want. I don't want you around here every day, maybe one or two days a week. I don't have the energy for a seven day a week student."

"Okay," I said.

"Also, I want you to promise that you'll do whatever I ask of you. There won't be anything that you can't do, but don't give me any kind of trouble."

"I won't."

"I don't think you'll be any trouble. I have a good feeling about you, better than any student I've had in a long time. Go into town and get settled. Get a place to stay and a job of some sort. When you are ready, come on out and we'll begin. Make it right after the first of the year because I'm going to be plowing some of these bushes and cacti out of here in the next few days. It is going to be dusty."

"All right, I'll do that, but you should know that I don't need to work."

He looked right at me unsmiling. "You need to work. Find something that you've never done before. And since you don't need the money, please give half of your earnings to a charity or poor person. Okay?"

"Sure," I answered.

"And," he continued, " I don't want you to tell a soul about giving the money away, even me. Just do it. I'll never speak about it again."

"Sure. Am I allowed to ask questions?"

"Absolutely. I expect it. There are only a few things I won't answer, but I'll tell you when and if you ask those questions."

"My first question then is, why shouldn't I tell anyone I'm giving away money?"

Paul got up from his chair. "Lets go outside while I answer that. I would like you to meet my helper around here." We went out into the sunlight and toward a man about 100 feet away. He said, "Because this work that you are embarking on is all inner. Everything is to promote understanding. I don't want vanity to rob you of what you are doing. It is work on the Inner Man."

"Oh, I see," I said.

We came up to a crouching Mexican man about my age. He stood up and smiled. Paul said something to him in Spanish and he put out his hand. "This is Arturo, Joe. He has been helping me since I got here. Arturo is an extraordinary worker. He only speaks Spanish."

We shook hands and grinned at each other. Paul led me back toward my car. "All right, young man, you are to take your time getting settled. When you are ready, come on out and we'll get started working on this place and on you, or rather in you."

"Thanks a lot Paul, I'll try my best."

"I know you will. While you are doing your business in Tucson, try to notice what you think about and who you talk to in your head. Make some notes and we'll talk about it next time I see you."

I pulled out of the long driveway flying high in my head. My mind was racing faster that my van as I headed back into town. Paul said to try to observe my thinking. Well now my thoughts were a jumble of bits of conversations. For a few seconds I'd be talking to Paul, then I flip and be pontificating to Barbara about my new life, and then over to Greg telling him about my episode with Paul, then back and forth at almost lightning speed. I was wondering if this is what Paul wanted me to do. It sure was weird. I couldn't stop this bouncy thinking. I don't remember driving at all, but in no time I was back near the University. I turned into a motel and took a room.

My mind was still racing when I went to bed that night. I had made some notations about the thinking I was doing and who I was talking to. Funny, but I found out that during that whole time; about nine hours, I hadn't let anyone else do any talking, just me blabbering on. I figured that when I calmed down I would get back to my old way of thinking, which was what? I don't remember ever thinking about how I thought. Shoot, I'm already learning something.

The next day I found a decent apartment about a block away and paid the first and last month's rent. I could move in the next day, New Years Day. All day I tried to watch my thoughts. It got kind of monotonous because it was more of the same thing as the day before. This is surely not how I always think? I wonder if everybody else thinks the same way? No, not possible. How could anybody get anything done always lecturing other people in their minds? Nope, I'm just going through something, I figured.

New Years Eve was a bust for me. I went down to the bar on the corner, checked out a few chicks and went home about ten. I think I was the oldest guy in the bar. I felt like the only adult. At midnight, I heard gun-shots, yelling, and general reveling. About fifteen minutes later my next-door neighbor brought home what sounded like two women. It was definitely two women. I wonder if he needs some help? No, I'm too sleepy. He'll have to manage on his own.

On New Year's Day I took a couple of long walks and watched the games on TV. I figured I'd move into my new place the next day. While I was walking I puzzled over why I couldn't tell anyone if I gave away money. I remembered in the bible somewhere; the New Testament, Jesus said something about people who pray in public already have their reward. I wonder if that's what Paul meant? I like that idea. It felt good. What am I thinking now? I'd better write all this down. Paul is going to be amazed.

I scanned the want ads to find a job I could do, but hadn't done. My eyes spied the words: "Taxi cab drivers wanted. No experience necessary." Cab driver? I always wondered about those guys. They seemed so low-class though. I looked further in the classifieds, but nothing appealed to me. So, that is how I decided to become a professional cab driver. I bet Barbara will be proud, I thought. Then I went off into a fictitious conversation with her in my head. She was aghast at how far I'd slipped. Then I thought I'd better write that down too.

After an informative two hour "seminar" on the intricacies of cab driving in the city of Tucson, I was given a nice certificate awarded to any participant who did not sleep through the whole thing. I was led out into the yard where they keep the cars when not in use. It looked just like a junkyard. Parts of cabs were scattered all over the place; front part of one cab here; back part over the other end of the yard. Doors and hoods and engines were stacked in different piles. I said to the guy who was showing the class around; "Are these the cars?"

"Naw," he informed me, "We make the cars from these parts. We got about 60 cars running and about 60 more in pieces out here. When something breaks on one of the cars in the field, we got the parts right here."

I whistled. "Nice operation."

"Oh, yeah, we keep these babies running all right. Hell, the average cab runs about 75,000 miles a year. It's hard to tell how many miles any one cab has on it because most of them are a conglomeration of cars. Hell, a hood and door may have 400,000 miles, the engine only 250,000 miles, but the front bumper may be almost new with 30,000 on it."

I was truly impressed, but that is not to be construed as a positive impression. It was sure a different world here. This was going to be some job. I was to report the next day at 5:30 in the morning to pick-up my car. I'd have to pay $42 for the privilege of driving for them, plus I had to have the gas tank filled when I came back at six o'clock that night. At least I'll get to know the city, I rationalized.

I was there at 5:30 sharp. I paid my money and waited for my car to come in, #14. Just before 6 o'clock, number fourteen came rumbling in. A giant of a man got out of it. He was about five foot ten and weighed in at about 400 pounds. I went over to him and introduced myself. "My name is Joe. I guess I'm driving this jewel." I noticed that he left the engine running.

He shook my hand and introduced himself as Big Ernie. I asked him why he didn't turn the engine off. "Sometimes this baby doesn't want to start, so I just leave it running when I can. But anyway, everything works except the heater and one of the windshield wipers; the right one—so it's okay."

"Did you make any money last night?" I asked.

"Oh, it was a pretty good night. I think I cleared about $58 after I paid for the gas and snacks."

Fifty-eight bucks, I thought, for twelve hours. He handed me the logbook and walked away. I looked in the cab and saw that the front seat was covered with candy wrappers. "Hey, Big Ernie, don't you think you should remove all this junk in here?"

He didn't even look back. "Naw, that stuff is always in there." And then he went around the corner. I took all of the papers and cups and donut boxes out of the front seat and threw them away. Then I got in and almost drove away. But the seat was all broken down; almost to the floor, and there were little blocks on the pedals.

The seat was pulled back to the maximum. His stomach must have been so big that he couldn't reach the gas when the seat was way back. I took the blocks off and moved the seat forward. Then I was all set, except I was so low in the seat that I barely could see over the steering wheel.

Anyway, I roared out of the lot ready to snatch my fortune.

I drove to a specific spot in town and sat with the engine running, waiting for a call on the radio to send me to my first assignment. It was real cold that morning and with the heater not working I was bouncing in my seat to keep warm. About 7:20 I got my first call. Someone said in a loud crackling voice, "Hey, number 14, you want a fare to Ajo?"

"Sure, where's Ajo?"

"Oh, just down Ajo Road a bit. Take the 10 and turn right on Ajo Road and just keep going. It's a good fare. The lady will give you $50."

I went to the hospital to pick up this lady and her son. The lady didn't speak English but the kid did. When they got in, he handed me a fifty-dollar bill. I took off for Ajo, whatever that was.

As I was driving I started noticing a strong smell. It wasn't pleasant at all. I turned off the I10 onto Ajo Road. It was kind of a dinky road, two lanes. Then I saw a sign that said: AJO-150 MILES. "What? 150 miles." I screamed. That is going to take me five or six hours for $50!" The kid and his mom were not moved by my outburst. That was why they already paid me. They probably heard it all before. Hell, I'll do it. Maybe I'll like Ajo.

The smell became unbearable. I finally figured out that it was from my seat. Big Ernie had perspired so much in here that the seat was soaked. I didn't notice before. I guess I was too disturbed over the other stuff. The two in the back smelled it too. The boy said, "It stinks back here, and it's cold. Can you turn on the heat?"

So there we were, stuck in the stink. We sometimes opened the windows and poked our heads out, and then, when we couldn't stand the cold, closed the windows and held our noses. I'm laughing now, but it wasn't funny then. After three hours I made it to the town of Ajo. It was a small place with a population of about 400. I went to the gas station and filled up with fuel. While the engine was running, I ran in and grabbed the lunch special of two hot dogs and soda for $1. At 2:30 I was back at my post in town, waiting for the next call. I don't think I ever spent a more miserable day. The smell didn't get any better. At 6 P.M. I stumbled into the taxi office. When I told the guys in there my troubles, they burst out laughing. "They gave you Big Ernie's cab? Nobody will take that piece of junk, just a rookie. That's some smell isn't it?" They roared. "Did you look at the back of your pants, buddy? They're soaked with Big Ernie's ass sweat." More laughter.

 I didn't quit. I think I had every right to, but I figured it was just a good lesson for me. Then I wondered what exactly the lesson was? Don't drive in a pile of sweat. Don't go to Ajo? I was so tired and I had to do this again in less than twelve hours. I counted my proceeds: I made $14. If I had bought a nice lunch, I might not have made anything.

 I peeled $7 off of my wad and walked out to the corner and gave it to some homeless guy. He thanked me profusely.

 I slept an hour on the couch. I woke up feeling depressed. I pulled the cord on the phone so I could reach it. I dialed my old home in L. A.. Barbara answered. "Barbara?"

 "Joe, is that you?"

 "Yeah, I just called because I wanted to find out how you are doing. I haven't seen or talked to you in about two months."

 "Oh, Joe, I'm glad you called. I would have called you, but I didn't know where you were. Where are you?"

 "I live in Tucson. How are you doing?"

 "In some ways good, but in other ways not so good. I've been hired as an anchor at channel 10. It's a great chance to move up in this damn industry. But my young boy, Chad, is driving me nuts. Did you know he's only 27? I thought he was at least in his 30's. The worst part is that he acts like a teenager. Joe, I've been regretting how I treated you. Will you forgive me?"

 "Whoa," I exclaimed, "this is a surprise. Yeah, sure, I forgive you. Actually, I think it was the best thing you ever did for me. I'm starting to grow up."

"Will you come back? I'll treat you much better that I did. I know I'm a fool—a bitch sometimes."

I looked over at the soiled jeans in the corner. " I don't think so, Barb, I really am enjoying my new life—in a perverse sort of way. Maybe in the future. I just don't know."

"I was afraid of that," she said. "Oh, Bert called and said for you to call him at the plant. He thinks maybe they've got a spot for you."

"Another surprise." I reached to the coffee table and grabbed the crumbled seven one dollar bills. "Naw, I'm making too much money here. Old Bert will have to do without my financial expertise."

"Oh, got a good job?"

"I'm a professional cab driver."

"Wow," she exclaimed in mock surprise, "I bet your MBA comes in handy there."

"Oh, yeah, I am a whiz at making change. I don't know how my colleagues do it without at least an MBA. And I get to meet lots of girls--well not girls exactly, but some very attractive grandmothers. I take them to the store, and who knows where that can lead?"

"Are you sure this is want to do with your life, Joe. I can get you into the industry."

"Barbara, I am happy for the first time in a long time. I don't know why, but I am. Driving a taxi has nothing to do with it, there is just so much more to it, I can't even begin to explain it."

She started sobbing. "Oh Joe, I'm so sorry that things turned out this way. Now, I'm not happy and you are. But that doesn't make me feel any better."

"I didn't think it would. I apologize for telling you about my happiness. Listen, I've got to go. I've got a heavy date with the washing machine."

"Well, okay. Give me your number just in case I need to talk to you."

After I hung up I just stared at the money on the table and the dirty jeans. I was numb from that conversation. Later I wrote down in my thinking-journal that I had no thoughts except bits and pieces for about an hour. I was confused. My wife wanted me back? My boss wanted me back? I could have my old life back?

I did my laundry. The next day I reported back to work as if I really liked it. They gave me car #22. The night driver seemed a little crazy. He showed me his 38 snub-nose pistol and advised me to get one. He said, "You never know when it will come in handy," pretending to shoot someone. I drove away in a relatively clean cab; no shell casings that I could see.

After five days of driving I got two days off. By that time, I had filled 26 pages of my journal with notes on my thinking, such as it was. I couldn't even call it thinking, just mental blabbering.

Chapter 4

Just before arriving at the property, I started wondering if Paul would be impressed by my efforts at seeing my thinking? What thinking? It was mostly just lecturing somebody about some nonsense. Would he consider me a dope or idiot that I wasn't doing any real thinking, or is what I do normal? He is making me think though, even if it is only about thinking. Am I thinking now? Maybe now I'm thinking. Man, this is real peculiar.

The property had a different look. They had it all flattened out. The bushes and cacti were gone. I parked beside the house and went to the front door. Paul yelled for me to come in. "Good, you are here. We are preparing to start the day's work. How are you, Joe?"

I sat at the table. He poured me a steaming cup of coffee and offered me some rolls. I took a small one. "Well, I'm good I think. I got a job as a cab driver in town and that is proving to be quite an experience." I handed him my journal. "Here is my so called thinking that I have been doing."

Paul took it and began to read it. He would read a little and then go to the next page and read a bit. After about five minutes he closed the book and looked up at me. "Were you surprised?"

"Definitely!" I answered. "Most of what I 'thought' is bull; just preaching or explaining."

"That's what I hoped you'd see. Most of what you and all the other humans 'think' is vain inner talking; not a dialogue; a monologue. Within each person's mind is a stage where we are the star and everybody else is relegated to the passive role of listener, and I might add—impressed listener. Also, if you noticed, for the most part, you can't think on any one thing for more than a few seconds. Our intellect is like a radio that keeps changing stations. You might think about a subject for only a few seconds and the station changes and you're on to something else for a few more seconds. We are so used to it we don't notice, but it is a circus in there. In your mind, did talk to me and was I impressed by what you were saying?"

"Paul," I answered with a smile, "you were my main listener and you were so impressed that you decided to let me be your teacher."

He laughed a good hardy laugh. "That is how we all are, son. It is ridiculous but true. I would like you to consider that it is not thinking at all, but something called 'imagination.'"

"Imagination? I thought imagination was good?"

Paul pulled another roll from the pile. "It is, if you are thinking about creative imagination. But this kind of imagination is useless fantasy. You can call it fantasy if you'd like. Sometimes I do. But I want you to be able to establish in your intellect what is thinking, which would include creative imagination where something is created, and what is imagination or fantasy, which is worthless."

"So, most of what I thought the last few days was worthless?"

"What you discovered is priceless, because not many mortals know what you just found out about yourself. It is life's biggest secret."

"Oh, good."

"Also, it is imperative that you keep observing your thoughts. It is the basis for understanding yourself. After years of work at this you will develop another kind of vision, an insight into your Self."

He finished off his roll. "Before we go out I want to give you an assignment, and this is just not for today, it is forever. I want you to try to be present as much as you can.

"Present?"

"Yes, present. Another term I use is self-remembering. What I mean by this is I want you to feel your body, or have the sensation that you are where you are, every time you can. For instance, as you sit there, feel you buttocks touch the chair. Also, notice that as you do that you can feel the room and your whole body."

"Yeah, I see what you mean."

"When you do that, you are in the present, and while you are in the present you cannot be in imagination; the two do not fit in the same space."

"Yeah, I see what you mean. It's pretty weird."

"But now you are not here, are you?"

"How did you know? I forgot."

"I know because everybody forgets. That is why I want you to work on it every time you can think of it, and do it for as long as you can. It will usually last only a few seconds."

"If I make up my mind, I think I can do it all the time," I replied.

He let out a snort. "We'll see, young man. We'll see. Okay let's go to work." We got up and went outside. Arturo was nearby with two wheelbarrows and two shovels. Paul said something to him and then looked at me. "We've got thousands of rocks around here. I'd like you and Arturo to load your wheelbarrows and put them in the truck. He'll haul them away."

"Okay," I said as Arturo handed me some gloves.

"And be careful of bugs that bite. The snakes aren't out yet, but scorpions are and I don't know what all."

I pushed the barrel about ten yards and looked around. I said to Arturo something about there being a million stones out here. He nodded. He pulled his barrel right next to mine. We began at the same time our picking and pitching.

I noticed something right away. Arturo was kind of lazy. He would help me fill my wheelbarrow to the absolute maximum, then when we went to filling his in, he would wave me off as if he could do it by himself just fine thank-you. He indicated that I should take my load up to truck and he'd finish with his. I could hardly push mine it was so heavy. Then I got to the truck, I strained to get it up the ramp. I made finally it, but then here comes Arturo with his barrow only half full. I was pissed as he zoomed up the ramp and dumped his load. I didn't say anything.

He was being real friendly as we went back to our spot. But

the same thing happened. Arturo insisted that I go with a bulging load and then followed me with his way-too puny pile. This went on like this for an hour. I was beside myself with anger. I frowned at him, but he seemed not to know what the trouble was with me. Pretty soon I was feeling the effects of the work. I was not used to manual labor in the first place and this was hard manual labor. To make matters worse, I could see that even after seven or eight loads, we had hardly made a dent in the work.

Finally, the back of the truck was full. Arturo drove it away. Since it was some kind of dump truck he could handle that part by himself. I stumbled back into the house and plopped down. Paul came in from the back and brought a couple of soda pops from the Frigidaire. "You look tired."

"Man, I don't think I've done so much work in my life."

"Isn't it good that you only have to come here a couple of days a week?" he asked.

"Oh, yeah, you are truly a wise man, Paul. But there is one thing that bothers me."

"What is that?"

I took a big gulp of my soda. "Arturo is kind of lazy. I've been doing about three times the work. You should see what he is doing out there. It is pissing me off and he acts like he doesn't know what is going on. Man, I've been mad for hours."

Paul broke up laughing. It took him a few minutes to stop. I wondered what was so damn funny. I wasn't in on the joke, that's for sure. I was morose. Finally, he said, "I told him to do that. I wanted to see what you'd do and what I had to work with."

I didn't know what to do. It had been some kind of test and I must've failed, or at least done something incredibly funny. "I don't get it."

"How much were you in the present?" he asked.

"I don't think I did that even once. I forgot all about it because I was too mad."

"I thought you made up your mind you were going to do it all the time?"

"Yeah, I guess I forgot about it."

"Joe, I want to tell you that you passed the little test. If you had hit Arturo you would have had to leave. I wanted to show you a number of things. First, that it is practically impossible to remember to be in the present, especially at first. You need a lot of reminders in your environment. Second, I wanted to show you something about energy, but I'll talk about that later. Just remember how you felt during the last few hours. Lastly, I wanted you to see that your imagination took completely over. You probably did all kinds of dastardly things in your head to Arturo."

"Well, that's true. He was killed several times." I was laughing at this point. "Paul, you are good. I can't believe it."

"Arturo is one of the best workers I've ever seen. He works hard here six days a week, ten hours a day. So, I am the one to blame for all this." He pulled something out of his shirt, a small band of some sort. "Here, put this over your watch and when you need to check the time, the wrist band should remind you to try to self-remember. It is just a reminder, not a sacred article or anything. I don't want you putting any more significance on it than necessary. Before long you'll find different aids to help you remember yourself, so this will just be your first one."

"Thanks," I said, in awe of what I'd just been shown about myself.

After awhile Arturo came back. Paul told him what transpired. As he came into the house he was smiling and holding out his hand. I shook it and laughed. Everything was fine. We worked the rest of the day and he pulled more than his share. In fact, I could hardly move at the end. He rolled both wheelbarrows up the ramp because I couldn't do it. We had picked up about half of the rocks.

Paul fixed a delicious dinner of fried catfish and potatoes, and a dessert of ice cream and cookies. I was glad he wasn't one of those rice and fake-meat guys. After Arturo left, he poured me a glass of white wine and we sat in the living room.

"Well, what do you think so far?" he asked.

"Paul, I am not so sure I think. But I do like what you're doing. I am a lot smarter about myself."

"That is the goal. I want to show you that this universe, from top to bottom, from the largest galaxy to the smallest sub-atomic particle, is one big machine. All of it operates as a stimulus-response mechanism. This includes you and I. Every thought, every action that you take is due to some stimulus. I'll take my time teaching you this, but once you get it, you will see the world completely differently."

"Paul, I am willing to learn whatever you know. Oh, I wanted to ask you something. Do you remember to be in the present all the time?"

He thought for a minute. "Most of the time, but I want you to know that it never gets easy. I have to work at it moment to moment, just like I expect you to do. Never let up. Every time you can remember, self-remember, and for as long as you can."

"It's hard. I already know that. I think I only remembered to do it about ten times all day."

"You have to fight, fight, fight to keep it longer and longer. It alone will change you like I can never explain to you. But eventually you will know it as I do. When you remember yourself you actually live your life. When you don't, you just exist like any other machine—a toaster or automobile, always responding to whatever life throws at you."

He paused for a long time, looking at me. "Also, I want you to try to observe yourself as much as you can; your thoughts, your actions, everything. I want you to just try to see what you are really like, but do nothing about it; just observe. This work is all internal and only incidentally external. You and every other mortal have a psychology that is a mess of contradictions and out of control. That is why we are so mean to each other, always arguing and at war on every level. But all of the work that you will be doing toward this goal is on the inside, in the realm of your intellect and emotions. You must know what is inside, and as of now, you don't.

"How long will that take?" I asked.

"That depends on you, fellow, but not soon. It will take many years at least. Think of this Work as growing an oak tree. It can't sprout and mature in a short time. Many things have to happen, and many things have to happen to you before you grow into your potential."

Paul rose from the couch. "All right Joe, I want you to go home now. I don't want you to come tomorrow. I don't want to kill you.

But I want you to do several things during this next week."

"Okay, what?"

"First, I want you to do some exercise this week, so you are not so out of shape next time you show up; lifting or running; something. Then I want you to read as much Plato as you can. Read it carefully and we'll discuss it. Last, but most important, try to remember your self and observe everything that you think and do as much as possible. It is very important."

"Plato, exercise and be present; got it boss."

He smiled a deep, kind smile and led me to my van. As I pulled out, I felt exhausted but somehow satisfied to my core. What else could I want, I wondered? A shower.

Chapter 5

I BOUGHT A BOOK on Plato's dialogues and proceeded to read every chance I got. I also put little things around to remind me to remember to be present. I hung a red ribbon around my steering wheel in my van and a white one in cab #22. I found the whole effort most frustrating. I really had trouble remembering, and when I did, it would last between two and five seconds. Occasionally I could hold on to presence longer, but not often and not for more than ten or twenty seconds. And I was the one who thought it would be easy! One thing I did notice was that after I started my presence, what would interrupt it was telling Paul about it in my imagination. I could not stop that, no matter what I tried.

I thought it was amazing that I'd never read or heard anything about what I was going through. Some books would refer to it, but I could see now they didn't know anything about it or how hard it was to be in the Now.

One afternoon I received a call on my radio to go to the hospital and pick up a fare. When I pulled up in front, a beautiful girl in a nurse's outfit jumped into the back seat. She was short with medium length dark hair. I figured her to be about 30 or 35.

"Hi, where you going?"

She gave me a piece of paper with the address. "You know where that is?" she asked.

"Ma'am, I'm a professional. Sure I know where that is."

I saw her smile in the mirror. "I didn't know I was in such company; a professional. I'm flattered."

"You should be," I said, "I've been doing this here job for over a week now and I really know my way around. I've been to Ajo. I've been to Craycroft and Speedway. I've been practically everywhere on the Tucson map. So I hope you will show a little respect for me and my professional acumen."

She smiled again. "Oh I will, I will."

I couldn't think of anything else to say, so I said, "I can't think of anything else to say and I want for us to carry on a conversation. Can you think of anything to say?"

"Look, you are funny, but I'm tired and I just want to go home. Sorry."

I was quiet for a while. "You want to hear some soothing music?"

"Sure, that would be nice."

I started singing a lullaby. Her eyes were closed but I spied a little smile.

Unfortunately, we arrived at her apartment house. I took a chance as she was preparing to leave. "Say, miss nurse, would you like to have coffee with me sometime?"

I turned to see her get mad. "Listen, I don't go out with taxi cab drivers. It is one of my rules. I'm sorry."

"But, I've got an MBA from USC, so I'm not your regular run of the mill cabby."

"Sorry Mr. MBA." With that she jumped out of the cab and walked into the building.

It took me about one minute to realize that she forgot to pay me. I turned off the engine and went inside, but once inside I saw that there must have been a hundred apartments and my chances of finding miss nurse were nil. I was stiffed for $5.10. Well, it was my fault really. This just meant that some poor person will be out $2.55.

When I got back to the station that evening the supervisor gave me a number to call, said it was some dame who said she forgot to pay me. The note said Liz and the number. I called when I got home. "Hello."

"Hello, this is Mr. MBA. Is this Liz, the nurse?"

She quit chewing something. "Oh, I'm so sorry. I was so tired that I forgot to pay you. How much do I owe you?"

"Let's see, I believe the grand total was $5.10."

"If you give me your address, I'll send you a check."

"No, I want it now. There is a little coffee house right across the street from you. I would like you to meet me there at 7:30 and bring the money, all of it."

She paused. I heard her chuckle. "You think you are pretty smart don't you Mr. MBA?"

"Call me Joe Peters, and yes I think I am pretty smart—I have an MBA don't I?"

"All right, I'll meet you at 7:30. No funny stuff though buddy. I've heard about you smart cabbies."

After hanging up I did a little dance around the apartment.

I couldn't keep my imagination still. I was telling Liz all kinds of things about me. Once in a while I would look at my watch and there would be that cover over it and I'd remember to remember. That lasted a couple of seconds and then I'd be back gabbing at Liz. I was disturbed that I couldn't control my attention at all. Paul said that no one can do it without years of work. That's almost unbelievable. All those smart people teaching in colleges and running businesses and they all day-dream all of the time and can't stop it, and don't even know they're doing it.

I got to the coffee house a little early. I took Plato to get some reading done in case she was a bit late. She didn't show up. I was disappointed and not a little miffed. I had counted on telling her all the things I had been practicing. At eight o'clock I got up to leave and in she walks. "I'm so sorry," she said, " I got in a heated conversation with an ex-husband."

We sat down and we both ordered decaf coffee. "So, you've had the experience of being married," I said.

"Yes, and I learned a lot. If you want to have a social life don't marry a doctor, and if you want to have any kind of life, don't marry a surgeon."

"I'll write that down for future reference." Our coffee came.

"So, here we are just as I hoped. My name is Joe, Joe Peters, and I've just moved here from Los Angeles."

"Well, welcome to Tucson. My name is Liz Lizetti and I've lived here all my life."

We carried on a lively conversation with a lot of energy. I kept wondering if my life of celibacy was going to come a sudden stop. Nice place to stop, I thought. At nine o'clock Liz said she had to go home to bed. "Need some help?" I offered.

"No, thank you. I've been climbing into bed by myself for months. I have it down pat now. But it was a nice clever try, big boy."

We were both laughing. "Say, I was thinking that maybe we could go to dinner sometimes. What do you think?"

Liz thought about it. "Well, do you have another car besides that cab?"

"Oh, yeah, I have a spare for emergencies, and this feels like an emergency."

"Okay, call me tomorrow night and we'll talk about it. Can you spend a lot of money on me?"

"Sure, Liz, I make a lot of money."

Liz gave me my $5.10 and I paid for the coffee with it. I left exactly a $2.55 tip for the waitress. "Why such a big tip for a couple cups of coffee?" she asked.

"I'm a big tipper, ma'am, when I'm happy, and I'm most happy tonight." I walked her across the street. I pointed out my spare car and she was very impressed. I tried to kiss her, but was rebuffed soundly.

I stopped making notations about my thinking. It got too repetitious. I pretty much agreed that my world is by and large a fantasy world, or imaginary world. Sometimes I was still amazed at how little else I do in my head but lecture people. I'd read a bunch of psychology books in my life; how come none of them ever said anything about that? Could it be that the psychologists are living in a fantasy world too and can't see it either? I bet. Ha! What a joke.

They're supposed to be the experts at this kind of thing. They must be the experts at pretending and putting on acts. I did notice that my list of people I would lecture could change instantaneously. Once a lady riding in my cab gave me hell about going too fast. When she finally got out I gave her a piece of my mind for the next five minutes in my imagination. Then I forgot about her. I guess I showed her.

I called Liz and asked her to dinner the next night. She said yes, but that she was only joking about spending a lot of money on her. I just told her to wear a nice dress. I asked around for the best restaurant in town. I got many different answers, but the one that seemed to come in first was at a resort hotel in the foothills. I made reservations.

We had lobster and something on fire for dessert. It was a remarkable dinner; the view was spectacular, the food excellent, and Liz was entrancing. I figured I was falling in love. "You know Liz," I said after dessert, "I think I'm going to be falling in love with you. I just thought I'd warn you that my intentions are noble, but sometimes my mind will be on your delicious body."

She laughed. "Well, Joe, before you go falling for me, maybe you had better call my two ex-husbands and interview them on the subject."

"That's a good idea, but I don't want you to interview my two ex-wives. They have a rather skewed view of my qualifications as a mate. They are mistaken of course, but just in case they are not, I rather you not talk to them."

"Some of the staff at the hospital are getting together for a cookout in the mountains this Saturday. Would you like to come?"

"I can't. Usually my weekends are taken up helping an old fellow do some landscaping out in the desert."

"Every weekend?"

"At least most. I have guaranteed him my labor for the next year. I hope that is not a problem. It is the most important thing in my life to go out there."

"Why," she asked intently.

"The man is a teacher and he is teaching me philosophy in

exchange for my labor. He is really an amazing guy."

"So, you're going to fall in love with me part-time? Every weekend I will be alone?"

"I don't have any choice. I made this commitment to him, and to myself, before I met you. It's for only a year."

She got up in a huff. "Well, maybe you should call me in a year." She walked toward the exit.

As we were walking down the stairs toward the van, I said, "So you have a nice temper, huh?"

"Yes, it is one of my most endearing qualities. If you talk to my ex-husbands they will confirm this fact for you."

"I like that in you."

"Oh shut up," she said, but she had a little smile.

I had her! "There is a new Woody Allen movie in town. Would you like to see it with me Monday evening?"

She walked in silence to the van. When we were driving out of the driveway, she said, "You are lucky I like Woody Allen. If it was anybody else I'd say no, but because it's Woody Allen I'll say yes."

"It has nothing to do with liking me?"

"Nothing!"

"Thank God for Woody Allen," I said. We both had slight smiles. When we arrived she was ready to be kissed, but only at the door to the apartment building. Her mouth parted as our lips made contact. As I walked away I said out loud to myself, "I made it to first base."

My life was full now. Being a cabby meant that I had plenty of spare time in the cab to read Plato, and I started exercising down in the apartment gym after work. Mostly, Monday though Friday was spent anticipating the weekend. I had a lot of questions to ask Paul. He and Plato had me on fire. I tried as hard as I could, but I couldn't stop talking to Paul in my imagination. Once in a while I'd take a break and talk to Liz, or Barbara, or Bert, in my dream world. I had a lot of sex with Liz, but again only in my head.

The next Saturday I was up at five and off to be with Paul

and Arturo. Even though it was still pretty dark, they were already outside looking at a pile of lumber that was stacked by the house. I waved as I drove up. "Good to see you, Joe," hailed Paul as I walked up to the pair, "Boy, we've got our work cut out today," as he motioned to the stacked boards. There must have been two or three hundred six by six square posts. I knew that we were going to build a fence this weekend.

"Looks like fun," I answered. I surveyed the mountain of wood and whistled. "Yeah, it looks like we'll be playing in the woodpile."

We went inside the house and sat for coffee and a coffee cake. "Well, how was your week out in life?" Paul asked.

"It was pretty nice. It took me about three days to get over being sore from last Saturday's rock job, but now I feel great. I also think I found a girlfriend."

Paul laughed. "That ought to provide a little friction for you. We can't do without a little trouble in our lives."

"I hope this woman is less trouble that the last two. They gave me maximum friction."

"You should know that the kind of woman you are attracted to is naturally going to rub you the wrong way," Paul countered.

"What do you mean?" I asked, "You mean I'm sunk before I even begin?"

"You are a very positive type, Joe, and the only females who really interest you are more contrary ones. They will disagree and push your buttons at every turn, and it will fill you with thoughts of having sex with them. Isn't that right?"

"How did you know? I keep thinking that I'll get one who will just want to please me and be placid and we can go through life without any waves, but I guess you are right. I never give that kind of lady a second thought. I guess I like steam in my life more than a quiet pool."

"There are two types of people on the planet, positive and contrary; about one half of each. This is not an absolute, but a continuum. Along this line at one end are very positive types and the other end are very contrary types. In between they are more or less contrary or positive. In life people usually notice them and call them nice people or disagreeable people.

The positive type is ever agreeable and hates conflict. The contrary type is interested in quality and will fight for it. They can't help it. It is mechanical behavior. Their favorite word is no. The positive type's word is yes. Contrary types have a job in the human scheme of things and they do it without realizing it, just like the positive types. I am not talking about being negative. You must understand that. There are contrary men and contrary women, but they are in no way more negative than the positive ones. In mating the two attract each other because they need to be whole. Two positive types, like you and I, will get along fine and can be great friends. If we brought in a contrary type, we'd have some problems, but it might be more fun."

"Hey, that sounds right. I can think of my friends and ex-wives and most of them fit one of those categories. That is remarkable."

"Once you begin to see it in people, you will never not be able to see it, and you will wonder why no one else does."

"Why don't they?"

"They are asleep, my boy. Not asleep like with the eyes closed, but in an hypnotic trance."

" I'm amazed," I said, "that if what you have started telling me is true, this world is nothing like I thought."

"No, it isn't and I expect you will continually be astonished as we talk further. The world, as we know it, is based almost entirely on imagination. It is full of illusion from top to bottom."

Paul poured us some more coffee. "I let you work with us precisely because you are a positive type. At this stage in my life I don't need anybody disagreeing with my every decision. I don't have that much energy."

"Well, yes, Liz is sure a contrary type. But now she makes me laugh when she's so contrary."

"That will change, Joe, don't worry. Sex energy makes everything bearable for awhile."

I knew he was right. I couldn't think of a girlfriend or wife I'd had who was not like that. I thought it was just women. I guess not. I changed the subject. "Paul, I read a lot of Plato the last few days, except for 'The Republic,' which is pretty thick, and I've got some questions."

"Shoot."

"Okay, I really liked the one where he dies, what's it called?"

"Phaedo," he said.

"Yeah, that's the one. It was a very emotional experience for me, but I read some place that Plato gave Socrates a smoother death than he really had because the poison he took is supposed to make a person writhe in pain. Socrates just died peacefully."

"Of course, Plato may have done that, but I don't think so. You must understand that for a true philosopher, life is all about preparing for death. Death is the final chance to show your mettle. To show fear or writhe in pain, no matter how much pain, is not consistent with what I know of the subject. Socrates was preparing to meet his maker in the best fashion and as bravely as he could. Can you grasp that, Joe?"

"Maybe. You mean that a philosopher spends his life thinking about death?"

"Yes, but it does not mean that a philosopher lives in fear. He lives his life to the fullest with an eye to his eventual demise. He also must court virtue and become conscious as part of the equation. When I say philosopher, I don't mean those people who walk around with Ph.D. behind their names. I mean a person who lives the life of a philosopher and seeks virtue and to escape from sleep; like Socrates."

I started thinking about that. I liked what he said because it made sense; a sense I wasn't used to hearing. Then he broke my reverie by indicating that the time for work had arrived. As we got up from the table, I could see out of the window the daunting mound of lumber that awaited us.

The job, as Paul explained it, was to build a three-foot wood fence around the entire property, which was 2 1/2 acres. The day before Arturo and Paul had staked it all out with string and red ribbons where the posts were to go. Each post was to be ten feet apart. There were going to be about 150 posts, which meant digging the holes with an electric auger and filling in around the posts with cement and dirt. It was quite a big job. I wished Paul had taken on about ten more students for this task. As soon as I thought that, I changed my mind. We can do this job by ourselves.

The three of us loaded the back of one of the trucks with posts, then as Paul drove around the property, Arturo and myself threw a post out at every ribbon. When we came back for another load, I asked Paul, as we filled the truck up again, "Can a contrary type ever change? I mean if they have everything go their way?"

"You don't understand, Joe. Positive and contrary types are born that way for a purpose, to keep things going. Without contrary types we would be in a fix because the world would have virtually no quality control and no tension, which is absolutely necessary. That's their job in the world, keeping us positive types in line. It would be a dull place without them. So no, they can't change any more than a positive type can change. You are always going to be agreeable, at least in most circumstances." He got ready to get back into the truck for another ride around the string. "Joe, this is a big subject. Start observing people in life next week from this perspective and you'll be able to answer some of your own questions. "Oh," he said, "the best way to see them is after a statement is made. A positive type will be in agreement and the contrary type won't, or will modify the statement in some way. There is much more to it, but I want you to discover all of the nuances by observation. One thing though, if two positive types marry, their marriage will be nice and friendly, but will lack fire. If two contrary types marry, their union will be nothing but fire and discord. They are not likely to have much peace. Although, I might say, some contrary people like it like that." He closed the door and we walked along side the vehicle until it got to where we left off.

It took almost two hours to set out all the posts. Now all we had to do was put them in the ground. Fortunately for my back we took a break before we started. Arturo put cokes, coffee and apples out on a table in the back patio. Paul sat down but didn't look tired, at least not as tired as I already felt. "Ready for another question?" I asked him.

"You don't even have to ask; just ask the question."

"You said that the world, no the universe, was a huge machine responding to stimuli. You said that even humans are part of this machine, or at least cogs in the machine. So, my question to you is: how can this be? Don't we have free-will?"

He chuckled. "Joe, do you remember when you said you were going to remember to be present?'

"Yes, I remember."

"What happened?"

"I couldn't do it, not even once," I laughed.

"That is how all things are in life. We have this illusion that if we just set our minds to something we can do it, but what happens is that we respond to our environment and that is completely out of our control. We are really helpless. Have you been able to stop your imagination yet?"

"No, not even close. Without the cover for my watch and a few other things I've tried I wouldn't have done it at all."

"It may be that after a person works on themselves for a very long time they can develop something like will power over themselves, but not over anything else. You may be able to remember yourself more and that takes a certain internal will, or you may be able to avoid getting mad when you ordinarily would've, and that takes will. But anything outside of one is always out of our control."

"Your job, if you are committed to this work, is to turn inward and develop that part. Life promotes the outside and sees it as the solution to its problems, building ever more elaborate machines and devices, accumulating more and more money and objects as the answer. Instead, the opposite happens: nothing gets solved and everything becomes worse."

"The idea of humans having will power or free-will is nonsense. Sometimes I think I can hear the Gods laughing as we humans struggle to explain how what we set out to do didn't happen, but the opposite did." He was smiling.

"Do you really hear Gods," I asked him seriously.

"No, I was joking. Please don't go into imagination about that sort of thing. I want to keep you down here with me."

Soon enough the break was over. Too bad, I thought, I was really getting warmed up to that subject.

As Paul drove the truck again, we would take this heavy, gas driven auger, and drill a hole two feet deep. Then we put it back in the bed of the truck and rode ten feet to our next destination. It was brutal work, but Arturo didn't seem to mind. He was a hard working machine. I smiled when I remembered how I thought he was lazy. He would constantly do more than his share of the lifting. I liked him.

The afternoon was a blur, but a slow blur; get out of the truck, drill the hole, get back in the truck, take a little ride, get out of the truck. I was trying to remember myself as much as I could, but I still could only do it for a few seconds. Every time I remembered to feel my body, I'd make up my mind to do it forever. Then I'd wake-up a half an hour later and realize I'd only done it for a few seconds. Very frustrating.

At the end of the day I was dragging, but when I looked around I saw what we had accomplished I was strangely satisfied. It wasn't pretty; just holes in the ground, but it was beautiful because I was part of it. As long as I lived I knew I was going to remember what it felt like to be happy like this. What is happening to me? I wondered. This doesn't fit with any script of my life I ever dreamed up, digging holes toward happiness?

Arturo cooked some enchiladas, piled high with greens and sour cream. Paul ate two. Arturo ate four. I ate six and would have had another one, but they were all gone. Food tastes a lot better when you've just worked your butt off. I refused the beer because I knew I'd fall right to sleep. I wanted to quiz Paul some more.

We took turns with the shower. When we were finished Paul and I sat at the table again for ice cream.

He started. "You know what I find especially appealing about the Socrates death scene—that his last words were something to the effect of arranging to have a debt paid. That was very moving for me. I understood that he was closing out his earthy affairs as best he could, leaving nothing to chance. He was going to his reward and wanted to go as clean as possible."

"You believe in heaven?" I asked.

"Joe, I have verified heaven. That is a lot different than believing in heaven. It is in here," he said, pointing to his chest, "not on the outside."

"How have you verified it?"

He got up from his chair and went to the couch and sprawled his long frame across it. I followed him and plopped in a big chair covered with an Indian blanket. Arturo, unbelievably, began to do the dishes. "That is one of those questions I can't answer, Joe, because you wouldn't understand. But if you will work hard at being in the present, in time I won't need to explain it; you'll know."

"I don't exactly understand why I'm trying to self-remember?"

Paul had a smile. "Okay, here it is: your real money in the world is attention. With attention you can get most things of real value. This is why they say, 'pay attention.' If you want something, pay attention. You can't see attention, can't measure it, but attention is the most important psychological food. People crave and need this food just to live. If you deprive a child of attention, he will wilt and die. Everyone in life needs it and courts it in a thousand different ways. It is the prime motivation in life. Next to it, paper money is worthless.

So, if you can understand that, maybe you can begin to fathom that the soul, a tiny nugget at birth, requires attention to develop too. Most people's souls are never developed because they do not understand the necessity of giving it attention. They do not even know about it. When you try to be in the present, you are giving some of your attention to life and the rest to your soul. If you give it enough, your soul will develop or wake-up and you can become enlightened or conscious, as they say. Understand?"

"A little I guess. I'll have to think about it. It doesn't seem fair or just that most people don't even know what they have to do to develop their souls."

"It may not seem fair, but it is. The signposts are everywhere, but it is too much work and the most people reject doing the kind of inner work necessary. All of the sacred texts, especially the Bible, are full of instructions as to inner development. In fact, the Gospels are the best psychological manuals on inner life, not history about events. You know how hard it is to work internally just from the little you've done so far, and you have not even scratched the proverbial surface. Life is fair. What would be unfair is to make people develop their souls who do not value their possibilities. That would be unjust."

While I was thinking about that, Paul fell asleep. Arturo and I helped him into his bedroom and onto the bed. He was exhausted. I went to my van and dozed off behind the wheel before I could even start the engine. I awoke when Arturo started his truck.

When I got home I spent some time writing in my journal about the ideas and events of the day. As I lay in my bed trying to sleep, I started thinking about the strange and wonderful world I had stumbled onto. My last thought was to whoever was listening: Thank you.

The next morning I woke before dawn when Arturo's truck rumbled to a stop in the carport. My body said No! Fortunately, I am more than my body. The other parts made me jump-up with a true jest. The two of us silently made coffee and Arturo laid out some Mexican pastries he had brought. Paul was making noises in the bathroom. When he finally emerged, he looked tired. I realized that he was an old man. I had forgotten that fact the last few weeks. He was so vital, not energetic or physical like Arturo, but he possessed an inner strength of purpose that I was just beginning to see.

His first word was, "coffee" as he held out his cup.

I poured. He took a roll and broke it apart. He brightened up after a few sips of java. "Today should be easy compared to yesterday. We need to treat the bottom two feet of each post so they won't get eaten up by termites."

"Treat?" I asked.

"Yes, it is some compound we will paint on. Then if we have any time we'll start the job of putting a base on the upper part of the posts so we can eventually paint them white. The next few days I will be in San Diego taking care of some left over business from my wife's death. Arturo can finish with preparing the posts to go into the ground then."

Arturo was already in the back getting the supplies ready. The guy was a fanatic. Paul decided we should work in teams. Arturo was one team and Paul and I were the other. Arturo took his can and paint brush and started on the west side of the driveway and worked around from there. We started on the east side. It was really simple. Paul held the post up while I slapped the liquid on the bottom two feet of the five-foot post. He then placed it in the hole to dry.

As we were working on the third post, I asked him about his wife. "She was the most remarkable woman I'd ever met and I knew it right away. Libby proved to be invaluable to me in so many ways. We were married 49 years."

"Did you consider her your soul mate?"

"I don't know what that is; some New Age designation that is supposed to mean something. I do know that I loved her to a depth unimaginable."

"Was she a contrary type?" I asked.

He laughed. "Of course, and I wouldn't have it any other way. We positive types need them. She kept me straight in areas that I didn't know anything about. She is the one who made the money for us while I was investigating my soul. She understood, and I can't tell you how important that is. Libby made enough money that I have plenty now for projects like this."

I thought it was a good time to ask a question I'd been thinking about since I first came out here. "Paul, why are you doing this? Why are you building a big ring of roses?"

"I've had an affinity for roses since I was a little boy. I thought that I wanted some day to be surrounded by them, and now I have my chance before I die. Also, Libby wanted it for me. So, it is a gift—for both of us." He wiped a tear away.

By lunch we had finished about three quarters of the work. As I expected, Arturo was way ahead of "B" team. After we ate, we stretched out the work to fit the day. At one point, I asked Paul about meditation. "Self-remembering is meditation and vice-versa.

It is all being in the present and that is the main thing. They are both hard to truly master. The way I am teaching you is difficult because there are a million distractions to overcome, but if you make every effort, you will develop muscles that can resist it and then meditate, or be mindful all day. Meditation, as it is taught in real schools, is useful only if you can do it long enough to penetrate to the soul. But it, too, is harder than most people realize. The Buddha, in order to become conscious, spent a long time concentrating under that tree before enlightenment came. It is a major, major sacrifice to attempt to be in the present no matter what method you use. It is just that I think for Americans; Westerners, it is more possible with self-remembering because we are an active culture and taking the necessary time to sit in one place for many hours a day is impractical."

"So they both can get you to the same place, but with self-remembering you can carry on a normal life with a family and job," I said.

"Yes, I think that's right. Mostly now in America, meditation is a pop-cultural thing for relaxation, which is fine, but not the real thing."

Before I left he gave me my reading assignments for the week. "I would like you to first read 'The Allegory of The Cave.' It is in 'The Republic,' book seven. It is important that you read about Plato's concept of our illusionary world. Then I would like you to read as much Shakespeare as you can. He was the world's premium genius and he was wise beyond anything or anyone in literature. Also, it usually helps if you read something about the plays before reading them. There is a book called 'The Meaning of Shakespeare' by Harold Goddard that is the best. Any questions?"

"No sir. I have enjoyed this weekend more than I can say, Paul. Thank you."

"And thank you, Joe. I'll look forward to seeing you again next week."

The three of us had big hugs and I left with a huge grin on my face. Man, I thought, no one from my old life would believe that I am working my butt off and loving every minute of it.

As I drove home I thought of all the people in my life and how they seemed to fall into that contrary or positive category. When I stopped to get gas and cokes, I made benign statements to three people in the store about the weather being hot. Sure enough, two agreed with me, and the third, a man of about 50, disagreed completely and told me how hot it is in Yuma. Contrary type.

Chapter 6

I was still pretty high from the weekend when I picked Liz up for dinner Monday. I told her as much as I could about Paul and what we were doing and why. "Do you think he'd let me come out and work on the weekends?" she asked.

I was surprised. "Liz, we work our butts off, at least ten hours a day in the dirt. Paul and I chat a little bit, but mostly it is just hard work."

She was indignant. "You think I can't do hard work? I can outwork you any day of the week. Plus, I pruned and took care of our roses when I lived at home. Nobody would touch them but me. I happen to love gardening and I especially love roses. So, there Mr. Work in the Dirt All Day."

"I'm impressed with your credentials, but it is more than that. He is a philosopher, a real philosopher. He takes on one student, and only one student a year and teaches them ideas. This year I'm that student. He does not take on two students," I said with finality.

She liked to argue and was not going to give up. "Look, I don't care about his philosophy. I just thought I'd like to spend more time with you and work on roses, which I love. Now what is the big deal if you ask. All he can say is no."

"Let me think about, okay?"

"Okay," she said. I loved her flashing gray-green eyes. During dinner I asked her about her family. She got serious and told me about losing her father in Viet Nam. He was a Marine officer and died early in the war. Liz described her life of longing for him when she was small and how she would work in the garden and imagine that one day he would show up and be proud of her roses.

Then it was my turn. I told her my story of Viet Nam and

how someone else had stepped on the bomb that should have been mine. I also told her the part which included me killing an innocent boy. I think I never told anyone in such detail how I felt during those months afterward. I was surprised when she took my hands in hers when I finished and softly cried. I don't know whether it was for her or me. I guess it didn't matter. Tears welled up in me too and I didn't know who they were for either. "Take me home," she said.

Liz was quiet during the short drive. I walked her to her door and she opened it and went in. I guess I was supposed to follow her although she didn't invite me. "Which way to the bathroom?" She indicated the direction without saying anything. When I came out Liz was sitting of the couch. Her white silk blouse was unbuttoned to her navel. I guess it was to spare the buttons. I was very careful with the rest of her clothes too.

I drove out to Paul's on Wednesday to see if it would be okay to bring a date. He had just arrived back from California. I asked him and told him why she wanted to do it.

He laughed a good hearty laugh. "So, you want a fly in the ointment do you?"

"I don't think she will be any trouble. I think we can put her off in a corner and forget her. She is like that; very quiet."

Paul really let out a laugh this time. He was in a good mood I guess. "Well, Joe, with your strong recommendation I'll allow it. But I don't expect her to be very quiet. You wouldn't pick a woman like that, but I've been around all kinds and enjoyed them all. Maybe she knows something about roses."

When I returned home I called Liz and told her. "I told him you were as quiet as a church mouse," I warned.

"Oh, don't worry about me, Mr. Peters, I'll do just fine. I won't embarrass you a bit."

All week I did my assigned reading with relish. First I read the Plato section in The Republic called "The Allegory of the Cave." Plato was saying that all of life is a big illusion, and anyone who tries to wake people up to this fact is not treated kindly. I thought about Socrates and Jesus. Then I thought about Paul. I wondered if he was in some danger. Maybe that is why he only teaches one person at a time.

Harold Goddard really made me appreciate Shakespeare. I couldn't stop reading his essays on the plays. He seemed to grasp the concepts like a true philosopher . I finished his work when Friday evening came. I thought I'd start on the plays on Monday. I must have read 12 hours a day. Cab drivers who don't care about fares can do that.

Liz and I spent a tender evening exchanging our life stories. When I told her about contrary types and told her she was one of those, she disagreed—and laughed out loud. "People have been telling me since I was a tot that I never agree with anything. I've got to meet this man who knows so much about me before he's even seen me." I slept until 5:00. Liz was already up and making coffee. As I watched her bustle about the apartment I thought she looked like an angel—a sexy one.

When we arrived I noticed bags of cement around the property. Planting day, I thought. We are planting wood. Paul came out to greet us. I introduced him to Liz. They shook hands and smiled warmly. Once we got settled with our coffee, he said, "The job today is putting in the posts. They've got to have about 12 to 18 inches of cement and the rest in dirt. We have to be careful to keep them lined up and at the same height. It will take about a day for them to set, and once they are set they had better be right or we'll have to do them over. But I don't think that will be a problem because Arturo has done this a few times before. Paul said something to Arturo and he nodded. Then Liz spoke to Arturo in Spanish. I was surprised to say the least.

"I didn't know you spoke Spanish," I told her.

"That was my major in college," she answered. "We've only been going together for a few weeks. You can't know everything yet. It might take a few years, if you stick around."

"I think he will," Paul answered for me. As we got up to go he and Liz walked out the back door. Arturo and I went out the front toward the cement and holes. We started mixing the cement in the wheelbarrow and pouring it into the first hole around the post. Arturo was very careful. We did some adjusting before it was just right. On top of that came the dirt. Arturo showed me how to pack it down.

After we had done a few of these, I looked around to see what had become of Liz. She and Paul were walking around the back of the property looking at the line of holes. They were in animated conversation. For some reason it bothered me a little. Stop it, I said to myself. Then I remember to try to be present.

I was glad I had Arturo as a partner in the cement job. I would have made a mess of it, but I would've been faster. It was taking us way too long, I thought, to do these. In truth, I had my mind on other things. I wanted to finish and get over to where Paul and Liz were and find out what was going on. I was jealous and I recognized it. I hate jealousy, especially in me, but there I was fretting that Paul was taking Liz from me. That's stupid, I told myself, Paul is 75 years old at least. What would she want with him? Then I answered my own question: He's charming. We kept working and I kept looking at my thoughts. They were not my best, but I couldn't stop them except for the few seconds I could self-remember.

We took a break about ten. I don't think they did a lick of work all morning; just talked and laughed. As Paul was coming out of the bathroom, I said to him out of Liz's hearing. "So, what do you think, boss? It was probably a mistake to bring her here, wasn't it? She just holds up the work."

He looked at me very seriously and said, "Joe, you are a very lucky man. Liz is so remarkable and she is so like my Libby; the way she looks; the way she talks and thinks. Yes, Joe, you are definitely fortunate."

"Thanks, Paul. I knew you'd like her." My insides were grinding. He is going to try to take her from me.

Then he said, "You fellows proceed with the work, Liz and I are going into town to look at some nurseries."

I was steamed. I could barely contain myself as they drove off in his truck. Arturo seemed to know what I was thinking and waved his figure at me and shook his head, as if to say, "Boy, this is another test."

Well, maybe it was, but that didn't help. I was hurting inside thinking of them entwined in a passionate embrace in some bushes at a nursery. Stupid, stupid, stupid, I kept saying to myself, but to no avail. I was jealous. I wish I'd never seen her. Here I was happy coming out here and then she has to come along and destroy everything. Even as I was thinking these things, I knew that I was being a child.

At lunchtime they still hadn't come back. I ate a sandwich in silence, but in my mind I was going off into angry tirades at Paul and Liz. Where did they go, Las Vegas? I went back to pouring cement and brewing trouble in my imagination. Finally, they drove up with a load of rose bushes. I went over and pretended interest in the roses. When Liz and I were alone, I said, "Well, what do you think of the old coot?"

She started laughing. "Paul said you were jealous, but I didn't believe it. Listen, Joe," she said seriously, " and listen good. I think Paul is wonderful. He is so like my father, or at least how I wanted my father to be. But you don't have to worry, I'm with you, and I'll stay with you. However, I do want you to grow up."

Paul was looking on while this was going on. "See what I mean by a fly in the ointment, Joe?" All of them were laughing, even Arturo. It was almost more than I could take, but I took it and smiled weakly. Another test, I thought, and I flunked this one too.

After we unloaded the roses, Liz played with them the rest of the day. The three of us men worked on the posts and cement. It was an exhausting day. Around 5:30 we stopped, having completed about eighty per cent of the work. My arms felt like cement and my shoes were covered with it. During the afternoon I kept thinking that, sure I wanted to "know myself," but not this stuff. This was too awful. I was truly a big baby and Paul had pointed it out so succinctly. I wondered what was next? I hated myself for that "old coot" remark.

Liz and Arturo prepared a dinner of thick steaks and baked potatoes. Afterward, Arturo left to go take care of his kids. His wife was eight months pregnant with her seventh child. Paul built a fire in the fireplace. At first I started resenting that he made a fire for Liz, but not when it is just us boys, but then I stopped myself short. "Idiot!" I screamed in my head. I decided to fight those thoughts with all my might.

Paul took the big chair and Liz and I sat on the couch. Paul started. "Joe, can you describe what happened to you today?"

"I'm embarrassed by it."

"Go ahead. You are here to learn about yourself, and I can't help you unless I know exactly what happened, or what your thoughts were. Incidentally, sometimes I call them 'I' s rather than thoughts."

"Okay," I said, "I don't know what happened to me, but I started thinking that you and Liz were going to run off somewhere. I felt terrible most of the day, but worse after I realized what a dope I was."

"You see the power of greed now, don't you."

"Greed? That's greed?"

"Emotional greed," he explained. "Greed is that feature in humans that wants to keep what it has at all costs. To your emotional mind, Liz is a possession, and I was a threat to that. Emotional greed of this sort leads to all sorts dastardly deeds; murder and mayhem, when someone tries especially hard to protect what he perceives as his emotional property."

"I thought greed was wanting to acquire money and wealth," inquired Liz.

"I think of that as avarice. Greed is wanting to horde. It is an emotion. Avarice is like an emotion, but not the same. Also, you can say that it is jealousy, which probably is man's most uncontrollable emotion. Many a murder have been done in its name and many, many more have been contemplated and carried out in imagination."

Liz looked at me. "Joe, I don't like you thinking I'm your property. I'm my own property."

"Stop Liz," directed Paul. He looked right at her with a wilting stare. "Joe and I are working this out. You have plenty of problems yourself that if you stick around long enough we'll discover. Now, I want to tell you that what breaks up more marriages and relationships than any other thing is meanness. The parties begin to get in the habit of hurting each other with their little comments. Each little hurting remark is a wedge that causes suffering and eventually the death of the relationship. What you said was mean and the way you said it was mean. That is probably what made your other husbands dislike you. I don't want to hear either of you being mean around me again. Is that understood?"

Liz was taken back. I was too. "I'm sorry Paul. I'm sorry Joe."

"Good," he said. "When a relationship begins, the people are overwhelmed with sexual energy and that makes everything seem just dandy, but soon enough that wears off and then the two get a good look at each other. I would prefer that when that extreme sexual energy abates for you two, you can look at each other with kindness, not resentment."

"I agree, " said Liz. "I guess you are right about my other relationships. I was pretty rough on them. I thought they had it coming."

"Nobody has it coming, Liz, even the worst of the worst. That's God's job. God balances all books. Besides," he continued, " negativity is what drives life the way it is and the only way it can be."

"I don't agree, " said Liz in a flash. "If people can just learn to cooperate and get along we would have a wonderful world. It is thinking like yours that keep people from even trying."

I felt a pang of embarrassment. She wasn't supposed to contradict our teacher. He only smiled.

"That would be true if the design were not just the opposite. People are designed to love their negativity, their hate, their pettiness and their worrying and fretting. We will always have wars and murders and the like because everyone is like that on an individual level inside. The more you look inside yourself Liz, the more you will see how true it is. Then your job will be to go against the grain of humanity and not be negative, even in the privacy of your thoughts. Negativity is violence and no one gets through the pearly gates with even a shred of violence in them."

"That is going to be hard. I have a bad temper." She paused, then said, "But the way you put it; 'God's job' will help me."

"Well, great. Now let's talk about something else. Joe, did you read any Shakespeare last week?"

"I read both of Goddard's books and I'll start the plays next week. But I did have one question about Shakespeare. I've read that many don't think he wrote the plays; that someone else did. What do you think?"

"When I was younger and cared about such things, I did research the question. I finally determined to my own satisfaction, from reading the sonnets, that the man who wrote the Shakespeare works was the Earl of Oxford, Edward de Vere. I may be in error but it doesn't really matter. Whoever it was had to be the most brilliant man in history. His grasp of the human condition was absolute. Much of my training came from studying his works."

Liz said, "But it doesn't make sense that he would give the credit to someone else."

"If you read and begin to understand his work," Paul went on, "you will see that whoever it was is both the greatest genius who ever lived, and a most humble man. He didn't need credit; he was a giant among men. Giants don't require acknowledgement from mere mortals."

"Goddard agrees with you about him being a genius," I added.

Paul was getting tired. He slumped in his chair. I thought I would get him to answer one more question before he went to sleep. "Paul, you spoke about the emotions. Is there a way to understand them?'

He perked up. "It probably will take you the rest of your life to fully grasp their significance and how exactly they work. There is an emotional brain, or center, that the emotions come from. It is divided into three general parts: intellectual, emotional, and mechanical. The mechanical part is the memory bank of the emotions and that is where we express emotions like gossip and other information about people. The emotional part is where we have those big emotions like you were having today. Violence and any extreme emotion come from there. A strong emotion to the positive side will always result in its opposite. What is called 'falling in love' is located here and if the expression of emotion is not controlled it will produce its opposite, anger and/or suffering of some sort. That is why there is so much anguish during normal courtship like what you experienced today. The emotional part of the Emotional Center packs a wallop both ways.

The higher part, the intellectual part, is where we can really learn to love; true love. First we have to wade past those initial battles in the emotional part. That usually takes years. Some older couples have reached that plateau of love. Appreciation, compassion, and gratitude are words that best describe it. People all have Emotional Centers and it is what makes us human. Most of the noble and ignoble things that man does come courtesy of the emotions. All of the parts of the Emotional Center are necessary. After many years of study, you may be able to distinguish and appreciate them for what they do.

Also, the Emotional Center is located in the middle of the chest and that is why people will touch their chest when they feeling emotional. They refer to the heart when they are talking emotionally because it is in that area of the body. Humans are the only animals who can put their chests together. We bring our Emotional Centers together when we hug or make love to another human."

"Wait a minute, Paul," said Liz. "Are you saying that emotions are good, or are they bad like most men think?"

"Neither, they are what is and we are chock full of them, even those men who say they don't trust them and so on. They are boiling over with them. They just explain them away as something else or excuse them or deny that they have them. It is all nonsense though. The higher game that we must play, or at least for those who would live to a deeper level, is to court and develop the higher intellectual emotions and control the lower ones, or at least know when they manifest. But like everything else worth having, it is a long and tedious task. But that is what we're here on earth to do, study and work on ourselves."

He got up and stretched. "I know it is only 7:30, but I'm ready for bed. I bid you young folks adieu." With that he turned and left our company. I looked at Liz and smiled. I offered my hand and we went out to our van bedroom.

When we were settled I said, "Liz, I'm sorry I was such a jerk today."

She put her hand on my face. " And I'm sorry for being mean. Paul is quite a guy isn't he?"

"What did you talk about today while you were out?"

She sat back straight against the back of our little bed. "A lot of things. He told me that he thought he was supposed to accomplish something in this life, but he is not sure what. He came out here in the desert to let happen what is supposed to happen."

"Seems like he is hiding," I said, "not waiting."

"Maybe he is doing both. I don't think he feels he can really hide behind a rose bush, but at least whatever his fate is, it will have to make itself pretty clear out in this forsaken desert.

He talked about evil for a few minutes and how it always offers itself in the guise of something good or pleasurable, and then it snaps the trap shut and you're stuck. Then he talked about roses and beauty. And then he asked me many questions. I was very impressed with Paul and how I feel around him."

"Yes, I know. I think I, no we, are lucky to have found him."

We made love, and it was especially sweet. Somehow Paul was making me see myself in a different light, a more pleasant light. I held Liz all night.

The next morning Liz asked Paul if she could be his student and he agreed to instruct her as he was doing with me. I think he was hoping she would ask. He told her about self-remembering and asked her to start watching her thoughts, or I's, and keep a log of who she talked to in her imagination or fantasy world. They had taken a walk after breakfast around the property and when they returned she told me about their conversation. I was delighted. Now I had someone else to talk to about the ideas I was learning.

When we talked later, she said Paul told her that our real goal on earth is to become a fully developed Man. That is Man without regard to gender. In the higher realms, there is no gender. He further said that human beings, or mankind, are a designation for a lower thing—an animal with the seed of a soul. Our job is to develop the soul and become a higher being—a Man in the fullest sense of the word. And then he added, "An angel."

Liz began digging around the house and putting in mulch in preparation for planting the rose bushes. I noticed that they were all yellow. Meanwhile, the rest of us continued planting the posts. About eight o'clock, a truck arrived and unloaded a couple hundred each of 2X4's and 1X6's. I knew we'd be doing a lot of hammering and painting yet before we even got to the roses. We finished before lunch with the posts. I offered to help Liz with her task, but she refused. "No, this is fun for me. You go off and find somebody else to play with."

At lunch I started telling Paul and Liz about the worst day of my life. This was the time a few months before when my wife and boss both released me from my obligations. "You say that was the worst day of your life?" asked Paul.

"Yeah, not including Viet Nam."

"Now that you have had more distance between then and now, would you still say it was the worst day of your life?"

"Well, now that you mention it, Paul, it may have been the best day of my life. Without it I wouldn't be here. I wouldn't have met Liz, either."

"Exactly," commented Paul. "We never know what is really good or bad because we only have one perspective at the time, but as situations change, former events take on a new meaning. So, what we think is good or bad can change back and forth many times every time we reconsider it in light of new material. Good and bad are not words that are very useful from a philosophic standpoint. From a life, or regular life, perspective they are fine because life is an illusion anyway."

"That is what Plato was saying in his story of the cave, right?" I said.

"Yes, he was pointing out that life as it is ordinarily lived is like looking at shadows on a wall."

"I read that once and didn't know he meant that all people

are like that," commented Liz. "But you are saying that we all are looking at these shadows even today. That is hard to believe."

"When you begin to look at how much your daily existence is taken up by imagination, which is made up entirely of fabrications, you will have an idea what a sad situation you and all life is in. The problem is that we are invisible people."

"Invisible," we both said.

"Right. We live on the inside, and only incidentally on the outside. Our psychological side, or spiritual side, is really what we are, not how we look or act. Our thoughts, moods, ambitions, emotions and so on are all on the inside and no one can see them and no scientist can measure them. We have a few indications of what a person is thinking but mostly it is wrong or much simpler than in actuality. The fact is; no one knows another and can only know themselves, but even that is a long and difficult process."

"I'm beginning to see that," I said.

Paul said something to Arturo as he went out the front door toward the pile of wood. "The funny thing to notice is that things never, or almost never, happen as you expect them. If you two want a good exercise to do, try figuring what will happen before you start a project or even a day. Then when it is all over, look and see what really did happen. I'll bet that you were not even close, especially on the details. Real life has its own agenda, which has nothing to do with our expectations, which comes from imagination. In fact, things often occur exactly opposite of our expectations. Reality is full of surprises and never intersects with imagination. My wife and I used to laugh how weird life really is."

He got up and signaled that the talking-time was over and the working-time had once again arrived. When we went out I saw that Arturo had put hammers, nails, and string out in front of the first post. While Liz watered her newly planted rose bushes, we began to measure with chalk and string where the 2X4's were to go. We were going to put two between each pair of posts as stabilizers for the 1X6's. After we had chalked six or eight posts, we began to hammer the wood planks to the posts. I looked around at the work already finished and realized how much we still had to do. This was a monumental job for a few individuals to do, but thus far I had received a lot of sustenance from my participation. I was glad I was there. I felt alive and became emotional like I don't ever remember experiencing before. Once, as I was working away, my whole chest and back filled with goose bumps. When I mentioned it to Paul he just smiled and said that I would lose it if I talked about it.

Once, while he was holding a post as I hammered the board to it, he whispered "Be present, my son. Heaven awaits your efforts." I looked up at him and nodded my understanding and thanks. Another time he pointed to my watch cover. At first I thought he wanted to know the time, and then I realized that he wasn't concerned with time; he was concerned with my presence.

Liz approached us when it was nearing dark. "Hey, you boys want a pizza for dinner?" She repeated it in Spanish for Arturo. We all nodded our approval. She drove off in the van, with a smear of dirt down her face. She was smiling.

Arturo took a couple of pieces and a beer and left before we sat down. I had a special feeling for him. He worked quietly and without fuss. He rarely smiled, but when he did his face was like a sweet light. He was patient with me, correcting my little blunders as we dug or hammered. I wondered if I could ever be like that. It was a goal worth working for.

As we were eating our food, Liz asked Paul to tell us more about the imaginary world. "We, and I mean the human race, think that we understand so much, but upon close examination, we understand practically nothing. This is why the world is in such disarray and always has been. We calculate our actions on what we think they will mean, but again, because we spend almost our entire lives in imagination day-dreaming, we can't know what anything means. Take for example your 'worst day' experience; you did not or could not have known what that meant. One of the things it meant was that today you would be sitting here in that chair eating pizza. And it will mean many other things too, but who knows what they will be. Every time something happens, it is like a rock thrown in a puddle; the waves go out on all sides affecting everything around it."

Paul finished his beer and got up. "Shall we repair to the living room?" We went to our usual places, Paul to his chair and Liz and myself to the couch.

"Okay," Liz said, "does that mean that my coming to here to work this weekend will have important implications?"

"Most assuredly, my dear Liz. And also, your coming here is linked directly to Joe's worst day. The thing is, we never know, or can know, where the links will show up. Something you do today may not have any effect for twenty years and then suddenly the link will be evident. If you know this and can watch it enough by being present, you will have plenty of entertainment to last a lifetime. Shakespeare said something about the world being a stage and that is one of the things he meant, life is a play and we need to watch it."

"I think I can see that a little," I said. "I'm already beginning to feel like life has some magic in it that I hadn't seen or felt before."

"Yes, observe, observe, observe. Observe yourself every moment and you can watch life and how it works; really works. You will see that life is a play on a stage to be viewed by the wise. When I say to observe your selves, I mean both the inner and the outer. Watch your thoughts, your emotions. Listen to your opinions; both the ones you express and the ones you keep hidden. After a time you will see that you are nothing like you thought you were. You will then begin to be on the road to self-knowledge.

Of course, self-knowledge is the same as self-consciousness and is a process that takes a long time. All of your life, you will be peeling back the layers of yourself. The more you see, the more conscious you will become, and vice-versa. Try to think of the body as a sort of hand puppet for the inner world. The outer world is a reflection of the inner. If you study your inner workings without judgment you will be closer to understanding yourself."

Liz shook her head. "Paul, how did you find all this out?"

Paul laughed. "It is too long a story. It would take me another 80 years to tell it, but I will say that after I met Libby, we traveled around looking for answers to questions. I was fortunate for two reasons; Libby was able to make money wherever we went. She was an astute in business matters and could sell real estate, insurance, or run a store of any kind and make money handily. The second reason I was fortunate is that Higher Forces led me around to meet the right people at the right time and led me to read the right material. Everything I did seemed to be geared to my self-development. Even Libby had the feeling that I was geared for higher things. That is why she was so supportive."

"Did your wife understand the things you were learning?" asked Liz.

"She understood our different roles. While I was off in the clouds, she was being grounded by the call of the earth, having babies and making a living. She was a saint in a way that I can't even explain."

"How many kids did you have?" asked Liz.

"We had four. One died right after birth. Our only girl passed away in a fall from a balcony while she was in college. The other two proved not to be like either Libby or myself. Both boys have engineering jobs in San Francisco. They have a normal life in every respect and they think their dad is a kook of the first order. And they had a life that was anything but normal too. We lived in odd places and did odd things. Once for three years, the five of us lived in a little village in Mexico. But they were resistant. They wouldn't learn Spanish, and when we moved back they forgot all that and became regular folks. I haven't heard from them since their mother died two years ago. She was probably their last link to me."

"I'm sorry." Liz said.

"Me too," I added. "Do you still love them?"

"They haven't given me much to love. I have five grand kids that they haven't let me see. So, I let it go."

"Paul, this has been a great weekend, but I think we have to shove off," I said.

"Yes it has been wonderful. I feel like I've been blessed." Liz said.

"You have Liz, more than you know," Paul answered. "All right, you kids take off, but I want to talk to you alone first, Liz." He looked at me with a smile. "And no jealousy out of you Joe."

"Don't worry Paul. I'm over that." I went out to the van and they stayed inside for about five minutes. She came out throwing a kiss to Paul who was out of my sight. A minute later as we were leaving the property, I reached over and grasped her hand.

"Did he give you a special assignment?"

"Yes."

"What was it?" I asked.

"None of your bees wax. What did he give you when you first came here?"

"None of your bees wax," I smiled. She bent over and kissed me on the cheek.

"I love you, Joe. I love you a lot."

Chapter 7

THE NEXT WEEK WAS different with Liz on board with me in the pursuit of consciousness or whatever I was pursuing. Maybe it was to become a true philosopher like Socrates and Paul. I wasn't exactly clear what it was I was after, although Paul did say it was about self-knowledge, to know my self. It was clear that I was learning that at least. In a few short weeks I'd seen some things about myself that I wouldn't have believed back prior to the Barbara/Bert day; my so-called "worst day." I was learning that I didn't have control of my thinking, my actions, or my life. What sad news, I thought. What more sad news is to follow, I wondered?

There was a definite change in Liz. She was just a beginner like myself, and yet I could see and feel her grasp on to Paul's teaching as well or better than I, with my two or three weeks more experience. She had taken to carrying a little stone in her hand when she could to help remind her to be present. She told me that Paul said he carried a stone for fourteen years in order to control his attention. We spent only two nights together the next week. She had other things to do that revolved around what Paul had given her. Still, when we were together, she was warm and dear. It was clear to me that we were in a relationship and that we had passed way beyond an affair. It must have been the magic of those roses, I thought.

One good thing about having her as a student was that she would tell me other things Paul told her when he was with her. Once, I forgot just when, she said, "Paul talked about life and how it always gets everything wrong and causes all of man's mischief. He said mankind is geared toward having its own way regardless of the circumstances. We, and by that, Paul means everybody, will be tyrants, sneaks, plotters, and wheedlers to have our own way. We spend all our energies toward changing circumstances, when the real problem is inside us. We need to change ourselves, not outer things, and definitely not other people. He said that we are the cause of our own suffering, maybe 99% of it, because we don't accept life as it is without trying to forever alter it to fit our little needs."

"So," I questioned, "this means that we should just give up—not do anything?"

"I asked the same thing. He said that we are always charged with trying to make things better, but that has nothing to do with the monumental self-pity and the dastardly actions we will take that goes with things not going our way. Acceptance is an earned virtue, but once we have worked on it and have some measure of acceptance and its parent, patience, we will see the world in an entirely different way."

"That is not what I was taught in school."

"Me either," she added. "It is a better way to look at life—refreshing."

My reading was going well. I read "Romeo and Juliet" twice; the second time carefully. Then I went to "Hamlet," which I read three times. I was in awe of Shakespeare's wisdom and his command of the language. I read somewhere that he invented thousands of words. Incredible.

Liz nudged me at 4:30 on Saturday morning. "Sweetheart, it is time to go have some more fun learning about our selves."

I made a grunt and rolled over. "All right dear, but didn't we just go to bed?"

"That was hours ago, or at least minutes. I can't sleep anyway. I've been talking to Paul in imagination all night. I might as well get out there and see what I'll really say, probably nothing important. Come on, I'll make some strong coffee and a good breakfast so we can be awake and strong today." She shook me playfully. "Come on, come on, let's go."

At breakfast I asked Liz how her log on what she thought about went during the week. She said, "I wouldn't have believed that mostly I do lecture in my imagination. I gave you hell a number of times or just informed you about roses or how to understand women and I don't know what all. But I caught myself talking to the doctors right in the middle of an operation on someone's brain, telling them all about Paul and his ring of roses. It was a crazy week. I couldn't keep my mind from wandering."

"Ha, that's nothing," I said. "I was telling the owner of the taxi company how to run his business better. I dare say that is more important than brain surgery."

She reached over and squeezed my forearm. "If people could overhear us, they'd think we were crazy."

"Yes, and they might be right because how can we be having so much fun talking about our illusions? It is strange, this world we've stumbled on to." We left my apartment building at 5:45. With no traffic my van got us there in thirty-five minutes.

On the way Liz confided in me that she had been able, for maybe the first time in her life, not to be so negative around the other nurses at work. "I have always kind of enjoyed watching them jump when I gave them a criticism. But last week I finally felt like I had a reason not to do that--it is mean and I don't want to be mean any more. I wasn't perfect by any stretch of the imagination, but when I was overly critical, I realized it and even apologized once. Janet, the one I said I was sorry to, was more surprised by that than by my little zinger. It felt good, real good."

"It makes me feel good to hear that, Liz. I have been able to assert myself a little more around work and with some of those creepy customers I get. That felt good too. I have always been run-over by anyone who was strong, or at least loud."

"Paul told me that each person had to work on different things," she said. "He called it working on oneself. Maybe you will end up telling me what to do."

"That would be nice," I smiled.

I felt a little joy well up inside of me when I left the dirt part of Rainbow Blvd. and bumped onto the slick black part. I reached over and ran the back of my hand down Liz's arm.

It was still slightly dark when we arrived, but I could see that the fence was finished. It was a beautiful site and made the place look like something special, not just a house in the desert. Cans of paint were stacked next to the driveway, so I figured out what we'd be doing for the next two days. Arturo and Paul were at the table in the kitchen discussing something when we came in. They smiled as we entered. "Arturo's wife had their baby on Wednesday. She came home Friday. I was thinking that maybe tomorrow afternoon we might all go on a field trip and visit the new baby girl."

"Oh, that would be wonderful," replied Liz. Then she spoke to Arturo about the subject while he was pouring us coffee. Both were smiling and laughing. She turned to me "He says that she weighed nine pounds, fifteen ounces."

"The mother?" I asked.

"No, silly, the baby. Paul please tell Joe not to be silly."

Paul just looked at the both of us and shook his head. "Did you see the paint cans out there?"

"Yes, I think I'll like painting better than digging," I said.

"Good, in a few minutes we'll fan out and start from either side of the driveway and work our way around with the base first, and then when we finish that we'll start on the actual painting. Liz, do you want to work with me?"

"Age and beauty, I like that," she said.

Just then, I heard a loud bang at the big window near the table. I looked up to see a bird drop to the ground that must've hit the window. Paul saw it too and jumped up immediately and dashed outside. I saw him in front of the window pick up the bird. He had his back to us so I couldn't see what he was doing, but in a few moments he lifted his hands and the bird flew out of them into the sky. He came back in and sat down.

"Wow, that bird was lucky," I said, "I would have thought he'd would have broken something."

There was a silence as if Paul had not heard me. He took a sip of coffee as if nothing had happened. Arturo looked at me and raised his eyebrows. Then Paul changed the subject.

"How did the reading go for you two last week?"

"We both read the same plays," I remarked; "Romeo and Juliet and Hamlet."

"I had read them in college," Liz said, "but never with the perspective of wisdom. I just thought they were okay in school, but now I saw much more in them."

"Me too," I added.

"Good, when we take a break we'll talk about falling in love and violence ala Romeo and Juliet. Liz, how was your work at remembering yourself?"

"I could hardly do it. But I did keep track of many of my imaginary conversations—very revealing and disturbing."

"I bet," he said. "It will be a little easier when you begin to understand that, as we are today, our imagination tells us what is real, but of course it isn't. Imagination, or fantasy, is on an entirely different track than reality. We deal with reality by escaping to our false world that we make up along the way to fit what we want. In it we are always right, or at least have a good excuse for what we did." We are never wrong in imagination. Remember that. We are always the star of our own day dreams."

"I don't exactly agree," said Liz." "I've been wrong lots of times and I've admitted it."

"Yes, I am sure you have and also had some real good excuse why it happened, like you were tired, or something, which made it all right in the end. You may not have even voiced it but you thought it and that is the most important thing. We are what we think, not what we pretend on the outside."

Then Paul stood up. "Enough of this for now. Lets fan out into our teams. And this is not a race. It is an experience. Try to remember yourselves as much as you can today."

As Arturo and I were moving toward the supplies, I put my arm around him as a gesture of good will. I tried to say something in Spanish, but my Spanish barely got past the "taco" stage. I told him "grande, grande" hoping he knew I was talking about the baby, not him. He did because he nodded his pride at producing such a big specimen.

We took our brushes and cans of the paint base and began one post apart, covering it on all sides and then working on the slats. It was pleasant work even though it was chilly that morning. Earlier in my life I would have daydreamed the whole time because it was such mindless work. Now, I was supposed to try to be present to it as much as I could. I would start off by trying to feel my feet while I dunked my brush into the liquid and continue as long as I could as I stroked the post or slat with my brush. Usually, I found that I could remember only until I got the brush up to the surface to be painted. Then I'd go off daydreaming telling Liz or Paul how much I was self-remembering. When I finally woke up from my reverie, five or ten minutes would have passed. I would have a little episode of discouragement and then remember that I wasn't being present and start again for another few seconds. The thing was, I didn't know when I went off into imagination, so I couldn't stop it. It was like falling asleep at night; it just happens. The morning passed with me painting and struggling to stay in the present. I thought if Paul could do this "most of the time" as he said, he was truly remarkable.

I would look over to Paul and Liz and I could see that they were involved in deep conversation. Sometimes I could hear Liz's clear laugh and I wished I could be there with them. I was stuck with a guy who I couldn't communicate with. Maybe it was better this way, I thought. At least I get to work on being in the present and seeing how difficult it is. We took a break around ten o'clock. I was stiff from bending over so I ran back to the house. Liz saw me and ran too. We arrived at the same time, had a hug and a kiss before entering.

When I mentioned my observation about going into imagination being similar to falling asleep, Paul spoke. "Let's forego the conversation on Shakespeare for now. There is something more important I need to explain to you. Going into imagination is sleep! It is just a different kind of sleep, a hypnotic trance. In the Bible Jesus says 'Awake.' This is what he means, 'come out of your day-dreaming sleep and pay attention.' There are several states of consciousness. The first state is when you are laying down sleeping at night. At that point you have very little awareness of what is going on around you. When you rise in the morning, you might think that you are conscious, and you are if you consider where you came from a few minutes before. But from another, you are just in a little higher state of consciousness, called second state. From the moment you open your eyes, you go off into a waking-state imagination. The main difference is that now your eyes are open. You are still not there in a real sense. Everything is automatic while you are in this state. You can eat and drive and function at life and still mostly be day dreaming."

He took a few potato chips from a bag and proceeded to speak. "The third state of consciousness is when we are aware of ourselves. Mostly this happens by accident. If you think back to things in your past you clearly remember, you will discover they are associated with some surprising event, like the time you fell off your tricycle, or when you crashed your car into a pole. Your memory will be more vivid; smells and colors are more likely to be recalled. This is because you are in a state of self-consciousness—a rare state indeed. There is a higher state than this, but it won't do me any good to talk about it because you are far from it yet."

"Is that what we are working for," I asked, "the third state?"

"Yes, you are working for third state. What you are doing now, self-remembering, is just practicing for third state. It will require much effort being present before you are really present in the third state. When it happens, you will know it."

He got up and went into the bathroom. Liz looked at me and said, "Good stuff."

"Yep, good stuff."

As she went out the door I watched her almost bounce along. She seemed extremely happy. I was a little calmer I thought, more contented than happy.

At lunch it was warm enough it sit outside around the picnic table in the back patio. We had sandwiches and chips and sodas. It felt like a picnic. "What did you think about 'Romeo and Juliet?" Paul asked Liz and myself.

Liz responded first. "I think it was about how two families can muck-up a perfectly good relationship."

I added, "And how the best laid plans go awry."

"Yes, the best plans are just wishes," Paul said. "No one knows what will happen, that is for sure, and so many plans are just so much drivel. And yet without a plan, nobody would ever know which direction to go and wouldn't realize how far they missed it. So, it is not without merit to plan ahead. But when I read that play I got the sense that Shakespeare is highlighting two things for us students of life. The first is that love as it is construed here is bound to fail, or at least cause much suffering. When I told you about the Emotional Center or brain, I said that there is an extreme part, called the emotional part. Romeo and Juliet were in this part, and this part always brings on its opposite. It is a law. They were so extremely positive that it alone caused things to go amiss. If you don't think I'm correct on this idea, spend some time and observe new loves that start too fast and too strong and see what happens. It may show you the nature of love, and that isn't it. It masks as love and people call it love, but it is infatuation and sex and produces misery in its wake. Love can happen out of this, but only after the difficulty is past and the feelings begin to mature. But this goes for any strong emotion. It will by its nature produce its opposite.

"I think you are right," said Liz. I've had several bouts of that and it was painful. I've made sure that I took it slower with Joe. I'm through with that kind of suffering."

"Ditto," I said. "When I was younger, I used to fall in love hard and it was terrible. What is the other thing you see about this play, Paul?"

"That violence and revenge never pays anything but suffering for all of the people involved. Everything would have been fine had not Romeo defended his friend's death. That set off the ultimate sad climax, which ended in more death and grief. Shakespeare goes back to this theme over and over again. He felt very strongly about vengeance of any kind."

"You mean that the justice system is all wrong?" asked Liz.

"No, no, Liz. I am only talking about an individual. Society has its own rules and does what it does. But whatever a person does within that society is held accountable by Higher Forces. Vengeance or violence of any kind by a person, no matter how justified he thinks it is, is judged harshly. You can see by observing life what vengeance brings. Romeo and Juliet being just an example. In real life it is just the same. Payment must be made."

As he talked, I began to have a strange feeling of being removed from the conversation and from the people. It was as if I was in another state of consciousness listening to them talk. I looked at Arturo off in imagination, probably talking to his wife, and I felt a deep love for him and when I looked back at Paul and Liz, the feeling was even deeper. It only lasted a short time, maybe not even a minute. Then I was back. As soon as there was a break in the discussion, I told Paul what had happened. "Is that the third state, Paul?"

He put his head down in his hands and stayed that way for what seemed like minutes. The rest of us kept quiet. Finally, he said, "I don't know, it could've been. The brain plays so many tricks that it might have been something else. See if it happens again and tell me about it. I'll think some more about it. When I was first developing, I had many such events and I still don't know what they were. One thing for sure, it wasn't bad if you felt tender when you were experiencing it. We'll see."

I was more overcome by his answer than by that experience. He was such a gentle man and his dealings with both of his students were gracious and truthful. He was teaching with everything he had. I made up my mind to be the best I could be in salute to him and his efforts.

Then he looked directly at Liz. "Liz, you've been experiencing too much of this extreme emotion I spoke about. Be careful. It will bite you."

She just stared at him. "I will."

Too soon lunch was over and we cleaned our mess and went back out to our places. This was going to be a beautiful place if I had anything to do with it, I thought as I picked up my brush. And then I remembered to be present. Then I immediately began telling

Liz something standing on my imaginary soapbox. When I realized it, I brought myself back again, but only for a moment.

At 4 o'clock we finished with that part of the job. Liz wanted to start the painting right then. She was still excited, but now a frown was beginning to form where a smile had been. Finally, as we were almost to the house, she stumbled on a rock or something.

"God damn it," she screamed. "I hate this God damned place." She shot a look at Paul with anger in her eyes. "And don't start with your stupid philosophy about emotions. Yes, I'm mad at this stupidity."

It was such a shock and she looked funny to me because now she was almost flailing her arms. I started laughing. "You should see yourself," I said. I was really giggling.

Liz turned toward me with a fury. Paul stepped quickly between us. "Liz, go take a long walk and don't come back until you feel better!" It was a command. She instantly turned and walked fast off the property. I quit laughing and looked in shock at her as she trounced down the dirt road toward who knows where. Paul went inside. I wondered if I should follow him or her. I went inside.

Paul went to his room without saying anything and Arturo went home. I sat and thought. At eight that night Liz came through the door. She was exhausted and plopped down on the couch.

"Where's Paul?"

"In the bedroom."

She struggled up and went down the hall. I heard a knock. She went in. After about an hour both of them came out. She had been crying. Paul looked at me and said, "Everything is alright now. We don't need to talk about it."

I took Liz out to the van where I cuddled with her. "I'm so embarrassed," she whispered. I decided never to mention it. We both fell asleep.

When I awoke the next morning, I came in and Paul told me

that Arturo was coming a little later so we could relax and have a leisurely meal and talk. I asked Paul about snakes while he was fixing a big breakfast for us. He laughed his good hearty laugh. "Arturo has solved that for us. He's got a dog, an unbelievable dog that hunts snakes. It is just an old mix breed, but his job is to find where the rattlesnakes are and bark like crazy. He was bit once when he was a pup and since then he sounds a loud alarm whenever he detects their presence. Of course, he can't tell the difference between a rattlesnake and any other snake, so he barks a lot. Most of the time it is a false alarm."

"Then do you kill them?"

"No, I don't like killing living things if I can help it. Arturo catches them and at the end of the day takes them out to the boonies and drops them off. We are lucky to have him. Otherwise we'd be in trouble. There are many rattlers out here. I think we caught 15 or 20 last year. We don't need our great snake dog yet. It is too cold out."

When Liz came in, she looked refreshed from her ordeal of the night before. I told her what Paul said about the snake dog. She was relieved because she said she was scared of snakes of all kinds. Me too.

During breakfast Liz asked what Paul visualized the place looking like when we finished. "I have spent a lot time thinking about it, over a year. I think that I'd like to have white roses in the front and red ones the rest of the way around. Then trees scattered around the property and grass over all the rest of it."

"That will be gorgeous," remarked Liz. "How about a little fountain someplace?"

'Maybe," he answered. "Of course there is a lot of denying force to deal with before we even get to that."

I glanced at Liz with a puzzled look. "Did you say denying force? What's that?"

"There are three forces in nature; in all creation," he began. "If you observe them long enough you will see them."

"I've never heard of that; three forces," said Liz.

"It is a law; the primary law of nature and rules everything we do or is done. It is called the law of three. Many references to it are made in ancient literature, including the writings in early Christianity. You've heard of the trinity?"

"Sure," I said, "I was raised Catholic, that is one of the mysteries of the religion."

"Yes, it is a mystery and I'm going to explain it to you right here in this little house. It is a most ancient idea, the idea that it takes three things or forces to create anything. The first of these forces, called first force or positive force, can be either seen as momentum or maybe it is what you want. This force is always moving forward, or trying to move forward. You are trying to do something, say build a large rose garden, and so you start, but soon enough the second force makes its appearance. Second force is a power that stops it or gets in the way. Part of this law is that to do anything of significance, negative force or second force must be a part of it. We can see it as trouble or the difficulties involved in doing something. Life is full of troubles because the world is full of people trying to do things and they do not realize that the two; positive force and negative force are part of the same equation. One says yes, the other says no. Does this make sense so far?"

Liz pushed the dishes off to the side of the table and pulled her coffee closer to her. "Yeah, sort of. You mean that the trouble people always have is a law and they can't escape it?"

"Exactly. No matter what you try of any significance, not just getting up from the table, but anything from getting a better job to becoming the President of the United States will have an appropriate amount of negative or denying force. Most times we are stuck because the second force is exactly equal to the first force. The world is an antagonistic place because of these two forces at war. Everything organizes around Yes or No. At any rate, second force gives us something to work against, something to overcome. But it is a good thing. Can you see what our world would be like without negative force?"

"Happy," I offered.

"No; sick. It would be a sick miserable place if everybody could have whatever they wanted. A few individuals have pretty much had their own way in life; kings, conquerors, famous people, and they became sick, sick emotionally because they didn't have enough denying force in their lives. So negative force is health giving, even though when you are up against it, it may not seem that way."

Paul glanced over to his easy chair. "Let's get more comfortable. We can do the dishes later." With that he led us to the living room.

"To continue; in order for change to occur, another force is necessary to break the tension between opposing forces. Third force, or neutralizing force, is vital because it alters the relationship between them. In fact, it is the essential element to creativity of any sort. This force is always invisible and you cannot predict it. It comes of its own accord. But once it arrives everything is different. It releases enough energy for things or situations to change and new views to emerge. Joe, you were describing neutralizing force when you told us about your wife and your boss giving you the heave-ho on the same day. They were both unexpected and they changed everything in your life."

"I'll say. But what was the first and second force in that scenario?"

"The first force was your life, the momentum of it. The second force kept you locked into it. You had a desire for change, a silent yearning, but were helpless to make your situation different. I don't know, but when this surprising third force made a visit, whether you wanted it or not, you had to change and a whole new life began emerging."

"That's interesting," said Liz, "because I've noticed the same sort of thing in my life but I didn't know it was a force, or a law."

"It is. If the both of you watch it from now on, it will become clear that the law of three is the basic law of creation on every level. In science third force is called by various names like catalyst, or not at all, but it is everywhere if scientists knew how to look. But if you watch your life with the help of self-remembering you will begin to see this, and once you do, it will be delightful to see how things really work. Of course, it is important to remember that whatever I teach you has many levels that you can discover only by studying them. Nuances will appear that only experience can teach. Life is the best teacher anyway."

"Oh, "I said," Liz said something about why we should try to self-remember that you told her; about Higher Forces? What was that?"

"I just said that when you are able to do be in the present, you sort of open the ramp for higher influences to reach you. They have no way in, except through the present. The past and future exists, but on a different plane. Only the present exists for us. Think of it as a place, not a time. Look around you. All that you see or experience is in this place called the present. By opening yourself to this place you also open yourself to the great fountain of grace from the Gods. You draw their attention; make yourself known in higher realms. The word gets out; that you are making efforts on yourself. When we are present, it is like a small bulb alighting. It attracts interest from above. It is how the Higher knows who is sincere.

Liz asked, "Paul, why do you keep saying Gods instead of God?"

"Well, sometimes I do. There is no reason why I wouldn't except that I feel more comfortable not using God; He is too high; too impossible for me to even think about. You must understand that there are many levels of invisible beings beyond our five senses, a whole hierarchy of souls right up to the highest level. The level right above us we call angels or Gods, or maybe we can call them anything, as long as it is with reverence. I sometimes refer to the higher as Higher Forces, angels, or higher influences. In fact, that is probably a better word; Higher influences because there are influences, fine energies, flowing to us at every second we can be in the Now.

In addition, I'd like you to know that each angel is unique, with a different essence and job to do. They all must work their way up the ladder, just like we need to work at our lower level. We are at the very first rung and an infinite climb through inner space.

When Arturo arrived we had the same teams and we did pretty much the same thing; paint the fence. The only difference was that now we were putting on bright white paint. I soon found out that it was taking longer because the paint had to be uniform and even.

It was more than just the slap job we were doing the day before. After completing just a couple of sections, the four of us stepped back onto the road. The results were startling. The sun bounced off the gleaming fence like a bright light. "Oh, my goodness," exclaimed Liz. That vision gave me the boost that I needed that morning. I attacked the job with more vigor and more presence than I had experience all weekend. I started humming.

Around 10 o'clock Paul brought a blanket and a basket full of sodas and pastries out of the house. He spread the blanket on the ground across the street from his property and we took our break appraising our work. It was quite moving, the four of us sitting together touching and being touched by the sight of what our efforts were creating. "Since I've been sitting here, Paul," I said, "I think I've been as present as I've ever been."

"Yes," said Liz, "the whole morning I've been in some deep state of self-remembering."

Paul touched his heart and said, "The energy to live in the present is in a high part of the Emotional Center . That is why all enlightened beings were so emotional; they needed it to be present, and being in the Now itself produced emotional energy. But may I add my young friends, 'You ain't seen nothin' yet.'"

"So, that means the more we can make ourselves emotional, the more present we can be?" I inquired.

"That is right, but not lower emotions, like those associated with aimless gossip, or those violent ones from the emotional part. Higher emotions are the ones to court. If you consciously put yourself around beauty and love and be ever gentle and forgiving, the intellectual part will lead you to a higher place where the Now exists. That is what Walt Whitman meant when he said in his last poem that he was going to the 'true songs;' that special place in the heart where we can live immortal."

There was a moment of silence, and then he said, "I think I'd like to call this place 'True Songs.' How does that sound?"

"Great," I said.

"I like it, 'True Songs,'" said Liz.

Paul was explaining it to Arturo. "True Songs," Arturo repeated with a surprising lack of accent. He smiled his agreement. Then

Paul said to us, "God sounds his trumpets through the medium of beauty. Train all of your senses to understand this fact. See and hear with your eyes and ears, but also feel with the heart. In fact, jump in heart first."

"Shall we go back to building 'True Songs,'" offered Liz.

"Yes, let's do. Let's do indeed," said Paul.

Later that night, I wrote in my journal, "WOW," I didn't know there was so much hidden in life, and it is all in my heart."

We worked until a little after noon when Paul called a halt to the day's labor. We had finished the front part and a couple of sections on each side, a nice morning's work. We carried our brushes and paint back to the house where we cleaned the brushes and ourselves. I suggested that since we were going to go over to Arturo's, we should bring food over for everybody at the house and have lunch there. It was agreed and on the way to Tucson, we stopped at a fast food restaurant and purchased a mountain of burgers and fries, enough to feed the little army at Arturo's house. As we drove I looked over at Paul, quietly sitting next to me. He appeared serene and content. Liz and Arturo were engaged in a whispered but animated conversation in Spanish in the back. That little van contained my whole life now. I felt like a most fortunate fellow to have so much.

It was an army. All six children were there. They introduced themselves to us. I only remembered the older boy's name—Jesus. The rest of the kids were all smiles and laughter, but Jesus looked grim and resentful. He was 15 and a big hulk of a young man. He looked like a gang member. The mother, Maria, and her baby girl, little Lisa, were the perfect picture of Madonna and child. Maria didn't speak English so Liz or the kids interpreted for me. Aside from Jesus, the whole family was a joy to be around. We shared the food, and with a combination of English and Spanish had a warm afternoon. Jesus wanted to leave but Arturo made him stay. He was not too happy about that and sulked.

The house was small and on the dilapidated side. The furniture looked like it was from "Goodwill" and the dishes were chipped and cracked. No doubt about it, they were poor. Toward the end of the afternoon, Paul asked Jesus if he'd like to work on the weekends with his father. He offered $6 an hour to start. "No," he said, "I'd rather hang with my friends."

Arturo was furious with him and let loose with a tirade in Spanish. Then Jesus turned back to Paul and said, "Yes, I'll do it. My father is making me."

"Well, great," replied Paul, "I think you'll like it out there, and you can see how hard your father works. You will be proud of him."

In answer, he went back into a bedroom and shut the door. With that exception, I was impressed with the joy and humility of the Garcia family. They were making a decent life and it wasn't easy on them. I found out that they came from Mexico seven years ago with four children and no money and were slowly pulling themselves up to where they could have enough food on the table.

Paul told us the story of how he met Arturo. The story was interpreted by Liz to Maria and Arturo. "I decided to build a house on the grounds that I bought. This was long before I thought seriously about the roses. Well, I was having a lot of trouble with the builders. They wouldn't show up on time, or not at all. And they were obviously making mistakes that even an amateur like myself could spot. I felt helpless because I was new to the city and didn't know anyone who could help."

"Then one morning, Arturo walks down the drive way. He said he was looking for any kind of work. He had five children and had just lost his job at a construction site in Tucson. I still don't know what he was doing out that far from town. I hired him when he looked around and told me some of the things the builders were doing wrong. When they finally showed up that morning I fired them all. I hired another contractor that Arturo knew and the house and everything else went fine from that day on. He is one of the finest men and hardest workers I've ever known. He truly is a God-sent."

Arturo and Maria were smiling. I pulled one of the little boys aside and told him to ask his father if I could speak to him outside.

The boy brought his father in the front yard where I was waiting. I told the boy to tell his father that I would like to present him a little gift in honor of Lisa, but that he could tell no one except Maria about it. Arturo nodded his agreement. "Wait here," I said.

I went out to the van and got my checkbook. I wrote a check for $5,000. I figured I had given my daughter that much and I knew she would waste it. Arturo and his family would make good use of it and deserved it far more. I folded it and when I returned I put it in Arturo's breast pocket. He took it out of his pocket, looked at it and then at me. He said nothing. He didn't have to.

As I was walking out to the van to go home Liz whispered to me, "I saw you give Arturo a check. How much was it for?"

"Bee's wax, my dear, bee's wax," is all I said.

As we started to pull out of the driveway, Liz asked me to stop. "Joe, I'd like to go back tonight and finish the painting tomorrow. Would you do that with me? I can call in sick tomorrow and the next day if it is necessary."

I was never in a position where I had to go drive a cab. In fact, it wasn't a job in the ordinary since of the word. I rented the cab each day I wanted it, and I usually got #22 if I got there early enough, but if I didn't show up they might not even know it because there were over 80 taxis changing drivers all at once. No, if I didn't show up, nobody would come looking for me. I said, "Sure, I'd like to finish the fence."

I waved at Paul as he was pulling out in his truck. I ran over and told him that we were going home tonight and get some more clothes and would be back to work tomorrow morning. He seemed pleased. I dropped Liz off at her place and said I would be back at 6 o'clock in the morning. She hadn't wanted to spend the night with me. She wanted some alone time, she said. I did too. I wanted to zone out on the couch and not have to deal with anyone, even someone I loved.

Beautiful Liz Lizetti, with her little overnight bag and a big yawn, was standing on the corner when I pulled up at 5:55. She jumped in and said she was going to lie down in the back and finish her sleep. "I was reading Plato last night until one o'clock. He's good, but he makes me sleepy this morning."

Monday was Arturo's day off, so the three of us began together down the eastern side of the fence. We were all quiet that morning. I was trying to concentrate on being in the Now as much as I could. When I wasn't doing that I was trying to keep track of who I talked to in my dream world conversations. Paul told me that was one way to find out who was important to me. He said I would only talk to important people in my imagination. I found out that I was talking to Liz the most, telling her things about my life. My next favorite target was Paul. I told him about Viet Nam and different things about my early experiences with my father. I didn't really speak to anybody out loud until about 10 o'clock when we came in for a break.

After we were settled into a bag of pretzels and a can of soda, Paul said, "I hope you folks don't mind carrying on for awhile without me, but I've got to go to the store and buy some food for the week. This is usually the day I do odds and ends."

"Go ahead, we got it pretty well in hand now," I said. "In fact, if you want to take the rest of the day off to do those odds and ends, it is fine with me."

"Well, we'll see," he said. He drove off.

"Liz, we haven't been very careful having sex. Are you worried you might get pregnant?"

"Not a chance. I was married twice before and I never got pregnant. Of course I wasn't very interested in having their babies. Both of them wouldn't made very good fathers, and I'm not sure I would have made a good mother either."

"Do you think you would now?"

"Maybe, if I had the right man. But I don't think I can get pregnant or else I would've by now. What about you?"

"I never had a real kid of my own. My only child is from some other man's seed. Neither of my wives wanted kids. Barbara was too interested in her career and how pregnancy might affect her chances at the top. Marge was pretty crazy, and I mean crazy. She had trouble dealing with Cindi as it was. I might like to have a kid now, if I found the right woman and if she could get pregnant."

Liz came around the picnic table and cupped her hands around my face. "Do you know you are a dear, sweet man, the best I've ever met." She kissed me tenderly several times and then proceeded to get me ready for some impromptu sex on the bench. We took most of the afternoon off. We also took everything else off.

We did do some painting. In fact, Liz pushed us to work until just before dark to make up the time spent having that long break which turned into a long lunch. She was energized by the earlier activity while I was a little petered out, so to speak. After Paul returned he spent the rest of the afternoon writing letters and cleaning house. That evening he fixed us a meal of pork chops with rice and salad. For dessert we had apple pie and ice cream. Afterward we took showers and came into the living room for our lesson from the master.

"You are just beginning to partake on an inner journey towards the stars," he began. The road to the stars, or eternity, is through the higher part of the Emotional Center. This is the part that must be developed to the highest point possible."

"How do we do that?" I asked.

"There are many ways. The first is by controlling your negativity. Try to control the expression of negative emotions by not letting them come out of your lips. This means when you feel a negative emotion welling up in you over something someone is doing, don't let it out. This is not to say that you have to 'stuff it' as the saying goes, but find other ways to deal with it, like self-remembering. A good trick I use is to express the opposite to the person. For instance, if you, Liz, are feeling hurt by something Joe said, go give him a hug or say something complementary. Your emotions will be in turmoil because you are in the habit of letting an offender have it with all of your negative energy, at least in your imagination.

If you do this enough, and I mean for years, you will tame the ugly beast, which is what negative energy is; a beast, a monster. Then you will have more room in there for the higher to manifest.

Negativity controls the world, more than sex, or power, or money. Man will give up any of those things, but hang on to the delights of being negative. It is a drug of the worst, most addictive kind. A person will have a million reasons why he should be mad, or jealous, or vicious, or have his endless complaints, but he never will face the hard fact that negative emotions are his most important psychological product.

If you are to get anywhere in the spiritual world, you must tame your negative words, deeds, and especially the final frontier, thoughts."

"But how do I stop Joe from doing what ever is making me mad?"

"Well, you could be direct and tell him. You can do that and not express negativity. You know the difference. You and the rest of humanity have been trained to think that only through the show of temper or meanness can a situation be controlled. Nonsense. It just creates more problems that may not show up right away, but will eventually. So, you may get your way then but pay in the long run as Joe, or who ever you've attacked, keeps an account of the incident. If, after you tell him not to do what is bothering you, he still does it, you have to figure something else out without being negative. You can't work on Joe, you can only work on yourself and you can only know yourself."

"Can I tell her if she is being negative toward me?" I asked.

"You can at your own risk," answered Paul. "Remember you too are working on yourself, not Liz. You can try it and if it is not received in a positive manner, back off. The most important thing to remember is to be kind. No one gets into heaven without a kind heart. That is another way to develop the intellectual part of the emotional brain, through kindness, charity, and mercy. It says someplace in the Bible about forgiving your offenders 7 times 70, no matter what they do. Jesus forgave his tormentors before he died. He said, 'Forgive them Father, they know not what they do.' That may be the most powerful thing ever said by a man, and an incomparable lesson to anyone who reads that line. Dedicate your lives, Liz and Joe, to a life of forgiveness and you cannot be denied a sweet reward after you leave this plane. I believe you will be judged after you die to this world not on your deeds, but what you are and how much you forgave. The accounts about others you take into the next world are your real black marks."

"That is powerful stuff, Paul. Any other tips to developing that higher part?" I asked.

"Try to self-remember always and everywhere, as Peter Ouspensky, a favorite philosopher of mine said. This will produce a potent holy chemical in you that will naturally feed your higher parts. You will be on the road to waking up, to developing a soul of heavenly proportions. Understand that life is opaque. We think we see it, but it is all distorted. Self-remembering clears up our sight."

He smiled at us and let us know that it was time for him to be alone for awhile. He got up and walked out into the dark. We got out the cards and played cribbage until 10 o'clock. Before we went out to the van, I could see Paul sitting on the bench in the patio in what looked like deep meditation.

With Arturo back and Paul working with us, we finished the painting by three o'clock the next afternoon. It was a pleasure to know that we had worked as a team to complete such a large job in what seemed like complete harmony. At lunch, Paul spent some time explaining how humans are designed to promote the imaginary world. "It is in the design," he said, "that people operate on a totally mechanical level. The lower parts of us are capable of taking us from the womb to the tomb without even once having, or doing, anything that is not mechanical."

"Even thinking?" Liz asked.

"Especially thinking. Our thoughts are not our own. They just come, sometimes we can trace them to some stimuli or another, but mostly they just arrive without invite. We have no idea what we will be thinking even a minute from now. If we are present, we may have a choice as to whether these thoughts can stay. If they do, we think them, if not, they evaporate. We must always have thoughts, but which ones get into our actual thinking is another thing. These thoughts are called I's. If an I takes roost, that is, if we accept it, it will attract other I's of the same ilk, or you might say, that original I, or thought, has babies and those babies will make up an attitude or maybe a little personality of some sort. The I's in this attitude will all support each other since they came from the same root. I's gathering together become a psychological powerhouse that can turn us into many things not very pleasant.

As we are in our ordinary state of consciousness, that is the second state of waking sleep, we cannot have any discipline of our thinking. A dog walks by and we have I's, or thoughts, about dogs. Then we associate away to all kinds of things, but all from the original dog I's. You have to watch your thinking for many years in order to grasp the significance of this.

In the second state we have many sub-states like anger, hate, envy, delight, and all sorts of attitudes and desires. These sub-states actually make up our lives. In a way, mankind is invisible. We think we see another person because we see their body. But the real person is on the inside, psychologically. Our body is like a space suit, a covering that helps us exist in this world full of gases.

Anyway, while we watch our thinking to see how automatic we are, we can also watch the space suit. This is our Instinctive Center, or the actual body. All of the inner functions of the body are automatic. We take a bite of food and we do not have to worry about what will happen because the body is on automatic pilot. We can then stay in imagination while the Instinctive Center takes care of things; heals us when we become sick or pumps blood to the various parts of the organism. It does a multitude of things we are never aware of in order to keep us functioning and able to live in our fantasy world."

"Ha," I laughed, "you talk about the idea of a conscious design and I'm beginning to believe it. Most of my life I've been dedicated to the non-belief of a God, and certainly not a design."

"My son, don't think in terms of belief. Think in terms of an idea. Then, if it is important enough, go about the business of verifying or understanding the idea. As I present you with the blueprint of life, see if that helps you in grasping an idea, for instance the idea of God. If you just consider God as if the concept is to be believed or not believed, you miss the point. It is like saying that you don't believe in nature. That would be silly because to a certain extent, you have verified nature, so you wouldn't say you believed or disbelieved. Everything in life, every concept, every idea, has many different layers on different levels. As you probe into the idea of, say God, you will be astonished by the how the layers and levels come together to create ever new and deeper understanding. The whole point of life is to create understanding, not beliefs."

"Oh," is all I said.

Too soon we had to leave. We gave hugs all around and vanished in a curl of dust as the van entered the dirt part of Rainbow Boulevard. My life had become, in just about a month, completely different. If it all somehow ended that day, I would never be the same or think the same again. I would never be satisfied with life without philosophy again, and without someone to explain it to me like Paul. What star did he come from, I wondered? And then I gazed over at Liz rubbing her little stone and looking ahead; what star did she come from to be able to make me so content?

As we were driving Liz told me something that Arturo told her about our visit to his house. "He said that his baby was born with a big red birth mark on her back. Well, after we left the birth mark had vanished."

"What? I said. "Birth marks, if they are real, never disappear."

"That's what Arturo said too, but he also said that he has noticed that Paul can do things."

"Things, what things?"

"Like cure things that are sick. I don't know," she said.

"Don't tell me that Liz, that makes me go into imagination big time."

"Me too. I just wanted you to know."

I let Liz off in front of her apartment after an almost tearful good-bye. For me at least, they were tears of joy. I thought I'd take the next day off again just to recuperate from the last four days of intense emotional and physical work. Maybe, I thought, I'll go over to the University library and visit their books. I love books and libraries. I was bothered about what Liz told me about Arturo's baby. Maybe I'd look up healers, or miracle workers.

I found a comfortable place in the library and spent seven hours reading the "New Testament" and The Merchant of Venice." It was the most relaxed I'd felt in years. I would never have taken such a respite from my responsibilities in the old days, the old days being a few months ago. I hoped silently that my new life would contain many such opportunities for study and reflection. At least now I knew that it was possible to live a different life. In those "old days" I wouldn't have known to want it. I was on the grind and in the rat race. Now I could watch the race and be present to it. I spent some time looking up people who were said to be able to heal. I came away thinking they were frauds. Maybe Jesus wasn't.

The following Saturday Liz and I were driving out to "True Songs" in the darkness of new morning. "This weekend is roses, Honey," I said.

"I know. I've been trying to keep my mind off of them, but I still keep looking forward to planting and trimming roses. It was such a pleasure to plant the ones by the house. They give me some secret pleasure that is deep down inside of me."

"Not me, I guess, at least in the same way. What gave me pleasure was watching you work with them. Now I know what a 'green thumb' really means. It is not about making things grow, it is about loving them and then watching them respond."

"You sound like Paul."

"I hope so."

I expected to see rows of rose bushes in cans when we arrived, but instead I saw shovels. Inside I groaned. "Oh Liz, I think we have one step first; irrigation."

"I forgot about that."

In the house Arturo and his son were sitting at the table drinking coffee. Paul came out in a cheerful mood. "Well, hello my dears," he said as he came over to hug us. "You remember Jesus from last week?"

I shook his limp hand and smiled. "I'm glad you could join us."

He didn't seem too enthused. "We are going to see if he likes to work with us. We've got to dig a little trench around the whole of

'True Songs' and on both sides of the driveway in order to lay some plastic pipe for the irrigation of the roses."

"The whole place?" asked Jesus.

Arturo answered him harshly in Spanish. I could see that a conflict was brewing. I wished Jesus hadn't come this morning. Paul went on. "We had a pretty good rain here Wednesday night and yesterday Arturo and I watered down the area we'll be digging in, so the digging will not be so tedious."

"How deep are we going to dig?" I asked.

"Between six and eight inches. We've got to keep measuring to make sure that the trench is at least six inches. Liz, you can be in charge of measuring and the depth and keeping us on a straight line."

"I can dig and do that too," she said.

We all had a good laugh over that. "All right, Liz, I don't want to cheat you out of the work," Paul answered with a smile. We finished the coffee and went outside and each of us took a narrow shovel and marched to the fence.

From the first moment, Jesus did not seem to get it. Why did he have to work? He didn't need the money he'd said. He wanted to hang with his buddies. Arturo told Liz that it was hard to keep him in school and out of trouble. Jesus had already been in Juvenile Hall twice for drug offenses. Father and son were working ahead of us several sections away, but we could hear them having words from the first shovelful. After about an hour in which the tension was palatable, Jesus threw down his shovel and stormed away with curses in both Spanish and English. He stepped over the fence and walked down the road.

I for one was relieved. I said to Liz, "So, you still want to have kids?" She smiled back and kept digging. Arturo might have been relieved too if it wasn't for his obvious embarrassment. He and Paul talked a minute. Paul had his arm around Arturo's shoulder, talking to him low. Arturo calmed down enough to resume work, but he kept glancing down the road where Jesus had walked, perhaps hoping to see him come back a changed person. He never came back.

I was getting so used to real work that the time passed swiftly.

It was time for break before I realized it. But I did realize that I hadn't been present much during that time. Paul said once while I was deep in imagination that the Moving Center was on automatic and when that happened it was difficult to stay out of the dream world. I asked him what the Moving Center was and he said he would talk about it at break.

Liz and I sat on the bench of our indiscretion of the week before and munched on cut-up oranges and apples. "The Moving Center is that part of us that moves, enjoys movement and thinks about movement and spatial relationships," he said. It has its own mind. In the lower part of that center is where we've stored our memory of how to do movement. The memory of how to ride a bicycle, walk, talk, drive, and a thousand other things is stored there. We just need to access that part and it takes over and we can go off in imagination while we are moving along. It is just like the Instinctive Center and its many functions.

It probably took a few minutes to put the shoveling into the Moving Center, and then off we could go into imagination, carrying on conversations with some one or creating scenes to play out. Until we put it into the memory bank, however, we had to be more present.

"Yes, I noticed that," replied Liz. "I hate it when I have to do five or six things that I'm not used to doing in the operating room. I guess I have to be more present."

"As you have already verified to some extent, the present is a difficult place to find, and difficult to remain once you arrive there."

"Okay, what is the answer," I asked.

"The same as always," he said, "work at remembering to self-remember. There is no easy way, and if there was, the result would not be worth it."

With those words, he got up and motioned for us to continue with our Moving Centers. As we made our way to the work site, I put my arm around Liz and said, "I love you." She repeated my exact words while looking at me.

I don't know how Paul did it, but he could work steady hour after hour without lifting his head up. Arturo was the only one that was clearly better than Paul and he was younger by about 30 years. It almost seemed like Arturo was designed for hard work. He was about 5 foot 8 inches tall and 190 pounds of solid muscle. I don't think I ever saw him tired, even after ten hours of digging. I, on the other hand, was not engineered to work that hard. I was going on emotional energy alone. I think it was the same with Liz. We were city people, bred to wear nice clothes and hold down clean jobs. But there was something out here at "True Songs" that kept us going way past our normal work ethic. It was the magic of the moment.

During the day a delivery truck dropped off a big pile of plastic pipe for the irrigation project. After a short lunch we worked without a break throughout the afternoon. By 4:30 we had dug the six-inch ditch all the way around the property. Without even a pause, we began on the two sides of the driveway. By six o'clock we were finished. "Liz, I'm going to the van and lay down," I told her. I woke up about mid-night with her arms wrapped around me fast asleep. I was hungry and thirsty. I untangled myself and went into the house and turned on the kitchen light. I opened the refrigerator and took out a pie and some milk. While I was rummaging around the drawers looking for a knife and fork, I opened a drawer filled with photographs. I took out a bunch to look at while I ate.

There was one with a young man, obviously Paul, standing next to a woman. What was startling was that she looked almost exactly like Liz. She was short with dark hair and beautiful. It almost could have been Liz's twin sister. It had to be Paul's wife, Libby. Then it struck me that both Libby and Liz were nick names for Elizabeth. No wonder he liked Liz so much. He had said that they looked alike, but I had no idea he meant exactly alike. I looked further and then I saw another picture of what I presumed were his three children. They all looked like they were in their early 20's. The two young men were tall like Paul, but without the look of character. They appeared too pompous to be his sons. The woman had a remarkable resemblance to Liz and Libby. I turned the picture over and their names had been printed on the back with peacock blue ink. The girl's name was Alice Elizabeth. I couldn't have been more dumbfounded. Liz's name was Elizabeth Alice. Then I looked for more pictures of Libby and found a few. On the bottom of a snapshot of her were the words, "Elizabeth Alice Martin-1950."

I took a few more bites of my pie and put the pictures back and washed my dish and glass. I felt strange as I walked out to the van. What the hell did all of that mean? Was it a coincidence or some something much weirder? And the part about Paul being a healer came into my mind. It felt like "Alice in Wonderland." Maybe I was going nuts, I thought. Maybe it is just a play like Shakespeare said.

When I arrived I curled up next to Liz with a lot of questions on my mind. I thought I'd wait awhile before I would tell her anything. I didn't feel like I was on very solid ground in my head. Maybe this self-remembering was something evil. Not a chance, I thought, and went to sleep.

At breakfast the next morning I asked Paul what the name of the child was that they had lost right after birth. "He died a few hours after he was born. We were going to name him Joseph Martin. Why?"

"No reason. Just wondering," I said.

As we were surveying the mound of pipe, I asked Liz, "Did Paul ever ask you what your middle name was?"

"As a matter of fact, he did on the first day I was here. Why?"

"Just wondering. He is a pretty inquisitive guy, that's all."

"Come on, tell me what you're up to?"

"Nothing, I swear." I moved away from her with a stack of pipe in my arms.

Our job was to lay the pipe all along the trench we dug the day before. It didn't look that difficult, but we would be spending most of the day on our knees. Around 9:30, the mail jeep pulled up to the mail-box and the man put a stack of letters in it. "Hey, who did that?" He was pointing to the fence from the road-side.

I was closest to the fence and I peered over the top. Two slats were covered with graffiti. "God, look Paul; Liz." The mailman shrugged and left. Arturo, Paul, and Liz jumped over the fence for a better look. Arturo was beside himself with fury. He knew that Jesus had something to do with it. He hadn't come home the night before. Paul appeared calm and instructed me to go get a paint can and brush.

Liz was talking to Arturo and Paul in Spanish when I got back. She came over to me while I was opening the can. "Paul is telling Arturo not to mention this to anyone, especially Jesus. But Arturo is not easy to control right now. He's embarrassed."

"Paul was telling us about forgiveness the other day," I said, "Well he is now practicing it."

Just then a car-load of Latino youths drove up in a beat up old car and stopped across the road from us. The four of them just stared at us with menacing smiles. Before we could react, another car pulled up with four more youths. Now there were eight tough looking gang members staring at us. Arturo started after them in a rage, but Paul stepped in front of him and looked him in the face and said something in Spanish. He then looked our way and said for us to take Arturo to the house now and stay there. I have never seen him so firm.

"I'm not leaving you here with those goons," I said.

Paul's eyes flashed, "Yes you will, I am your teacher and you will do as I say or get off this property this instant."

"Okay." I grabbed Arturo by the arm and with Liz on the other arm, led him away down the drive. When we reached the porch, Paul turned and went across the street to the two cars. The eight boys jumped out and surrounded him. "Oh, shit," I said.

But Paul seemed unconcerned. He was talking to them in Spanish in a most friendly style. One of the kids was right behind him almost touching him. Suddenly, as if by magic, one of the kids in front of Paul broke into a big smile and said loud enough that we could hear, "Paul!" The threatening circle broke up and everybody was in front of him now. He was shaking their hands one by one. I was transfixed as I watched them become almost joyful. Then they all walked over to the fence and a couple of the boys grabbed the brushes and prepared to paint away the graffiti. Paul waved us over.

The boys all shook our hands and said they were sorry for the mess. One of the youths, Artie, said that Paul lived in his village in Mexico when he was a child. He said his mother still talks about how Paul helped her family put on a new roof after a storm. He also said that in that part of Mexico, everyone thought Paul was a saint and a healer. Artie couldn't wait to get home to tell his mother that Paul lived here. "She will come to him and thank him for all he did for her family."

While they were painting and talking, I had that strange feeling come over me again. It was like I was watching this from another place. My body was a mass of goose pimples. I saw my hand go out to one of the boys as he offered it to me as a way of saying goodbye. Everything was in slow motion. They piled into their cars and drove off. Then I came back from where ever I had been.

Arturo was talking a mile a minute and pounding on Paul's back. Liz just looked at me. "A saint and healer?"

Paul said, "That is a bunch of nonsense. I don't want to be a healer. One time I visited a child with malaria and she got better the next day. There was nothing to it except their imagination. Now let's all go back to work."

At lunch Paul acted as if nothing had happened. Finally, while we were eating the sandwiches, Liz asked him to tell us about Mexico. He clearly did not want to, but after a time of silence he said, "I spent about three years in a little village in Mexico. I won't give you the name because I don't want you talking about it, even after I'm dead. Libby and the kids went with me. Libby started a business exporting some of their goods, while I began helping who ever needed it. I organized the repair of their mission and then I worked on people's houses and helped them pave their main street. When I wasn't doing that, I spent time out in the desert meditating. I was attracted to their simple way of life and thought it would do my kids some good to be around such humility. Unfortunately, toward the end I got to be known as a healer and people from all over the district came to call with their sick children and relatives.

It was very unpleasant for me, and especially for my boys who hated Mexico anyway. So, one night we left and went back to San Diego. That was about 13 or 14 years ago. And that's it; end of story."

"They still remember you though Paul," I said. "You must have made a good impression."

"Maybe I did, but I couldn't take all the attention. That is one reason I moved out here, to get away from my reputation. It was getting too heavy."

"We will keep your secret, Paul," promised Liz.

"You mean you can't heal people," I asked.

"I don't want to be known as a healer. I just want to spend my life raising roses and staying away from the limelight. It is all a play anyway," he said. "What will happen will happen. Our role is to just watch it unfold. Actually it can be quite entertaining and even humorous. Sometimes I have burst out laughing when I realize that a situation turned out exactly opposite of what I planned. It is the God's way of keeping me humble."

I noticed that he didn't answer my question. I decided not to pursue it and give him his privacy instead.

We finished the whole job by day's end. I was reluctant to leave because it seemed like "True Songs" was an enchanted island. But Paul shooed us away. He said he needed to be alone. As we were backing out of the driveway, Paul came running toward us waving. I stopped. When he got to the window he said, "If I set up that spare room as a bedroom, do you think you'd like to sleep there instead of this bus?"

"Of course," we both said. "We'd love it," Liz added.

As we were driving to Tucson, I told Liz about what I had found in the drawer the night before and about the name similarities. She was silent for a long while; maybe ten minutes. "I've had the strangest sensation since I first went out there that I belonged. Now this just confirms it."

"But what do you think it means?"

She shook her head. "I don't know. I don't know. But it is not bad."

"Sometimes I have a feeling like I should kneel down to Paul.

He is like a holy man."

"You better never do that. He'll kick you off the place or at least tell you to stay out of imagination."

"Yeah, I know." We laughed.

Tuesday evening when I got home from my job, Liz called me and asked me if I'd like to have dinner with her and her mother and stepfather. They were in town for the day on their way somewhere. I said sure and agreed to meet them at the restaurant in their hotel. When I arrived they were all in the foyer of the restaurant. Liz gave me a kiss and introduced me.

"Joe, I'd like you to meet my mother, Mary, and her husband, Jim Parry. Mom and Jim, this is Joe Peters."

We shook hands. Jim said, "Call me Big Jim, everybody else does." He was big all right; 6 foot 4 inches and about 260 pounds. He also was a jovial guy. His handshake was firm and warm. Liz's mom was about her daughter's height; 5 foot 2 inches but was heavier by about forty pounds. She had the look a woman who got her way most of the time. I was pretty sure I wouldn't cross her.

We made our way to our booth. Even though I figured Mary was the boss of that little family, Big Jim was the entertainer and host. "Will you let me order that wine for tonight?" We all nodded agreement. The waiter was standing there and Big Jim spoke to him in wine language and he scurried off.

"You two live in Phoenix now?" I asked.

"Yes," he replied. "I'm the owner of Parry's Audi, and Big Jim's Foreign Auto Mart."

"We live in Scotsdale," Mary added.

"Joe used to be a manager of finance at Big Missile in California," Liz said.

"I got laid-off a few month's ago," I added.

The wine came, and after the obligatory ceremony of tasting, he gave a toast to Liz and I. "Well, son, I might have something for you up in Phoenix, something real good; manager of finance at the Auto Mart. It would pay better than you think."

I smiled at Liz. "Thanks for the offer, Big Jim, but I'm kind of happy right here in Tucson."

"What do you do now, Joe," Mary asked.

"I drive a cab."

Big Jim let out a roar. "Whoa, I thought you said you drove a cab."

"I did. I love it too."

That dumbfounded both of the oldsters. He said, "Well, if that's what you like." Then he burst out laughing again.

I wasn't mad at all. I understood that what I was doing wasn't exactly normal. Liz was irritated. "Jim, you are a boor. Mom, control your man, will you."

I waded in with a laugh. "What you don't understand Big Jim, is that I'm well off financially. I don't need to work at all. I'm driving a taxi for the fun of it. Most of the time I get to read. Then every once in a while I get a call and go pick somebody up and drop them off and go back to reading. On a good day I make $80, on a bad one I pull down almost $20. Plus, I met Liz driving a cab. Now I'm not going to do it much longer, but I'm enjoying myself while I'm doing it."

Big Jim calmed down and got sincere. "You know Joe, that doesn't sound half bad. I work six days a week, 12 to 14 hours a day. I'm tired most of the time and even though Mary and I go to parties all the time and I act like I'm having a ball, I'm bushed and frazzled worrying about lawsuits and the feds. I made a million dollars last year after taxes, but I have wondered if it is worth it. I mean how much money do we need really?"

"But Jim, you wouldn't quit now, not when you are on top," Mary said.

"No I guess not," he answered. "Say, the crab is great here. Can I order for all of us?"

The dinner was pleasant. Big Jim and I spent most of the time talking about life and what it means. He was very interested in our work in the desert with Paul. "Sounds like it cleanses the soul."

"It does. It does."

Chapter 8

Roses! As we drove up that first Saturday of February there were rows and rows of white roses. They were a delight to see. They made "True Songs" come alive just sitting there in those five-gallon cans. We walked around the rows. I looked at the labels. They were "Ever Blooming" roses, which Liz said meant that they flowered almost all year. There were two types both white hybrid tea, "Sheer Bliss" and "Grand Final." They both had a strong sweet fragrance and had large blooms. Liz was beside herself as she dipped her nose into one rose after another. "Ah," she would say, "smell this one." While we were thus occupied, Paul and Arturo were looking on appreciatively.

When we went into the house, surprise of surprises; there sat Jesus on the couch. "Jesus, you came back?" I asked.

"Yeah, my homies talked me into it. They said that I should help my father. Then I started thinking about it and thought I'd give it another try. I'm sorry for the way I acted last week."

I raised my hand as if to say, "No problem." We all gathered around the table in the kitchen to drink our coffee and share some rolls. Paul asked us to remain silent for a moment while he said a little prayer.

"Dear Protector, bless these decent people and make 'True Songs' a good and sacred place."

"Amen," said Liz. Then she asked, "Does prayer really work, Paul? I never thought it did. I figured it was so much baloney."

"Yes, and no," was his answer. "No, if it is just words. But definitely yes if it is done with presence. Then the window is open and your words are at least heard. Higher forces won't give you temporal things. They've assigned nature to do that and it is written into your individual plays beforehand, so don't waste good prayer on silly things. However, for things like grace or wisdom of God's creation, that is another matter. Inner opportunities will be granted by using prayer, but remember everything comes at a price and wisdom is the highest priced item on the menu. The price is suffering and/or work."

"I am willing to work, Paul," I said.

"You have certainly been given the opportunity, son. I don't know what is going to happen in the future, since that is closed to all human eyes, but I have a feeling deep within me that something is cooking and you are likely to be in the middle of it."

"That doesn't sound good," Liz said.

"Nothing is bad. Everything, no matter how awful seeming, is only a mask for a better place to be inside. Remember that. Now kids, let us get started on the work right in front of us."

I said, "How do we proceed this morning, Paul? I'm anxious to get started."

He took the last gulp from his cup. "We have to work together on this. I am glad there are five of us to do it. First we have to dig holes about 24 inches deep, put in some mulch and then cut the rose cans away and place them in the holes. Our next step is to fill the holes with dirt and pack it down. Also, in two or three places around each bush, we want to plant a clove of garlic."

"Garlic? I asked.

"Garlic is the best protector of roses there is," said Liz.

"Yes," said Paul, "apparently garlic keeps many pests and diseases away. This is what I am told by my two rose specialists on site, Arturo and Liz. Anyway, Yesterday Arturo and I marked where the roses go; three between each set of posts."

"How many bushes do we have out there Paul?" I asked.

He thought a moment. "Let's see. I ordered 125, but I think we only need 120 to do the job. That's along the front fence and then on both sides of the driveway. It is a lot of work."

"We can do it," Liz said.

"I know," Paul answered.

Jesus was a different worker than he was the week before. He handled the shovel with a hardy grace copied no doubt from his father. The father and son team were the diggers, Liz was the mulch and garlic girl, and Paul and I the planters. Sometimes, Liz would get up and wield a shovel if she was waiting for a new hole to be finished. Paul kept whispering to me as we crawled around the ground, "Be present, Joe. Be present. You are feeding your almighty soul." His saying that was strong medicine for me. Whenever Liz came close he would whisper something to her. I presumed it was the same thing.

At 11:00 it started to rain, not hard, but enough to drive us indoors. We decided on an early lunch, and if it wasn't too muddy we'd resume later. Arturo and Jesus combined to cook us some special pork tacos with rice and beans. The pork was fried crispy. They were especially delicious. After we ate it started raining even harder. Paul told Arturo and Jesus they could go home because we weren't going to be able to do any more work that day.

We went into our new bedroom and saw that Paul had gone to some expense getting it ready for us. The queen sized bed and chest of drawers were new and made of oak. The mattress was solid, and the bedspread, sheets and pillow cases had a red rose pattern. On the night stand was a vase full of white roses and a card that said "Welcome to True Songs—Paul." When she read it Liz hugged Paul for a long time and sobbed softly. I was overwhelmed too.

I walked out to the patio and thought about this new life of mine. Nothing made any ordinary sense. I was busting my ass off here digging and crawling in the dirt, and working as a cab driver in the city and giving half my pay away. But in return, I had the most decent and loving woman I had ever known, and as my friend and teacher I had a guy who defied description. A saint he was. I often felt awed in his presence even when he was doing nothing. He was humble and smart and I don't know what else. He was making me see everything from a different perspective. From the other side of the screen door he called, "Do you play chess young man?"

"Yes I do," I said, "I played on the chess team in college."

"Good, perhaps you will teach me something this afternoon."

I should have known that Paul was good, but he suckered me into thinking he was a bump on a log. He kept making what I thought were amateur moves. Then when I took his queen after about twenty moves, I smiled a wicked grin at him. As I was grinning he said the words "check and mate." I looked down in complete surprise. I had been so stupid I quit paying attention to what he was doing. "Again?" I asked him.

"Sure," he smiled slightly. "Maybe you can teach me something this game."

But this time I was on to him and gave him a good game. He still won, but at least I played better. "Where did you learn to play?"

"One of my early students was a grand master. He taught me a few things."

"How many students have you had," I asked, "and what are they doing now."

"I have had a number official students. I don't remember exactly, maybe 20 or so. I've had more than that who started but ran away after a short time, finding either me or the knowledge too bizarre. Of the ones I had for about a year, many have taken what they know out into the world to try to bring some consciousness to humanity. I've given two permission to teach—one in Germany and one in Canada. We keep in touch."

Liz had been watching with amusement, but not listening because she was on the other side of the room, said as she walked over closer, "Okay, master, how about teaching us some philosophy?"

"All right," he said, "but before I start I need to go to the bathroom and get a glass of water." He got up and went to the bathroom. When the door closed, I turned to Liz and kissed her hard on the lips.

"I can't wait to try that new bed for its buoyancy," I said with mock passion in my voice.

"Well, while Paul is in here with me why don't you go in and bounce around awhile and tell me what you think. I'll tell Paul you're in there having sex by yourself. He'll understand."

"No, I don't think he will. He can see you are beautiful. He'd think I was crazy."

Paul came in and we retook our dignified philosophical postures; ready to receive the Word. He passed us by and poured some water into a glass full of ice. While he was doing that Liz whispered in my ear, "You're cute. I'll test that bed with you later."

Paul sat in his chair, smiled at us and began. "I'd like to tell you about something called considering. It is very important to understand this because it will explain why humans act the way they do. Considering comes in two forms: 'internal,' also called 'inner considering,' and 'external considering.' Almost all of the considering that humans experience is inner considering. This type of considering comes from our attitude that we are due special attention from everyone we come into contact with. It is a deep emotional reflex that goes to the core of our own feeble state and is the root of selfishness. We have high expectations of how others are supposed to treat us. We internally demand that people pay homage to how intelligent, thoughtful, and decent we are, even if we aren't any of those things. We are constantly taking offense at other people because they do not value us enough. Someone cuts us off on the highway and we are incensed that they would do such a thing to *us*. A clerk in a store takes a little too long waiting on us and we are beside ourselves with anger. How dare they! This goes on every day of our lives and covers not only real events, but also our imagination of how others are thinking of us. We think that they, whoever they is, had better be thinking good things about us. We are forever prepared to take offense and rehearse our responses from an absurdly vain posture. The thing is, we like to talk about others and do it often and in the meanest and most judgmental ways, but hate it when others talk about us for it might be bad, because that is what we do. We skewer those around us in a variety of ways, but they better not be doing that to us, and if we ever get a scent that they are, we are insulted. This is even though that is exactly what we do."

"I do that," said Liz.

"Everyone does it," he went on, "but this low comedy of judging other things is aimed not only at people, but at all kinds of other events and objects like the weather, politics, our car, or the traffic. We take it personally when traffic lights stop our progress, or when the law prevents us from some activity. We spend countless hours in imagination lecturing traffic engineers, politicians, policemen, and clerks about our special status and how they ought to change everything for our benefit. After all, we have just pointed out their stupidity for not doing so. We even pray to God to change the weather for our sake, for a picnic or our general comfort. And the real funny part is that when something goes our way, we smugly think that God has given it to us, and then with false humility we thank Him."

"You make us sound pretty silly," I said.

"Yes, of course silly, but all of this comes from the notion that we are of tremendous significance; the very center of the universe, and that's the silliest part. No matter who we are, everyone feels exactly the same way. It is one of the attributes of being human. This is the reason that how we appear is more important than who we actually are or what we do. We expect each person we come into contact with to pay homage to our image. If they don't, or don't appear to, we take it quite personally. We have developed elaborate acts to convey exactly how we wish to be treated and thought about. A person who has a special position in society, like a mayor or a wealthy businessman, puts on a certain act of being regal and will develop the habit of talking down to those under him or her. It is all smoke though, and they have no fire in them."

"Well, does anybody have it together?" I asked.

"Only someone who knows his or her self. They alone realize the folly of such parading around in image. They've seen it and are horrified by it. Most people never even get a glimpse of their real self."

Liz got up to go to the bathroom. "I keep thinking you are talking about me personally. You should see how I act at the hospital. I'm a terror. Even the doctors watch it when they are around me. I'm beginning to see that I'm awful."

"Yes, Liz, you have the opportunity to see yourself in a different way now. The thing is, when you get to work again, those I's will want to do the same thing. Don't try to stop it. Just observe it and after a time, if you see it enough and see it for it's ugliness, it will go away of its own accord. If you try to stop it, it will just wait until you are not paying attention and rear its horrific head again, only worse the next time. That is the magic of observing yourself. We cannot change by willing it because we are not able to do anything. We have no control. Self observation, that is dividing yourself in two; the observer and the observed, will be the vehicle we can use to make changes, and they will be natural, not by force."

Then he got up and stretched. "Let's finish this after dinner. I want to go to the little store and make a few phone calls."

"Why don't you get a phone put in here?"

"I've been thinking about it. It would be easier."

Before Liz came out, he left in the pouring rain. "He's gone for awhile," I said.

She sat in his chair. "He understands human nature so much. I wonder what he was like when he was young?"

"From what he said, he and his wife started the search when they were pretty young. He might have always been like this."

"Joe."

"What?"

"You know what really turns me on?"

"What?"

"A man without his shirt on."

"Like this?" I said as I pulled mine off.

"Yes, that did it."

We really didn't give that new oak bed a decent trial. Right in the middle of everything, Liz remembered about the pictures. I tried not to take it personally, but when she exclaimed, "The pictures!" the lovemaking was over and I was left sprawled atop the love bed. After she dressed she scrambled out into the kitchen and spread the photos out on the table. She just stared at the ones I told her about. "God, oh God," is all she said.

"Well what do you think?" I asked.

"I think that we are in something special; a play, like Paul says. In some ways it is kind of creepy, but since I know Paul, I know he wouldn't be involved anything like that. I don't want to go into imagination on this. I want to be grounded and just watch what happens."

"It adds another dimension to this place and our place in it."

"Let's not say anything to Paul about it and just see what happens, okay?"

"Okay," I said as Paul's truck came rumbling up.

When he came in he brought some fresh fish from the store for the evenings meal. We all involved ourselves with the preparation. It was raining hard outside. After we had worked cutting and breading the fish for a while, I asked Paul if he believed that higher beings were helping him on earth. He stopped and looked at me a moment. He turned and ran some water over his flour-covered hands. As he dried them with a paper towel he said, "Joe, for me it is a fact, not a belief. If I tell you much more of how I know this, you and Liz will go off into imagination and I may never get you back. Suffice it to say that I knew I was safe from those boys last week. They couldn't have hurt me if they wanted to. They could've hurt you and that is why I got you out of there."

"How did you know?"

"Liz, I knew because my role is something different. I have something to do here before I go, and it is not to be killed by a bunch of boys. I am not going to live much longer. I don't know how much longer I'll be here, but not long; not more than a year.

My life has been full of the most bizarre coincidences, almost from the first. Most of them I can't even explain or understand. Many of them have indicated that humanity is coming to a climax of some sort. Higher Forces are ready to make some changes here on earth. I don't want to be part of it. I've run from this notion for many years. I may not have any choice."

We just stared. "What are we doing here?" I asked.

"I don't know, but something important that is for sure." He threw the paper towel in the wastebasket and went outside. "I'll be back in a few minutes."

A few minutes turned into an hour, and would have been more but I had to call him in for dinner. "I'm sorry I talked in that way to you. I won't do it again. I don't want you to feel like I'm some mystical being because I'm not. I just get carried away. I'm sorry."

After a quiet dinner he began again to tell us about considering. "All right now, where were we? Oh, I know. There are many facets to inner considering. One that is interesting is that each of us has our own special justice system. This system of right and wrong is entirely subjective and grounded in our whimsical presumption that no matter what we hear or read about a situation, we have all of the facts necessary to pass judgment. Never mind that there are always many sides to every problem and that every side has a multitude of sides and sides of sides. We still feel a moral right to pass judgment based on the smallest amount of information. Not only do we make a ruling on the situation, we almost inevitably pass harsh judgment. Mercy is not in our normal make-up. That extreme part of the emotional brain is the culprit most of the time.

Of course, most of this goes on in our imagination and is never seen by anyone. This way we can maintain our image. In our imagination we are judge, jury and executioner and everyone should get what's coming to them, except us of course. We imagine our own innocence no matter what the crime or what the evidence and plead our case in the fantasy courtroom of our minds.

We are so immersed in our own inner considering that we are unable to see the world objectively. We have, in our interior world, a hierarchy of worth among people of various stations. Big businessmen, church officials, rich people, and famous people head our list, with the poor and sick last. We live in a world of comparison and are taught by society who is important and who is not. Then we treat people based on these judgments; again mostly in imagination, but still enough on the outside to create a skewed society where spark and spangle are more important than intelligence or depth. We suffer from this extraordinary high opinion of ourselves that is a plague to us personally and to the larger society. Christ said, 'Blessed are the meek for they shall inherit the earth.' The meek here means people not so full of inner considering that they can see the true nature of things. Further, it means to be without resentment and has nothing to do with the outward act of meekness. To be without resentment means not to inner consider, to be balanced in our view of the world, to take all things on their right level.

Another way to see inner considering is realizing how much we fear other's judgment of us. Many of our actions in life are geared entirely to fit within imaginary parameters of other people. It does keep us in line within a society since we act based upon our fears of what other people will think about us. However, for us personally, it limits our creativity and keeps us fretting about other people's opinions. 'What will people say,' is what controls us as a society."

Paul was silent. We were silent. I was thinking about how I had spent my life putting myself in this hierarchy he spoke about and worrying about what others thought about me. "How do we change this?"

"By being in the present. It is the cure-all for all our ills." He got up and kissed Liz on the cheek and without another word went to his room.

It began to rain hard again early on Sunday morning. I sat up in bed and looked out the window at the deluge. Big puddles of water were everywhere. I knew that we weren't going to be doing any planting that day. Liz looked up from under the covers. I said, "sleep," and crawled in with her snuggling against her front. She made a grunt of displeasure and turned around so that we were like spoons in a drawer. In one minute flat Liz was breathing the deep pleasure of well-earned sleep. At 9:30 my eyes opened again. The rain had stopped. Liz was now facing me with her nose in my neck.

I rose slightly to look at the clock on the wall. "Honey, it is 9:30."

"What." She was up like a shot. "Oh, my goodness, Paul must have been waiting for us for hours." She put on her housecoat and went out into the hall. As she opened the door I could see Paul's door open and a pajama clad man wave like a little boy. "I'll make coffee," she said as if guilty for something.

"Great," he said. "Look outside Liz. It looks like another play day for us."

I got up and showered and put my work clothes on, just in

case. When I sat down to coffee, Liz gave me a peck on the lips, said, "Love you," and was off to the bathroom. By 10:15 we were all sitting at the table where I had placed a platter of scrambled eggs, bacon and toast.

As we were eating Paul asked if we'd like to go with him to visit the San Xavier Mission. "I'd like to go. I've never been there," I said. "How about you, Liz?"

"I'd love it. It is such a peaceful place."

We drove out in my van. On the way Paul gave us a run down on the Mission and its history. "It was first built in 1700 with Father Kino overseeing it. I believe he placed the cornerstone. Kino was a saint. He brought Christianity and a sense of order to the Pima Indians. He humbly worked among them for 24 years. His main contribution on a higher plane was love. He showed all who ever had contact with him how to love.

Later, after the Jesuits were expelled by Spain, the Franciscans took over and rebuilt it in their style. And then in, I think 1886, an earthquake pretty much destroyed it. It has since been rebuilt again. Now there is a major restoration going on. What I like about it is that it feels like a sacred place. I've been there many times to worship."

"Are you a Christian?" I asked.

"Not in the usual sense. But you don't have to be a strict Christian to worship. I've had some amazing experiences inside that church. I feel a holy presence there."

The Mission was on an Indian Reservation 20 miles southwest of Tucson. It sat like a ship in a desolate sea of desert. The reservation was poor, with run down houses scattered about. There was a place that advertised "Indian Fry Bread," about one hundred yards from the church. The mission itself was in a somewhat state of disrepair. Once inside, I could feel that it was indeed special. I'm sure I couldn't feel the things that Paul felt, but it was powerful nonetheless. Paul whispered to us, "Feel this place with your heart," and then signaled us that he wanted to be left alone, so Liz and I joined the rest of the tourists walking around and touching the walls and statues. After about fifteen minutes we were ready to go to the gift shop off to the side of the church. We looked for Paul. We found him kneeling in a pew in front of one of the side altars. His eyes were closed. We decided to leave him alone.

After about an hour and a half we left. Paul invited us to a well-known Mexican Restaurant in town. We ate in this noisy family filled place while Paul gave us bits of information about some of his former students. "One woman, with six children came to my house and demanded I take her on as a student. She had all six kids with her," he laughed. "I wondered if she just wanted day care, but she proved to be an excellent pupil. I don't know how she managed it, but she took care of the kids and a very demanding husband, and still spent quality time with me learning the same things you are learning. I finally started going out to her house every day and ended up doing housework and changing diapers while we talked about Shakespeare." He had a most happy smile on his face.

"You've given a lot of service in your life, haven't you?" asked Liz.

"You have to my dear. It is the path to heaven."

Before we arrived back I asked Paul to explain how he thought the universe started, or what caused it to start. "I am teaching you a different way to think about things because the old mechanical way leads nowhere," he said. "In fact, the most necessary thing to do in this work is to think differently. Christ said it many times in the gospels but it was mistranslated into 'repentance.' Until you can totally change your thinking you will be stuck with this flat earth with its flat way of seeing.

"One of the ways to look at this issue is that nothing starts and nothing ends. Everything is and has been in constant flux. It is a perpetual transformation machine, even us. We are transforming and being transformed at this very moment. This means that what you might describe as an ending is only a change of some sort. A beginning is a change from something else, but still containing the seed of the thing from before. You take a bite of food; it is gone, but it is being transformed into something else. The universe is in continual metamorphose, always being remolded. Life gets the idea that something begins or ends from its paltry vision and understanding. Shakespeare said in one of his sonnets, 'Everything holds in perfection but a little moment.' He means that after that brief moment it starts to become something else."

So when you hear about the 'Big Bang' or some such absurdity, just know that the universe is and was forever. It is a living being with many beings within it. The earth is just such a being, with its core serving as its heart, pumping blood-like lava out onto the surface to renew itself. We have a very narrow conception of what living means, but everything that exists has life on its own terms."

"That makes sense, but it is not logical, at least I don't think," I said.

"Logic is low thinking and doesn't contain a speck of understanding, which comes from our Emotional Center. Life presents logic as something high, but at best, it can only be an aide to something high. The idea of beginning and end is an example of logical thinking, but for the purposes of understanding anything deep, it is useless."

"What about when people say there is no God because the world has too much suffering?" asked Liz. "That is what I always said and believed."

Paul was sitting in back and had been leaning forward with his arms on our seats. After Liz asked her question he moved forward and seated himself between us. He looked squished, but his slender frame just fit in the slot between our seats. "That's right, the world is full of pain. One philosopher called it a pain factory. What must be understood here is that suffering is money in heaven. Now I'm not talking about unnecessary suffering. That is the kind motivated by worry about the future or fretting about something in the past. The constant bellyaching that humans engage in is just so much unnecessary suffering. I'm talking about real suffering; sickness and hunger and all of the other torments humans are subject to. This is heaven's currency, but only if it is used right. Quiet acceptance is the way to convert suffering into money for heaven. Being in the present while you are suffering is using this money for all its worth. To suffer in silence is golden.

Life thinks it is a curse to suffer, but all life suffers and always will. As long as hardship and trouble are considered something terrible and must be avoided, it cannot be used as currency. It is a gift I tell you. It is a gift for you if you accept it. So, when people say that there is no God because there is too much suffering and a merciful God would not allow his people to suffer. They don't understand. Nothing is free my children. Everything must be paid for and if the reward is heaven, the best payment is in the money of real suffering, but only with presence, otherwise it will be wasted.

This does not mean that you should find way to make yourself suffer. You will be given just what you need for your evolution. So, don't go looking for it, it knows the way."

We pulled into the driveway. It had started drizzling again. I was thinking about what Paul said. I had never heard anything like it before. It was good stuff, I thought.

Liz tried to go out and work in the mud, but Paul wouldn't let her. He gave us a choice of going home or hearing him talk a little on self-love. We picked hearing him talk. Liz got out her little pad to take notes. At first Paul had not wanted that, but then when she said please, he relented. He's a sucker for her too, I thought. We got all settled on our couch with sodas. "We are madly in love with ourselves. We are the center of everything in our minds. One of the worst things a person is asked to endure is an insult. It penetrates right down deep into our vanity. The person who has received such an insult will be like a roaring lion, if not outwardly, as least inwardly. He or she will do the most dastardly deeds in their imagination trying first to hurt the insult giver, and then to excuse their own actions in some way. The heat from one little negative comment has enough energy in it to last for days. Watch your imagination especially after you have been told something you don't like, or that is somehow derogatory. It will be good theater, and funny too if you can separate from it and look at it while it is happening."

This also leads to another aspect of inner-considering, and that is that we develop an elaborate system of 'account keeping' on people's behavior. In this system we remember who we treated well and expect certain treatment in return. This is not a monetary situation, but an emotional one. This idea that someone is indebted to us can span years or decades. The opposite is also at work, our account keeping extends to those who were not so nice to us. We may spend a considerable amount of time paying the person back, even if it is only in our fantasies. This psychological principle promotes complaining and an attitude that the world owes us and should be nice to us no matter what we do."

"Can you give me an example that I might be able to see?" asked Liz.

"Well, at work does everyone treat you like to want?"

"Are you kidding? Even though I'm kind of a difficult person to be around to most of the staff and they treat me with respect, still a lot of those high and mighty surgeons treat me like some kind of servant. One or two of them really get my goat."

"That is inner-considering. You are keeping accounts on how they should treat you. Even if you never say anything to them, you will waste energy day-dreaming about showing them up, or telling them off. Do you see that Liz?"

"Okay, got it. So, you are saying that everybody does that?"

"All of the time. It is how the world works."

"And the only way out of it is to self-remember?" I asked.

"Yes, that and observing yourself. And don't forget, you can only work on <u>you</u>. Life will never see it in the first place, and it is too perversely satisfying to stop it even if they did. Account keeping makes people feel real in an unreal world. Everybody gets to be on their own illusionary soap box or in a pulpit."

He seemed tired, although all that we did was ride around and talk. But then he did most of the talking. I figured that teaching must be a drain on him. While Liz tidied up the bedroom, I loaded up some stuff to take home.

On the way home I said to her, "You know I've only known you for a little over a month now but I feel like it is year at least."

"At least. We are on the fast track, I guess. Next thing you know we'll be living together."

"Do you want to live together now?"

"No, it's too early," she said. "Maybe next week," she added with a smile.

I became a substitute teacher that next week. The pay was only $46 per day and that was about what I was earning driving a cab. I didn't have to quit my old job. It wasn't that kind of position. I just never showed up again. Nobody knew the difference. We weren't that close of a group. I presumed that substitute teaching was teaching. But after my first day on the job, I found out it was more like nothing. I walked into an English class figuring I would teach the freshmen all about grammar or writing.

The note from the teacher said, "Take roll. Allow only one student out at a time to the rest room. Good luck." But what was I supposed to do I wondered?

As the kids began to pile into the room the place was filled with glee. "A substitute, a substitute," they kept saying. I thought it was because they didn't like their teacher and were relieved to see another adult.

No, that wasn't it. They were happy because it meant party time. I had a hard time getting them to sit down, and when they did sit down it didn't look like the seating chart at all. A couple of girls were sitting on boy's laps, several desks had been rearranged to face each other and no one was in their right place. And noise; they were laughing and cussing and somebody had their stereo on high. Finally, I yelled to get their attention. It worked--for a couple of seconds. Then it was back to chaos. Several girls started to leave. I stopped them. "Where are you going?"

"To the nurse," one of them said. "We have an emergency." The others nodded that this was true. "We'll be back before class is over. It is only a one period emergency."

Everybody was laughing at me as the girls left. I started thinking about the calm, sedate taxi. That day I had five periods; two of them were from hell, one from purgatory, and two were from earth. No heavenly classes that day. When I tried to talk to several teachers I was given the cold shoulder. Finally toward the end of lunch an elderly lady came up to me. "I can see that you are a sub too. Sometimes the staff is not too friendly. It is just because they don't know you. They have many of the same problems you do, only they have stay here every day."

"I thought something was wrong with me."

"There is, you can't get a job, so you're a sub. A lot of the teachers think we are losers. Not all of them, but some of them."

"That's interesting. To heck with them," I said. "I'm here for the big bucks, not their approval." I laughed. I wasn't going to inner consider these people. They had to put up with those students every day. What a torture.

In the five days I had five different assignments with five different high schools. It was pretty much the same with the teachers, although each school was different as far as students were concerned; some were much more attentive than others. I decided to only go to those schools since I pretty much had my choice. I almost felt like calling Big Jim and telling him of my significant career move.

Liz told me during our drive to "True Songs" on Saturday that she did much better inner considering her doctor bosses. "It is almost a relief not to have to be concerned how they treat me."

"How did you do on the other end of the scale? How did you treat some of the other nurses; the ones you said you deride?"

"Better; not perfect, but noticeably better. They think I'm in love or something," she said. "Well, I am in love; in love with you and in love with my own possibilities. That sounds funny; in love with my own possibilities, but it is true. I feel so much more alive now."

"Me too. I felt better all week when I did something that I would ordinarily inner consider, and have the thought; 'be present' instead."

"Me, I feel like an apostle. I am the first woman apostle." She smiled broadly and winked at me.

We pulled up to "True Songs" and were surprised to find most of the white roses planted. They must have worked like crazy, I thought. Only one row down the driveway needed to be finished. It was a beautiful sight.

In the house I saw that Jesus was back again. As we started our coffee ritual, Paul told us that we should finish the white roses today and that a truck was delivering 100 "Mr. Lincoln" red rose bushes sometime this morning. We could then start on them as soon as we finished with the whites. He said that we would eventually need about 300 red bushes. We were going to keep the remaining four white bushes in case some of the ones we just planted died.

The ground was still saturated with water so the digging was easy. Digging is never easy, but in comparison with what we did the week before this was a snap. I suggested that Jesus, Arturo and myself just continue making holes after we finished with the ones along the drive way. Paul said it was okay, so the three of us diggers became a well-oiled team. Jesus and I were the lead diggers with a hole each and then Arturo came behind us and measured the hole and made corrections as needed. Jesus was more like his father than I thought. He really got into it and matched me stroke for stroke.

My arms ached at lunch. Jesus was rubbing his too. After we finished eating Arturo took his son out to look at something in the back. Then Liz surprised me. She told Paul we had seen the photos in his drawer. "It was shocking to see how much I looked like both your wife and daughter, and the name thing really sent my head spinning."

Paul put his fork down on his pie dish. "You can probably figure out how shocked I was when I first saw you. I was having trouble controlling my feelings, and that is truly rare. I don't completely understand it even now. I think that Higher Forces are giving me a gift. Liz, you have no idea how much you act like Libby, and in some things you act like Alice. I told you my life has been full of coincidences. Well, this is just an example."

"Do you think this place is sacred?"

"I don't know, but with you here, Liz, it sure feels like it sometimes. And Joe, my son who died had your same name. I still don't know what it means, if anything. I doubt it means nothing. I feel a storm coming inside me and I'm glad you both are here with me.

America, this land of the free and home of the brave, is at its core a mean spirited, spoiled, war-like country. We make war with the thinnest of excuses and march around like we are heroes. In times of trial, like hunger or want of some commodity that we are used to having, the people of this country will turn outwardly vicious. We've already armed ourselves with millions of guns. We are ready, and many are hoping for the worst so that they can use those guns. Many people in our country are in love with being self-righteous and rude. They are subtle sometimes and always have an excuse to cover up their cruel intentions, but it is a perverse pleasure to say or do something hurtful. I think the Gods have had enough of this foolishness and are preparing a storm for us."

"A storm?"

"Yes, Joe, like I said before, something big, but I don't know what yet. I just get a powerful feeling that whatever it is will be payment for the way we acted over the last 50 years or so. We've got to be ready kids, and the only way I know of is to be present and finish the roses."

"Well, we can start right now," said Liz as she was opening the door.

Liz took the conversation literally and she was going to do all she could for this peculiar man who affected us so. I think that she just needed that little extra boost to give her absolute all to the project. It was love that propelled her into this new mission. She loved Paul like a father; like the father she never really had. But this was even better because Paul was a super-father, kind and wise, powerful but in a gentle way. I wasn't jealous of this. I rather admired her for it. As for me, I personally couldn't work any harder. I was trying my best as it was. As I was digging after our conversation, I kept coming back to the thought that something big was afoot. The last two months or so had been so strange and wonderful that anything he said I believed. Paul was the most sincere person I'd ever met; like Socrates or Jesus. I don't think he could or would lie to me. He might be mistaken on this one though. I hoped he was. I didn't fancy being in on something big. I was just a substitute teacher.

We finished the white bushes just before lunch. The advance digging team of Arturo, Jesus and myself were well on with the holes on the west side of the property. We had finished about ten when we went in to eat. Just as I was walking in the door the truck with the red roses arrived. I met the two burly delivery men and asked them if they would drop off the cans all along the line we were planting instead of in one big bunch by the house. They said no, but I offered them $50 a piece to do it. They changed their mind. This was going to save us at least a few hours just not having to lug those heavy pots around. As I walked back to the house, I felt like I had made a contribution to our cause and it only cost money.

We laughed about my experiences as a sub during lunch. I told them about one boy who was copying from a girl next to him during a test. He was so mindless that he copied her name too. "We do the same thing all of the time," Paul said. "We have a part of us, in our Intellectual Center that is called the 'formatory apparatus' that just copies what others say or think. That is why life is always repeating the same things in the same way. They pick something up that is a nifty way to express something; 'weapons of mass destruction,' for instance, and everyone says it. Of course, that is what we call the other guy's weapons. Ours we call 'nuclear deterrent ' because it sounds more palatable. Obviously no one gives credit to whomever they heard those phrases from because that would be ridiculous. But in many ways it is the same thing as what that young man was doing. Life is on automatic. We drive, eat, emote, and a thousand other things while completely asleep, and we don't even know it. But it is God's design so that only a few stout souls will find the way out of the cloud of unknowing."

I went out to pay my special workers before they left. Everyone followed and went to work building "True Songs." Thinking about it, I thought when this thing was over I'd like to commission a statue of Walt Whitman with his quote about "The True Songs' on a plaque. Around three o'clock I couldn't dig another shovel full of dirt. I sat on the turf for fifteen minutes before joining the planting crew.

I could see that Liz was tired when we finally came in around 6 o'clock that evening. I sent her in for a nap while I helped Paul fix dinner. He was quiet while we peeled the potatoes and made the veal patties. He did look up once and say in the most sincere tone. "Joe, if you can work hard enough on yourself, you may be able to enter the Now. It is an incredible place."

"Can you describe it?"

He thought for a minute. "Just the fact of being here with your whole self is what is special. To feel the room around you and to see things from many perspectives all at once is hard to describe. But you are here; here deeply and emotionally."

"It is like taking drugs?"

"No. Being in the Now, the present, is very different."

"Would you advise taking drugs as an experiment?"

'No," he said most emphatically. "They are poison. For whatever you get out of them they take double in payment. I don't care what people told you, they are a bad medicine."

I woke Liz up for dinner. She seemed revived from her exhaustive state of an hour before. She told a story about a doctor the week before who made an error in an operation and the patient died. "He was beside himself. He was not a bit worried about the woman who had just passed away. He tried to get promises from all of us who were there to cover for him. I would not make such a promise and I told him. 'But,' he said, 'this could end my career.' My question to you Paul, is should I tell on him?"

"That is a strong moral question, Liz. It is not clear to me so I can't help you with it much. If you think that by telling something good will come of it, fine, do tell someone. But if it was just a mistake that was not his pattern at all and it won't help for him to go through the business of lawsuit and all the rest, maybe you shouldn't volunteer. It sure won't bring back the woman. I will say one thing though, if you do it because you don't like him, that would be wrong. Your decision must come from a higher place, not from inner considering."

"What if all of the above are true; that I don't like him and would like him to suffer for his mistake, and he is a fool that makes many such mistakes and never accepts criticism or changes. What then?"

"Two things," my dear, "the first is that it is yours to decide, but you must accept any consequences that come of it. If he can turn it around and blame you for instance, you may be the one that suffers, even if you are innocent. Once you do something, it may have all kinds of consequences that you never intended. This is not to say that you shouldn't ever do anything, especially what you think is right, but you be prepared for the unexpected outcomes."

"You said there were two considerations," she said, "What is the other?"

"The second is that we really decide nothing. We are compelled by forces not in our control to carry on our lives in a certain manner. No matter what you 'decide' today, it may not be what happens. It is really out of your hands except in your illusionary world. This is a much harder concept to see, but if you get it, it will make you humble; as well you should be."

His remark made me think about humility. "Why should we be humble?"

"The Gods accept no souls to the higher realms unless they have gotten rid of all of their poisonous vanity. To a great extent, they help us when we get old by taking away one function after another and making us unattractive. This should help us leave pride and vanity behind with our youth, but too many times it doesn't work. Most times vanity is the last to go, right with the body's demise."

"Wait," said Liz, "I want to know more about this idea of things not being in our hands and yet we have to suffer the consequences. First of all, don't we have free will? Or is it all a big play, as you have told us, and everything is out of our hands, except the consequences? That sounds wrong."

"It is a rather difficult idea to grasp," he started. "It is a play being performed in this big theater of the world. This big machine called life just turns out all of our situations and events mechanically and it is a downward spiral back to the brutish world we started with. So, it is not so much written as set into motion. However, that being said, Higher Forces have provided that individuals with some measure of real consciousness can pull the rest of humanity up. They, and only they, have Will, with a capital W. But it is not a Will that can control outside events, which are mechanical. Conscious Beings, or the Enlightened, can control their selves and can be used by Higher Forces for their own designs. Consciousness is like a shot in the arm for the earth. The Gods can direct and use such a person to create all sorts of beauty; to bring light and understanding through philosophy and various forms of art to our world and keep it from completely descending into a hell on earth. We have tottered toward that state many times."

"When you two," he looked at us both for a few seconds, "make efforts to be in the Now, you are saying to the Gods, 'Use me.'"

"Do you know who these Enlightened Beings were, or are?" Liz asked.

"I'll prepare a list for you later and give it to you. I only know some of them, but if you study them and read their writings, you will get a picture of what I'm talking about. They all are heading in the same direction—heaven, and they will take you along."

We were all silent. It started raining again. We all walked out into the patio to watch. "More denying force," Paul commented.

" I've never seen it rain so much this early in the year. Our rainy season isn't until July at least. Is that good or bad?" I asked.

"Neither," is what he said as he walked back inside.

He sat at the table and wrote letters for the next two hours. Liz and I read on the couch. I read Whitman and she read Emily Dickinson. Occasionally we would show each other something of what we were reading. They were both writing about the same thing in different ways, the soul and God. Paul took Liz's copy from her hand and sat down in his chair. He looked at it for a moment and gave it back to her. "Dickinson had an invisible role. She stayed to herself and wrote these noble poems about esoteric topics. They discovered her work after her death. Whitman, who lived at the same time, led a big life full of turmoil and hardship. They are both in heaven, yet got there in different ways."

"Walt Whitman's poetry was big and brave," I added.

"Yes, he was writing an opera; the opera of America and the soul. Whitman was a big fan of the opera and he got much of his early inspiration while being overcome with emotion in an opera house in New York. He called his poems songs, and they were, they were great arias from a great singer."

"Emily Dickinson seems so quiet compared to the blood and guts Whitman," Liz said.

"Soothing is a word I think of when I read her. She has calmed readers since her little packets of poems were discovered by her sister."

"You still read both of them?" I asked.

"I have owned those books for over forty years and visit them often. They are for different moods and for different times. Emily's letters are a joy to read. She had such a mastery over the English language it overwhelms me. I have made both Walt and Emily my friends, and like all good friends, they are there when I need them."

We got some work done the next day. We started planting in the holes we had already made the day before, but by 9 o'clock it started pouring again and we had to go in. Paul let Arturo and Jesus go home after paying Jesus for two full days work. We sat around the house and played cards, chess, and talked. Paul spent most of the time giving us examples of inner considering and then after he was sure we understood that concept, at least intellectually, he talked about the other considering; external consideration.

"The only way out of the human snarl of inner considering is through external considering. This requires effort of a different sort. It means working to be passive to others, to not respond to people's behavior. At first, this means pretending that you are unconcerned. You will judge an incident, but try not to indicate this in your outer manifestations. It will be a formidable trial to control this demon, but it is the first step to mastering inner considering which needs to be conquered in order for the purer external considering to take its place. The strength of the unpleasant judgments in imagination will become clearer as you try to self-remember each time these judgment I's surface. These I's have a ponderous amount of energy with which to be in imagination, and it is a royal battle to dissipate the energy. The only way to do this is by self-remembering, being in the present. At best it is a slow and torturous process. And also exhilarating."

"You mean by pretending that something that bothers you didn't bother you?" Liz asked. "Won't people take advantage of you if they know you are not going to get mad?"

"Maybe, but remember you are working on yourself. What they do is on them. I don't expect you to be a sucker, but wise. Somewhere in the New Testament, Jesus says for us to be gentle as a lamb and wise as a serpent. But the only reason that we would do this is to change ourselves and not be subject to the heavy laws nature has saddled us with. Internal consideration is a law of nature and everyone dances to its tune. It does not have to be this way however. There is another tune.

In its pure form, external consideration means putting yourself in another's place. Start from the other person's viewpoint and act from his attitude; not yours. Ask yourself what his requirements are and how you might help him. This does not mean giving away all of your money or time; it means not to judge, not to inner consider, and not to manifest according to your selfish view. It also means enduring the unpleasant actions of others without protestations and without inner revenge.

Real external consideration is not superficial like a waiter in a fine restaurant who takes care of your every need for money. It is deeper and the reward is the development of humility and it is the true path to humble empowerment."

I looked at Liz for a moment. "You mean the first step is to be passive to other people when they push your buttons, and then when you have mastered yourself to the point where it doesn't bother you, you can be active and think like them and help them?"

"Pretty close, only I think that some people will always bother you. Many still bother me. The thing is to never show it and by not showing it you will be able to resist those I's that wish revenge. External consideration is a magical formula that purifies the Emotional Center and can make you holy. It is not a weakness to give in when you do not want to. It is not a weakness to be polite to someone who has done something detestable. It is not a weakness to ignore an insult. On the contrary, this type of effort is for the strong; the real heroes of life."

I sat for a moment in silence. "We should go, Paul"

"All right. Do you want to come on the patio and pray with me?"

"We'd love to," answered Liz for the both of us.

As we stood in a line outside looking at the rain, Paul told us to hold hands. "While we are reciting this prayer try to keep focused on your body and the prayer at the same time. If you can do both you will truly be praying." He close his eyes, raised his head slightly. "Our Father, who art in heaven, hallowed be THY name..."

During that minute of worship I had another strange feeling as I entered the present more than ever. I welled up inside and imploded. That is not a very good way to explain it, but that is the best I can do. I seemed to see the roses on the side of the house in a new way. They came alive. Well anyway, it only lasted a little bit of time, maybe a second or maybe a minute. I lost all sense of time. I also felt Paul beside me as a holy presence. It was a very powerful minute.

The month of February was the rainiest month in twenty years in that part of the country. Liz and I went out every weekend but I think we only actually worked planting roses two full days and a few hours here and there. But it did give us a chance to spend more time with Paul in the house talking. Arturo still came around every day and even when it was raining managed to keep busy. By month's end the ring of roses was almost complete. Fifty remained to be planted. I was thinking that when we got finished, we would have planted 430 rose bushes. That was a remarkable accomplishment for the four or five of us. It was hard, hard work, but small payment for what I personally was getting from the experience. I think I know what the apostles must have felt like being around Jesus. I was quietly but continually in a higher state when I was around Paul.

In March Arturo brought out the snake dog to live at "True

Songs." We called him "Spot" because of two big patches of black on his otherwise white body. Watching him work was the most amazing thing to witness. Arturo took him on a long lease to survey the property every morning and just before dark. When Spot discovered a snake he backed up and let out a yowl and started barking. Arturo came over and picked the snake up with a long implement and placed him in a burlap bag. They did not catch a rattlesnake until they had been hunting a week, but lots of little snakes were bagged. The non-rattlers were taken a100 yards away and dropped off. Arturo took the poisonous ones way out somewhere and dumped them on his way home. I think that's what he was doing. He might have been killing them, but he never said he was and he wasn't supposed to.

On the morning of the 12th of March, Liz patted down the dirt on the final red rose bush, a brilliant red Chrysler Imperial. While we sat in the dirt around the bush, Paul went in the house and brought out five glasses and a bottle of red wine. He filled our glasses with wine and poured the rest of the liquid around that last plant. We raised our glasses and Paul made a short statement. "I dedicate this ring of roses to our Heavenly Father and all his angels who have been a part of this effort. I humbly thank Thee." With that we clicked glasses and drank.

Part II

Chapter 9

Things changed after that. The intensity was gone. There still was much work to be done, but it didn't feel like there was a time schedule. We were planning to put in a large patio in the middle, clumps of yellow roses around that. A number of trees and grass was to be planted. This would complete the project. And of course, the roses needed tending. Pruning and keeping weeds from choking them was going to be a major undertaking, but Liz was more than delighted to lead that task. I used to watch her sometimes when she was pruning the yellow ones by the house and she seemed to become part of each bush as she smelled and touched them. It was an affection I didn't understand, but one that I respected.

To be in the ring of roses was a most unusual feeling. Sometimes when I was alone and tried to be present and look around me, it felt like a church made of flowers. Later, it would seem like a fort protecting us from the onslaught of the outside world. But in those first heady slow days of March I thought of nothing but roses, Paul, Liz, and my own contentment. On April 1st, I asked Liz if she would become my wife. We were sitting alone in the patio. "Liz, I wonder if you would consider being my wife?"

She touched my cheek. "I would consider it, but aren't you still married?"

"Not for long. I think by the end of this month I will be a single man again."

"Would you like an answer today; on April Fools Day?"

"Well," I said, "I would like it anytime I can get a positive answer. The Fool in Shakespeare was usually the wisest person around, so it might be a good time—but only if the answer is yes."

"Yes."

"Yes?"

"Yes."

"Oh, God. Oh, God." We embraced and I could feel her tears roll down my neck confirming her commitment. After a couple of minutes we went inside and told Paul. He took both of us in his long arms and we all sobbed like little babies.

Before we left we decided to be wed in the middle part of May at "True Songs." By that time the big patio would be finished. Paul was a minister of some obscure church and said he would be happy to perform the ceremony. We drove away that evening holding hands trying to stay out of imagination.

The frenzy started anew for Liz. I don't know what it is with women, but the ceremony of marriage is a lot more important to them than to men. She went about the business of organizing the wedding in addition to her duties of rose gardener. Liz and Jesus had become closer over the past month as she showed him how to work with the roses. He took to that task with a rare gusto for a teenager. Arturo and I did all the other little tasks around the property. We watched the patio go up in a week's time. It was done by the same people who had built the house the year before. It was 40X30 feet with a grill in one corner and a retractable awning on the south side. Liz and Jesus planted yellow rose bushes around the outside.

While a backhoe came and dug 12 holes for trees, Paul, Arturo and myself repainted the trim on the house yellow to match the roses. On the 30th of April we helped two other employees of a nursery plant two eucalyptus, four sycamore, and six oak trees. During that month I noticed that Paul seemed to lack his normal energy. He would work with us for a few hours and have to rest in the house. When Liz showed concern, he just said that he was feeling his age.

I called my mother to invite her to come to the wedding but she told me her corns were acting up so she couldn't come. But she was sorry, she said. My brother said he couldn't come because he was too busy in Germany with business. Marge, my ex-wife, wouldn't tell me where I could reach Cindi. Just as well, I thought, she wouldn't have come anyway, and if she did, I wouldn't have enjoyed her company. Liz, on the other hand, invited everybody in her hospital and some of her old school chums. The total was going to be 100 guests, all on her side. She relayed to me her conversation with her mother about the wedding.

"Mom."

"Yes, dear, how are your doing?"

"Joe and I are getting married and we'd like you and Big Jim to come to the wedding in four weeks."

"The cab driver?" she asked.

"Well, he is a substitute teacher now. It is quite a bit better, mother."

"Oh, I hope so. I don't think I'd approve of you marrying a taxi driver. What future could he give you?"

"As usual mother, you are right. That is why I insisted he quit that job and become a professional substitute teacher."

"Good dear, I'm glad you put your foot down. Sure, we'll come. Where is it?"

While she was telling me this we were laughing at the way she put her foot down. "Wait 'till she finds out that a substitute teacher makes less than a taxi driver, I said."

"We won't tell her," Liz said, "and Big Jim will probably envy you."

"He didn't seem all happy working himself to a frazzle."

"Mom says he talks about selling out and retiring all the time. He should, they have all the money they could ever spend, but mom likes the social circle."

As the wedding day came closer, Liz became more concerned about Paul and his lack of energy. He was less active than ever and spent much of his days reading or contemplating. One night she took his temperature and his pulse. They were okay, but that didn't allay her fear. "It is not normal to lose your energy like you have in the last month or two."

"Why, Liz? The big job here is done. Just let me be an old man now."

"Well, okay, but if you get worse, let me know."

"I promise. Now the two of you come sit down for a while. I want to talk to you about this thing called energy." We sat on the couch ready for one of Paul's lectures. Liz curled her legs under her and leaned back in the corner while I did near the same thing in the other corner, except I couldn't curl my legs up like she could. "We eat food," he started, "and the Instinctive Center takes it and creates energy, or potential energy, in the body. It takes a lot of energy to just run the body under normal circumstances. The heart beating, breathing, digestion and all of the rest of it takes energy. The Moving Center uses energy too with all of our movements like walking and chewing. But most of the energy is in reserve waiting for something to release it.

It requires a psychological component to release energy beyond what is necessary to sustain life. That component is impressions."

"Impressions?" I asked.

"Yes, anything coming in the five senses is an impression. Depending on how we interpret the impression is how much energy we will automatically let out for our response. In other words, if we see a rattler crawling in the living room here, that will release a certain amount of energy to deal with it. But if a baby was crawling across the same floor, the energy would be of a different type and come from a different place depending on what we wanted to do; pick it up and cuddle it or protect it if that snake was there. Another example might be you taste some food that is spoiled, you instantly have the energy to spit it out and go over and throw it away. There are thousands of examples, but if you think about it our responses will be fueled by the impression themselves. Our Emotional Center expends much of our available energy. Anger and other negative emotions take a lot of energy. If you hear something critical that someone is supposed to have said about you, you throw a fit and expend a mountain of energy. This is so even if you heard wrong; they were talking about someone else.

The thing of importance here is what you 'thought' they said. That is an impression.

Each impression has the capability of releasing only so much energy, depending on how big and important the impression. If you see a car accident on the corner it will liberate energy, but after you think or talk about it for a time, the energy will be used up and you won't want to think or talk about it any more. On the other hand, if the impression is more important, like a loved one passing away, the energy that is generated may come for many months and be of a more intense nature because you will keep replaying the impression in your mind. Once the energy finally dissipates, you will be said to have gotten over the incident."

"So what happens if you don't receive any impressions?" asked Liz.

"Well, that is not likely, since we are bombarded by impressions by the thousands everyday. We can only respond to a few of these or we would quickly go into overload, but our system will not allow that. But in the case of being in a place where limited or no impressions are coming in, we would die. Food, air, and impressions are the things we absolutely need to survive. Take away one of those and the other two do not matter. Also, we have one place to intake air, one to take in food, and five for impressions—the five senses."

"Is that what fuels imagination?" I asked.

"It fuels everything we do psychologically, and especially our imagination. Our fantasy world depends upon things happening so it can go and create the endless scenes and conversations that humans spend their lives in. This is why, by being in the present, you can short circuit this waste of energy and it can be used to create your soul."

"Now some people have a lot of energy while others are like slugs no matter what happens. How can that be if they all are responding to the same impressions?" I inquired.

"Two things," Paul said. "The first is that different people have more raw energy to draw from than others. Certain types have a tremendous storehouse of energy to use while other types have little to use, no matter what the impression."

"Types?" Liz said.

"Yes, types. There are different types of people on the earth. I haven't told you about them yet. Maybe I will later if I think you can use the information for your evolution. But let me not get off the subject of energy. The second thing to know about energy is that having energy, especially too much energy, is not comfortable. The normal human drive is to get rid of their energy. If a person has a lot of energy, they will be driven to expend it as fast as they can. They will walk fast, talk fast, and when they talk, they will expend energy in just the way they talk; more plosives and more words emphasized. Plus, they are likely to talk more. Talking and imagination are the prime releases of emotional energy. Western culture has more high-energy people than Eastern cultures. That is why Americans are driven to build and do things and succeed in life. All of that takes great quantities of energy.

On the other hand, persons with a low amount of energy will have a different take on life. They will be more patient, do more sitting and resting, and have tomorrow as a goal to get something done. Many Eastern cultures are like this and their religions and other social organizations will reflect this fact. Their worship will be sitting quietly and meditating or chanting, no big building projects for them. There is nothing wrong or right in either way. They just have their root in how much energy is available to them as a people. This is why, for instance, the German people are so different in almost every way from the Polynesian people; energy."

"So does this mean that we are trapped in the kind of life we can have by the amount of energy we manufacture?" asked Liz.

"Also, does this mean that high energy people and societies are better?" I added.

"No, I don't want you to think formatorily on this subject. By formatory I mean in a yes/no mold, or a logical way. In the first place high energy is not better by any means, nor is it worse; it is just different. We in the Western world tend to think of accomplishments like creating big mechanized societies as better, but they are not. In many ways they are a detriment to our inner development. We are not as able to stop and look at the mess we are creating with our busybody schemes. There is no invention or project without a corresponding downside, and many times we are blind to the down-side or we don't give it enough importance. So, because a person or a country does not have great quantities of energy means virtually nothing in the real world of the soul.

Liz, in answer to you, since energy is released by impressions, it can also create energy in a matter of speaking. The raw energy in the body can manifest in many different ways in many different places, at a football game or at an opera. With the knowledge I am giving you now, you can, by simply putting yourself in places of higher impressions, bring forth a higher type of energy. Great works of art, fine architecture, classical music, awe inspiring literature, or decent and good friends will release in you an energy that is finer and easier to use for your own higher purposes. If you choose to be around wrestling matches, loud friends, or other low impressions, you will tend to be that. In a way, each person is a totality of their impressions. Do you two understand what I'm talking about?"

"Yes," I answered. Liz nodded in agreement. "So" I asked, " a person who stays away from lower impressions will become higher as a result?"

"I think that is right, but remember that everyone is around lower impressions much of the time. It is not possible to escape that, but you can learn to separate from them so they do not do damage to you."

"How?" Liz asked.

"By being present to them and intentionally not letting them in. In other words, suppose a co-worker is yelling at you. Now that is a low impression, but if you are present, you will realize that she can't hurt you or make you mad. If you respond in kind, the low impression got in and did some damage. The whole answer to this and many things is in increased self-awareness.

Strive always to have as much beauty in your life as possible. There are all kinds of beauty. Graciousness is beauty of behavior. Virtue is beauty of the spirit. Wonderful art and music are rich food for the soul that helps in the transforming process from beast to angel, from horns to wings. Remember this my dear friends; beauty's purpose is to make us beautiful, so bring beauty, beautiful impressions, into our being via presence. Jump in heart-first. I read somewhere that nature has so ordained that he who seeks divine images will find the divine."

"You've given me a lot to think about," I said.

"Yes, do think about it and watch yourself and impressions closely. The whole area is amazing to behold once you begin to grasp it. Life will not seem the same because the veil will be lifted a little and you will begin to become beautiful while you change inside."

Liz and I left and talked about the idea of impressions and beauty all the way home.

Liz's mom came down the week before the ceremony to help her get ready. As a result, I didn't have much access to Liz that last week, but that was okay because every day after work I went out to "True Songs" to prepare the grounds for the onslaught of over 100 people. We rolled out giant rolls of grass to give the place a warmer feeling and put up an iron curved sign over the entrance to the driveway that had the words: "TRUE SONGS." On the Friday before the wedding we had everything looking good. I cut roses most of the day and put them in a trellis over the little stage where Paul was going to marry us. Arturo watered the grass and did general clean up. At three o'clock Arturo and I went into town to pick-up our tuxedos. I also drove out to the airport to purchase our tickets to London.

Liz and her mom stayed at our apartment while I stayed with Paul at the house. As it got dark I went out to the little patio. Paul followed me. "Well, son, how are you doing with all of this?"

"Well, I'm pretty nervous. This whole thing has come on so fast. I mean the whole thing. Seven months ago I was happily married to another woman, settled in a long-standing, good paying job. Now all of this is so different and sudden I think I'm still in a little bit of shock."

"You should be. When the Gods act, it is decisive and fast. Really, you had no choice. They had been preparing you since you were born for what is now and what is to come. It has just seemed quick because you had to take such an abrupt turn."

"I guess. Oh, I am happy about everything. Don't get me wrong. You are the most remarkable person I've ever met. Sometimes I get a little depressed because I can't stay in the present much and am afraid you will find out and kick me off this land."

"You are quite normal my son. It seems simple to self-remember, to feel your body and know where you are, but it is the hardest thing in the world to do. I know you are having difficulties. If you weren't, you could teach me."

"That is a relief," I said. "I'm not doing very well, but that is good enough for now."

"I appreciate you and Liz more than you can imagine. I need you in my time of trial which is coming—which is coming."

"What do you mean, Paul? Are you going to die or what?"

"We all die. I'm not concerned with dying. In fact, I will welcome the day I leave this old bag of bones. No, I feel that I'm going to be called upon to take part in a great play. I've prayed for the cup to be passed, but to no avail. This is what I'm here for."

"What is it?" I asked.

"If I knew the details I wouldn't tell you, but I don't. I only have a few hints and it seems to be involved with my former life. But I don't want to talk about it." With that he got up and walked out to the new patio and sat on the stage. I went to bed a couple of hours later and he hadn't moved.

Saturday was a bright and sunny day. "The True Songs" was a sight to behold. The roses were in full bloom and seemed to swallow us in beauty as I looked out from the house with Arturo early that morning. The wedding was to be held at 10: 00 before it got too hot. At 9: 00 the guests started arriving. Jesus pointed the cars to park along the road. As each group of guests entered the property I saw their eyes light up as they looked around. The place was truly stunning. I was standing on the porch and shook everyone's hand and welcomed them into the house where they put their presents down and got a refreshment. Many kept saying, "Wow, this is some place. I've never seen anything like this out in the desert."

At 9:45 Liz and her parents arrived in a black limousine that pulled up to the house. I was already in the patio so I didn't see her until the ceremony began. The music began and she and Big Jim marched down the aisle between the chairs. I came from the side and Big Jim handed her to me. I was clearly startled by her radiant beauty. Liz wore very little make-up usually, and most of the time wore none, so this was the first time I'd really seen her in full make-up and surrounded with a sparkling white satin dress smiling her biggest happiest smile

Paul stood before us in a white suit, white shirt with yellow highlights, and a yellow tie. He looked like a saint to me, with his kind face and little smile. He started speaking in his deep voice about how he met us and how what decent, delightful people we were. He went on to read some prayer I'd never heard, maybe he made it up. Then it was my turn to talk and I turned to the audience and told them the story of how I met Liz in my cab. It was a funny story and when I ended with "and it was the best fare I ever had," the audience laughed. I bet a lot of them didn't know I had been a taxi driver. Liz told how I always made her laugh and how I'd taught her to laugh at herself. She ended with the sonnet that Paul had recited for us the month before; "Let me not to the marriage..."

We turned around and Paul had us exchange rings. He put his hand on ours and said, "With all the power in me, I bless this marriage and I bless you both. I now pronounce you husband and wife. Go in peace, but first Joe, please kiss your new wife." I did and we turned to the applause of the audience. We were both crying for joy.

At the reception, which took place in the house and the patios, I spoke to everyone for at least a little while. Big Jim gave me an envelope and offered me another job. I refused but thanked him for his kindness. I went to the bathroom and opened the envelope. There was a check for $10,000 and another little envelope addressed to me. I opened it. It said, "Joe, I admire you. Sometimes I envy you your life and even your job. If I can ever help, let me know." He signed his name.

We left in the limousine at 12: 30 to the airport. Our plane was leaving at 2: 00. As we drove away we looked back. "Beautiful," she said. I kissed her and said, "Yes, and we helped build it too." I turned around and thought to myself, now what?

With a stopover in Atlanta, it took 14 hours to reach London. Paul had suggested that we not have a strict itinerary so we could feel freer to do whatever presented itself. With that in mind, I made only a two day reservation at the St. James Hotel. We both were too exhausted to go out so we slept or lounged around on the very large and very high bed. We made love the next day for the first time since we were married. I fell into Liz's open arms like a hungry bear and took my time loving that gorgeous woman.

At breakfast Liz pulled out a sealed letter that Paul had given her to open on our honeymoon. It was short. "Dear Joe and Liz: As a wedding gift I have decided to have my will redone to include the both of you. Upon my passing, you will inherit the property known as "The True Songs" as well as the 2 1/2 acres on either side and the 7 1/2 acres directly across Rainbow Blvd.. I have done this because I love the both of you like my own two lost children. Sincerely,..." It was signed Paul Martin.

Liz just shook her head. "That dear, dear man. I don't know what to say."

"I talked to him recently. He thinks he is in for a difficult time soon. He said he will need us then. Paul wouldn't say what it was that was going to happen, but he didn't sound pleased."

"I've had this strange sense of foreboding sometimes when I look at him when he is alone. I keep thinking that he is a Christ-like character. One time when I got up to go to the bathroom in the middle of the night about a week ago I saw him out the window kneeling out by the patio on the hard ground looking up at the sky. He was praying. I went out to him and just stood 10 feet away. He looked over at me and said, 'Have you come to watch with me?' I didn't know what he meant at first, then decided he meant self-remember. I just said 'yes' and we stayed that way, me standing and him kneeling, for another half an hour. Then he got up and we went back into the house. "

"Maybe he is scared."

"No doubt about it, she said. "It is scaring me too. We are going to have to be there for him."

"We are his two apostles," I answered.

"I'd laugh," she said, "if it wasn't so serious."

Neither of us said anything for a while. I got up and looked out the big window overlooking the Thames. When she joined me I said, "This is silly. Paul said for us to think of nothing but each other on this trip, and I think we should obey that commandment, don't you?" Liz smiled and snuggled me her agreement.

We liked London and made arrangements to stay at the hotel for three more days. We got a newspaper designed just for tourists to find out what was going on. That night we went to see Shakespeare's "King Lear" in a local theater and the next night we went to the Royal Shakespeare Company's production of "Merchant of Venice." Since we had read both plays under Paul's tutelage, we saw and I think understood more than most people in the audience. The third night we watched an insipid modern musical about rats and cats.

During the day we made love, went to breakfast, walked around London, visited a museum, had tea, and went home for more love and a nap. What a vacation. I think I'd always had attractive women for girlfriends and wives, but Liz was movie star beautiful. Liz made me feel proud, and especially so because she was devoted to me and showed it.

When we checked out of the St. James, I rented a car and we took off for Stratford-on-Avon. There were a few scares while I tried to maneuver that pint-sized auto out of the city. It was hard to remember to stay on the left side of the road, and it was especially difficult when I had to make a turn in traffic; I invariably ended up on the wrong side of the roadway with irate Londoners honking and waving their displeasure. I think God was on my side. Otherwise, there was no way we could've come out of the first few minutes of confusion alive.

Stratford-on-Avon was Shakespeare's birthplace so I was looking forward to going there and touching the things he touched. When we were taking a tour of his house I remembered what Paul had said about him. After we came out I said to Liz, "Paul says he thinks the man who wrote the plays was not the man named Shakespeare who is buried here."

'Well, if that is true," she said, "we just paid money to be in the house of an imaginary hero."

"But then, most things are imaginary aren't they? At least that's what the teacher says."

"That is hard for me to grasp yet. But even Shakespeare said something about life being rounded by a little dream or something like that."

"I think," I said, "I remember him saying that sort of thing many times in many different ways. I do know that I consider you a dreamboat, baby, and I don't want to wake up out of this honeymoon dream yet."

We stayed at an inn in town and went out to the grave of Shakespeare and paid homage just in case he wrote the plays. In the next five days I don't think we drove more than 100 miles each day. We kept stopping and visiting the shops and little taverns. We did spend a night in Oxford, just so I could say "I went to Oxford" in case anybody ever asked about my educational background.

Coming back into London to drop the car off was a snap compared to how I left. I was practically and expert at making turns and staying on the left side of road. We took a train out to the airport and waited four hours for our flight. We were both honeymooned out. Liz had showed her negative side a few times during the latter part of the trip. I found out that she did have a solid temper. Fortunately, it never lasted long. She had Paul's influence to help her control herself. Good thing: I don't know how much screaming I could take. It reminded me of the good old days with my first wife. Of course, I was no saint either. I caught myself doing little things to irritate her and to get her goat. I guess we were both a little tired of being on our absolute best behavior. We were ready to go back to reality; whatever that was going to be.

Chapter 10

WE CAUGHT A CAB to our apartment when we got back to Tucson. The place was full of presents from the people who were at the wedding. Before we settled in for the night I called Paul and told him we were home and to thank him for his present. I said that since Liz did not have to go back to work for a few days and school was out, we'd come over later the next day after we unpacked and got settled. He seemed delighted. After dinner, Liz and I opened the presents. There was nothing unusual; toasters, table cloths, and a variety of do-dads that come with every wedding.

The next morning we slept until 10:30. The time difference was eight hours from London time so I knew we'd be out of whack for a few days. We drove out to True Songs in the early afternoon. Paul was jovial when we arrived. He hugged us and told us how much he missed us. It was like he was truly a father to the both of us. Arturo did a little dance of joy when he came in from the roses in the back. It felt good to be home. Within minutes of arriving I looked around to see Liz going out the back door heading for her roses. I asked Paul how he had been feeling. "Oh, I guess I'm really feeling my age now. I don't seem to have any of the old zip lately."

"Maybe you just need to rest," I offered.

"Well, I am getting more of that."

Liz fixed a dinner of spaghetti and salad. As we were eating I mentioned to her that Paul was feeling tired lately. "Well," she said to him directly, "as a surrogate daughter, I am ordering you to go to the doctor."

"All right, Liz. I think that's a good idea. Do you know any doctors in town? I am without medical insurance of any kind."

"What, don't you have Medicare?"

"I have never applied. In fact, I haven't been to the doctor in maybe thirty years. I thought I'd never have to go."

She seemed taken aback. "Tomorrow, I'll take you to see my ex-husband. He's a general practitioner in Tucson. He'll see you and I'll make sure he doesn't charge you. He owes me."

Paul laughed at her seriousness. "All right Liz. We'll go tomorrow."

Later he asked us if we wanted another little lecture. "Yes," we said in unison and plopped into our places like two kids ready to get candy.

"First, I wanted to tell you that all philosophy, if it is real philosophy, is a gift from the Gods. It is a way to contemplate the Higher and to set up a method of adoration that is not rote. Jesus taught a philosophy called the 'Word' and it was the highest we have. But at their core, all philosophical doctrines, as expressed in the great religions, has the same root. They may use different terminology and have come at different times and different places, but they have two central ideas in common. That is 'know thyself,' and the idea that we mortals are asleep and must awaken in order to move into higher realms. Philosophy has nothing to do with arguing about intellectual positions or about whether there is a God or not. It is only about the love of wisdom, and that wisdom is the wisdom of God. Further, a philosopher is not one who teaches other's philosophy, but one who lives philosophy moment to moment. Plato, Seneca, and Jesus, were philosophers. They lived what they preached."

"You are a philosopher?" I asked.

"Yes. For many years I resisted that title, but the last 15 years or so, I realized I am living the life full time. But this is getting off the subject I wanted to talk about tonight. I want to talk about something called 'vanity.'

Vanity is this out-sized love of our selves that comes with being human. It is so anchored in our hearts that we can never consider for a moment that we can be wrong in any manner whatsoever. We put ourselves into little cocoons safe from all criticism. These cocoons will buffer everything unpleasant that may come our way.

Suppose we make a mistake. We will have a ready-made excuse handy; prepared in advance and practiced perhaps countless times in our dream world just in case. If we were caught red-handed we will still spend considerable energy making it seem less than it is, or blaming another person or the circumstances; trying to wiggle out. But imagination is where we never can be wrong and no one can dispute it.

We love those who will feed this part in us. I would say that marriage would be a dead institution if people courting each other did not feed vanity in the other person. Also, we tend to despise those who insult us or even tell the truth. We don't want the truth; we want flattery even when we know it is a lie, especially if it is a lie.

The reason I brought this up is to tell you that you must observe yourselves and your vanity. It is necessary to rid yourself of this devil because it prevents you from becoming conscious. Consciousness is our goal here at True Songs."

While I was thinking about what he said, the doorbell rang. Paul got up and opened the door. "Anna," he exclaimed. He spoke in Spanish and two adult Mexican women entered with a young boy in tow. He made introductions. The other lady's name was Juanita and the boy was Jose. They all sat down on chairs and Paul explained that Anna was from the village where he used to live in Mexico. She was the mother of Artie, the boy who stopped by here a month or so ago. Juanita was speaking to Paul about her son, who was about seven or eight.

Liz said, "She is asking him to heal her son who has leukemia and may die soon." Paul looked perturbed. He answered her. "He is telling her that he is not a healer. He can't heal Jose. She is saying that you healed many people in Chihuahua. You are famous down there. He is saying that was a mistake. Anyone who got better was not because of me, but because of other things." Juanita got down on her knees and put her hands together in prayer. "Please, Mr. Paul," Liz continued, "at least pray on Jose. He will die shortly anyway. Just pray on him."

Paul put his hands up to his face and covered it. He came out of a moment's repose and nodded to the mother. He waved

Jose into the kitchen and sat him on a chair. Paul pulled a chair in front of him. We could see plainly as he put his hands on the boy's head and face. He closed his eyes for a couple of minutes in deep concentration. He then took his hands away and smiled at him at spoke to him softly. They came back into the room with the boy smiling. Paul refused the $100 bill offered by the mother and said something in Spanish. Liz told me he asked the two women never to tell anyone else where he lived. "Please," he said in English. They both agreed with big nods and smiles. In a minute they had left.

Paul turned to us after he shut the door. "Now it starts," he said with sadness. He walked out into the dark toward the big patio.

Early the next morning Liz called her ex-husband and asked if he'd see Paul that day. He said yes, he'd see him before normal office hours and for Paul not to eat anything in case they would need to do some tests. Liz got Paul out of bed at 7:30 and they were out the door within a half an hour. Paul looked around at me as he left. " I'll finish our discussion from last night when I get back."

Arturo and Jesus were driving up as they were leaving. "Where are they going?" Jesus asked.

"Oh, they are just going to the doctor. Paul has not been feeling well lately."

"We both noticed that he has not been strong. He mostly sat around when you were gone."

They each grabbed a donut and were off to their jobs around the property. I thought that these two are becoming closer because of Paul. Jesus actually seems to enjoy the work. I had the temptation to just sit around and read while Liz and Paul were in town, but I decided instead to go ahead and work; I was getting too much from the experience. I grabbed the hose and pulled it out to the trees to water them. After I finished I swept the big patio and settled down to pulling weeds from around the roses next to the driveway. Before noon Spot discovered a big rattlesnake in the back. I saw from the driveway how efficiently Arturo handled the situation. He was a jewel, I thought.

Liz and Paul returned at 2: 00 that afternoon. He was smiling. She was not. "I am taking him in for a CT scan tomorrow morning. Jeff thinks that he might have prostate problems; maybe cancer."

"I told her not to worry, Joe. What ever it is the Will of God. That means it can't be bad."

"Paul," she said earnestly, "you worry about your soul. I'm going to worry about your body if I want to."

He went into the house with a little smile. "I am worried about him, Joe. My ex said that from his exam, it doesn't look good. But this saint we have here doesn't seem to care if he dies or not."

"I know. He told me several times that he would almost welcome death. He said he's tired of everything."

When we walked back in he was frying two hamburgers. "That's the reason you are having so much trouble now, Paul," Liz said. "You eat too much fat and sugar."

"You do too," he countered.

"I know, but I hold you to a higher standard." She was smiling.

When he finished his meal, he started talking about creation. "Liz asked me on the way to the doctor about creation and all the talk about the 'Big Bang' and the idea that scientists work with called 'survival of the fittest.' I told you Liz that I would think about it, and so I have. Scientists have at least one major handicap when considering how this world came about. They can only measure from the five senses and must deduce everything from the data they can sense. This puts them in a difficult position, whether they realize it or not. In the first place they only have a tiny part of the data possible, and also because they lack all the information from the invisible world. The inner world is a vast place that reaches to infinity and wholly inaccessible to measurement. The visible world is only a shadow of the invisible universe.

The world of thoughts, emotions, attitudes, desires and drives of every kind are all part of this invisible world. And that is just with us here on earth. In other realms; higher realms that are inhabited by invisible creatures, they cannot even imagine. All that scientists have is some little bit of information to connect the whole universe. The Big Bang may have happened, but I doubt it. At any rate, it was only a part of a much larger event. Everything is in transformation at every moment. We are being transformed at this very time into something else. It is impossible to destroy anything, even an atom. We can change it into something else, but then that is transformation. So, if the Big Bang happened, it was something else first.

The whole solar system is geared for and around the birth of souls. Many eons ago, angels from some other part of our galaxy were sent here to develop a place to harvest little souls—God's ultimate desire to share his bounty with those who are worthy. The angels did not know how to go about this task, so they had to experiment, or create by experimentation, everything to support souls, including these amazing bodies we possess. One of the tools they used was a dimension called time. Time is limitless and the Gods used it to build nature from the ground up. While they learned and created, the angels were serving their God in complete joy.

You must understand that humans are an experiment on this planet. The universe is replete with experiments of this sort, and all of it has the ultimate aim of the development of souls.

Finally, in this experiment, they had the human body ready for the implantation of the soul, a glorious event. But this creation was not like we think. The bodies they created were perfect physically, or as perfect as nature would allow, however, mankind was also designed to have a number of severe handicaps in the software. He was drawn-up with a psychology in disarray and confusion, and then was cast into a deep hypnotic sleep. He was further impeded from knowing himself, always being in imagination about himself and everything around him. Humanity is truly in sad shape psychologically, which is to say spiritually.

As I said, this was all in the blueprint because heaven is not free. Man has to devise ways to surmount the difficulties presented. Higher Forces have sent many messengers down, or rather developed them, to give us clues as to how to earn a heavenly reward. But even with their best efforts, only a few people can make it. It is something like many acorns falling to the ground, but only a small number will ever become oak trees. It may not seem fair, but it is how it is and there is nothing the acorns can do, or we can do.

We have difficulties and even horrors to go through in this life, but they are all designed to help us, not hinder us. They can make us stronger; more able to grow heavenly roots."

"So, should I be glad when I have problems?" I asked.

"If you develop your self enough, you will be glad. But that is a long way off. First you have to have many hours of work on yourself before you learn appreciation. Appreciation, or gratitude, is an earned virtue. You will have to become deeply emotional in the right way first."

"Does this mean that I have wasted most of my life hating my difficulties?" asked Liz.

"No, but it does mean that you need to get to work right away self-remembering, observing yourself and at the same time, not resenting your difficulties. Your time is limited, but your possibilities aren't. Try to have the thought that each day, each moment, is a beginning. 'Always be a beginner.' Rainer Maria Rilke said that. He is an angel now."

The next day, Saturday, Paul and Liz went into Tucson for his test. I went out with Jesus and worked pulling the weeds that seemed to grow so well around the bushes. Arturo started up the new mowing tractor that Paul had purchased while I was away and began to cut the huge lawn, now at about one and a half acres. I asked Jesus why he had made such a radical change from the gang-banger he was just a few months ago.

"Artie, one of the guys who marked up the fence, told me that Paul was some kind of great man and that he was afraid to do anything against him. He really was a different guy after he came back from out here. Then I started thinking that maybe I was a little stupid to act like I was acting. I decided to give it another try."

"I'm glad you came back. We really need you."

"Now that I got over that resentment of my father, I am loving it. It is so peaceful here."

"Do you still see Artie?"

"Sometimes. He's always asking me how Paul is doing. Last night he told me that he cured a kid they brought here. The whole neighborhood is talking about it."

"Cured him? How do they know that?"

"He's playing baseball."

"Oh. Paul is afraid that people will come out here all the time looking for cures," I said.

"They can't help it. That's all they are talking about. Artie's mom said that in Mexico he cured many people."

I shook my head and got up to get a drink. I was thinking about what Paul said about something bad that was going to happen. This must've been what he was talking about. Then I started wondering about being a healer. Was he really someone who could actually make people get better from cancer and other diseases? That is an incredible power.

When they got back from the hospital, I told Liz what Jesus said. We decided not to tell Paul. It might upset him. She said that they'd know what the results of all the tests on Paul were on Monday. They had another appointment with a specialist that she knew. Liz was worried, even if Paul still appeared unconcerned. "It is all been planned out eons ago, my dear," he had told her.

On Saturday night, Paul beat me easily two games of chess. We tried to show Liz how to play, but in frustration she announced, "This is a dumb game," and went back in the bedroom.

"How do you feel, Paul?" I asked.

"I feel fine, Joe. Please don't ask me that any more. It promotes self-pity in me. I have spent my life fighting that negative emotion. I don't want it to overtake me now when it will do real harm."

"What do you mean?"

"Self-pity, no matter if it is justified on a life level, is a minus as far as the soul is concerned. The Gods want us humble, not wallowing in vain self-pity. Self-pity is announcing to the world that I am real important and look what has happened to me. Poor me."

"Oh—even if it is something we don't deserve?"

"We are not to decide that. We have to just take what comes and still try to be present. That makes the Gods smile. Then they know they can test us even further. No one tastes paradise without passing many tests, my lad."

I thought about it. "They are going to test me too?"

"Most assuredly. That is how the Gods show their confidence in you. Don't worry. They won't give you anything you can't handle. They haven't me."

With those words he got up and went out into the night. I walked back in the bedroom and took the book Liz was reading away and announced, "I need a hug."

Chapter 11

Arturo and his son took off to take their family on a picnic that Sunday. We all slept late. I was up at 9:00 and I decided to read the Bible out in the patio by the house. I read some of the parts about Jesus doing his miracles. He drew huge crowds wherever he went because of this. I'm sure it wasn't just to hear his preaching. I was thinking that it was his healing power that made people take notice when he was crucified. Otherwise, there probably wouldn't have been the Christian Church and all the rest of it. So, it was the healing that won the people over in the first place and at least gave him a reputation after he died.

I heard Paul and Liz bumping around in the kitchen so I went in to join them. "Morning," I said.

"Good morning," replied Paul. Liz poked her lips out to be kissed. I complied. "I heard there is a Bach concert in the park in Tucson this afternoon. Shall we go?" Paul asked.

We both agreed that that would be a nice way to spend a Sunday. Paul stopped and perked up his ears at something. He got up and pulled back the drapes. There were six automobiles in the process of parking on the side of the road in front of the property. Out stepped about twenty Latino men and women with two small children. As we watched from the window they gathered in front of the sign "True Songs." They were not sure what to do from that point. "Joe, will you go invite them back to the big patio. Tell them I will be out in a few minutes."

"You sure, Paul?" asked Liz.

"Yes, Liz, as sure as I've ever been. I can't hide from this forever. I decided that last night."

I walked out to the gate accompanied by my wife of under a

month. "Hello," I said loudly. They gave a variety of greetings in English and Spanish. "Can I help you?"

"A man in his fifties stepped up. "We would like to see Paul, please."

"He told us to tell you to come back to the patio and he will be with you in a little while." I held my hand out indicating they were to follow us. The visitors were all smiling as we made our way to the patio. There were only a few chairs and two benches, so about half of them had to stand. After about five minutes Paul emerged from the house and walked toward us. He had shaved.

As he got close to us he opened his arms in a sign of welcome and started speaking Spanish. Eventually, they brought a girl of about twelve and an old man in his seventies or eighties. He walked back into the sun to get away from the others. He spent about five minutes talking to them before he put his hands on them and prayed silently. After Paul finished with his praying, he came back and asked if they would pray with him. In Spanish, he led them in the Lord's Prayer. Then it was over. They started walking back to the cars. The whole ceremony took no more than 12 or 15 minutes.

When we got back to the house he sat in his chair. He looked tired. "Will you move into this house today. I think I'm going to need your help and support."

"Today? Sure." Liz looked at me. "Okay?"

"Okay with me. We'll leave right now and be back in a few hours."

"No, please only one at a time. I don't want to be left alone again."

We decided that I would go in first and get what I needed and then Liz would go later. There was a sense of urgency to the whole affair so I left right away. I packed my two suitcases and filled my van with the rest of my things. I completed the task in about 45 minutes from the minute I arrived. When I returned Liz helped me unpack and then jumped in the van and drove away. It wasn't even noon.

I asked Paul what he told those people. "I told them that I didn't consider myself a healer, that doctors were the best. But if they wanted me to pray with the two they brought me, I would be glad to that."

"I heard that you did cure many people in Mexico. Is that true?"

"I don't really know. Some maybe got better, but I don't take credit. They must've gotten better naturally. That happens all the time without somebody praying over them." "Jesus told me that boy you saw the other night is playing baseball now."

"Well, I didn't do it, but maybe the angels work through me for their own purposes. I do feel a powerful tinkling or buzzing when I pray over someone. It is getting much stronger now than when I lived in Mexico."

"Well, those folks sure believed in you," I said.

"Son, you don't know what you've signed on for here. And I can't help you. You must be present as much as you can. That will be your only shield to all of this."

"I'm trying Paul. I'm trying."

Monday morning Liz drove Paul to the doctor's office. She had asked for another day off work and it was granted. Arturo and Spot searched for trespassing serpents while Jesus and I began cleaning the beds around the house of assorted weeds. Around ten o'clock a string of cars arrived again. I ran out and told them that Paul was gone for a while. I ask them to come back in three or four hours. They seemed mollified and left.

I told Jesus what had occurred over the weekend and he relayed it to Arturo, who just raised his eyebrows.

After lunch Liz drove into the driveway. From my vantage point on the porch, I could see that she was giving Paul the business about something. He was stoically looking ahead. She jumped out of the car and stormed into the house without a word to me. I opened the door for Paul. He smiled and said "Hi," and went into the house.

Liz was coming out of the bathroom. "You know what, Joe?" The doctor told Paul that he has prostrate cancer and that it has spread beyond where surgery can help. Then this world famous cancer specialist begins to set up an appointment to start chemotherapy and Paul here says, 'Thank you no. I don't want that.' Can you believe it Joe?"

"Yes, I can believe it. Why don't you want to get better Paul?"

Paul sat in his chair and stretched his long lean legs out. "Well, dears, I don't want to live any longer than necessary. I'm tired and this is my chance to get out. I know you can't understand it, but you may if you are given enough time. I'm sorry if I've upset you Liz, but it can't be helped."

She sat down and cried. "Just when I get my life set with my two dream men, you go and want to die. Paul, live for me if you won't for yourself."

"Liz that is self-pity. You told me you don't have that problem," Paul said.

"Oh, shit," she spat out as she went back to the bedroom and slammed the door.

"So, Paul, we are going to watch you die?"

"I'll try to teach you through my dying. Remember how Socrates did it. I just hope I can match up to his example."

"How can you die when you can cure other people?"

"It is my time, son. I don't care about this old body of mine anymore, especially since we've finished the rose garden."

I put my head in my hands trying to be mature and be in the present. I kept repeating to myself what Paul had told me, "Know where you are at and feel your body." Then I remembered about the people who were coming to see him. "Paul, a whole bunch of people came to see you this morning. They'll be back in a little while."

He smiled. "Good, I want to see them." He said this in an almost jubilant manner. He sure was a puzzle. He is so happy he is going to die that being a healer for a time doesn't even bother him. "I'm going to rest until they come." He got up from the chair and laid his frame down on the couch.

A composed Liz and I led the new contingent out to the patio. Arturo and Jesus had set up chairs, but this time there twice the number of people, so there still were many who had to stand. Paul came out and duplicated his performance of the day before. There were five children of different ages with different ailments. He spent longer talking, giving them what sounded like a sermon, although I couldn't understand any of it. After they filed out and were driving away, Paul said, "That takes more energy than I thought." He went back to the couch and slept until dinner.

While he was sleeping Liz told me the doctor gave him three to six months to live if he doesn't have any treatments. "The doctor warned him that this kind of cancer can be pretty painful and asked him if he wanted any pain medication for when it starts. Of course our healer here refused it."

"Hey, I just thought of something. He could heal himself."

Liz shook her head. "Didn't you hear him? He wants to die."

"Oh yeah," I said. "He wants to show us how to die."

"Don't you think that's ridiculous?"

"No, I think he will be living his teaching."

We had installed our little TV on the table in front of our bed. I turned on to the 10:00 P.M. news as we settled into bed. Toward the end of the broadcast, the pretty lady said, "Oh, here's an interesting item. Many people in the Old Pueblo have reported that there is a 'healer' that lives west of Tucson. They say he has cured many people of incurable diseases."

The older gentlemen co-anchor made a face. "We had one of those in Denver about ten years ago. He is now in jail for fraud."

The pretty lady made a face. "Well, who knows? Maybe there is one who is not a fake. We'll see." They both smiled their best TV smiles.

I sunk down under the covers. "Oh, no. We're going to be besieged by reporters tomorrow. This is awful."

"I guess I'd better call in again tomorrow. They are going to run out of patience with me," Liz said.

"I think you should go into work. Eventually we will need the money. Besides, I can handle it around here tomorrow."

"Don't tell me what to do, Joe. We just mixed our checking accounts.

I haven't told you about my investments. I didn't come out of two marriages to doctors without some compensation you know. Besides, I got a stinking rich mama. No, I don't need to work."

"I thought you enjoyed your job?"

"I do, but that's beside the point. I'll take a leave of absence until this nonsense is over." She gave me a dirty look. "So, don't tell me what to do, mister big shot husband."

I started laughing. "And I thought I was going to be the boss."

She grinned and said, "shut-up," and dived under the covers with me.

Paul made her go into work. I guess he was the real boss. She left at seven. I fixed breakfast for Arturo, Jesus, and Paul. There were already people milling around outside the property. Paul told Jesus to go tell whomever comes that he will see them at nine o'clock. He told Jesus to work around where the entrance was for the whole day. After we ate Arturo took our wonder dog out for a tour and I did the dishes.

Paul called me into the living room. "I've decided that I'm going to teach you whenever I can since I'm not likely to be here for your full year of instruction. So, it may not be under the best circumstances but I will do my best. I expect it to be a little chaotic around here."

"It was on TV last night."

"America is so efficient. This is going to be a big deal before long. That is the American Way. Our country lives on big deals."

"Okay, tell me something I need to know?" I asked. "We have a little time."

He shifted around in his chair and looked out the window, I presumed to see the people who were on the outside waiting to get in. "Joe, look out the window at all the beauty around us; the roses, the trees and the grass. Some of what I'm going to say to you I have verified; some I have not, but strongly suspect. God, the soul, beauty, and love come from the same root in another dimension. I don't know how to tell you what dimension it is: 4th, 10th, or 20th, if there is such a thing. But God exists in that place and the soul is part of God. The food for the soul is beauty and love. They actually may be the same phenomenon seen and understood by different senses. Certainly, I can't tell the difference sometimes when I am in a very high state. They meld together in a mystical way.

Each person is conceived with a soul, or maybe the nugget of a soul. It is our job to feed this little nugget until it becomes a life unto itself and can enter the higher places in the other dimension, which we call heaven. The odds of this happening are minute. It is hard beyond comprehension. The royal food that I told you about, beauty and love, is gained only with much work and right suffering. The most important work is the effort to remain in the present, whether it be by meditating, prayer, or self-remembering. Right suffering is by not buffering your life from its realities. Maybe this evening I'll explain buffering when Liz is here. It is an important idea.

To finish up, the soul is what gives life. Without this seed there is no life. It is the Real 'I'. When it goes away, the body passes to the worms. Souls become developed to different levels, all the way from the level of Jesus or Shakespeare down to a minus state as with some of our more famous human beasts. Jesus, the highest being to have manifested here on earth, said that most people are dead; that is, they walk around but have already lost their chances to evolve."

"Do souls get another chance to develop in another life?" I asked.

"I don't know that. I think so, but I don't know it for sure. Some religions in the East have that as a principle, but I have not been able to verify it. One thing for sure; you and I have this life to make ourselves conscious beings. Who knows after that."

"Very interesting. I'll tell Liz tonight what you said. Thank you, Paul."

"Well, I'm going back in my room to rest and meditate. Please come and fetch me at 8:55, will you?"

"Sure, Paul." He walked back and closed his door. I looked out the window at the large crowd gathering. It was 8:25.

When I knocked on his door just before nine, Paul opened the door with a flourish. "I'm ready." We walked to the window. As we looked out at the hundreds of people who had gathered, he gave me instructions. "Joe, I want you bring about 20 or 30 at a time back to the patio. After that group leaves, wait about ten or fifteen minutes before letting another group in. Try to put the press off as much as you can. I am not interested in talking to them or having my picture taken. You be my spokesman." He paused and then went on. "I hope we can maintain some order to this. If we can't I don't know what's going to happen. We may get trampled to death. Oh, tell them that I will speak Spanish in the morning, and English in the afternoon."

As Paul walked out the back door toward the patio, I took a deep breath and went toward the mass of seekers. They were quiet when I reached the gate. "Ladies and gentlemen, I'll lead about 20 at a time to see Paul. When he has seen those and they have left, he'll take a little break and then I'll take another group to him. He will speak only Spanish this morning and only English this afternoon." When I finished, a women who was obviously from the press moved over to me, but before she could speak, I gave her a sign and said, "I'll be back in a few minutes."

I led a group down the drive way and across the walkway to the patio. Paul was sitting in a chair as they entered under the roof of the patio. I waved to him and went back to the main gate. The woman and a man with a TV camera were standing in front waiting for me. "My name is Barbara Gomez from Channel 8 News. We'd like to come in and interview the healer, what's his name, Paul?"

"Yes his name is Paul, but he does not want to do any interviews and he doesn't want to have his picture taken."

She was perturbed. "Do you understand that we are from the media? We have a responsibility to report any news that the city would be interested in."

"Go ahead and report what you want, but it has to be without the benefit of Paul's help. I'm sorry."

They faded into the crowd and began interviewing people

who were standing around. I saw them talking to a couple of other reporters. They all shook their heads in disbelief. After about 20 minutes, I turned around to see the group coming back up the drive. They were all grinning. I looked at my watch. "In ten minutes, Paul will take another group." Everybody was talking at once as the group entered the mass waiting by the gate. Oh, man, I thought, this is going to be some day.

And it was. Helicopters flew over all morning and trucks arrived with equipment to record the event. Several guys constructed a tower on top of their truck to get a better view. From time to time, another reporter made their way up to where I was standing and demanded, requested, or pleaded for and interview. I always said no. I did answer a couple of questions. One man said that some people were saying that Paul wasn't really a healer. "Paul is not a healer. He doesn't say he is. But he does pray over some people and if they get better it is not because of him." To another who yelled out something about even if he wouldn't give an interview they would dig and still discover what his gimmick is. I yelled back, "Well, start digging, my man."

Another, an attractive woman, asked if Paul was a Catholic. I said, "No, he is of no particular religion, but is friend to them all."

After the fifth group had left I told them that Paul was going to take an hour for lunch. Then he would be speaking in English. I walked back toward the house to see an exhausted Paul sprawled on the couch. "Tough work?" I asked.

"The toughest," is all he said and he was asleep.

At 1: 30 I let the next bunch in. I went up to a reporter who I had seen before on TV. "How come there is this big deal over some guy in the desert. I've never seen anything like it."

"There wouldn't been if a few reporters hadn't checked out some of the cures this Paul was supposed to have done. They said that they seemed valid cures. About an hour ago, they had a physician on one of the channels who said that a kid with leukemia was a 100 % better."

"Do you know that Paul denies being a healer or anything else?" I asked him.

"Yeah, well what the hell is he doing now? It looks like he's doing something."

"I don't know what he's doing. He is just praying with these people and they think they are better psychologically or something. I don't know."

"Getting cured from leukemia isn't psychological you know," he said.

Paul had told me to tell the crowd that he was only doing two more groups today. That he would start again tomorrow at 9: 00. I asked several men who were standing around if they would help me control the mass of people who seemed ready to bolt toward the patio. They gladly agreed and took on a righteous power that was almost frightening. They were on the side of God. I remember Paul saying that righteousness of this sort could become a most evil and destructive thing. He said righteous originally meant to be balanced, but it had become a monster in the hands of so-called religious people and an excuse for all kinds of cruelty and killing.

It was hot that day, reported to be 106 degrees. Many people fainted from the heat and had to be taken to the hospital. The sound of sirens was disconcerting, especially to those who were coming to be healed. After Paul sent back the final group, I made another announcement about it beginning at nine the next day. Most of the people had already left, having been driven away by the heat and the lack of water. Just the reporters remained with their trucks and equipment. When they gathered around me, I made the same announcement about Paul not doing interviews.

About that time Liz pulled into the driveway. "Hey, who are you?" someone yelled. She ignored them. I said nothing and left them. My helpers kept the media from following me.

Liz ran into the house. When I got there she was kneeling down beside Paul on the couch rubbing his head with a damp cloth. "What went on here today?" she asked as I walked in.

"It was crazy."

"It must have been. It is on every radio station. He really is curing people, Joe; really making people better. The town is going wild. That is all anybody at the hospital is talking about."

Paul looked up from his half-sleep and just shook his head. "This is just the start, my dear."

"Paul, I quit my job. So, you can't make me go back to work."

He smiled weakly and patted her arm with affection. "Thank you, Liz. I do need you. I also need a drink, Joe."

I snapped into action and brought over a pitcher of iced tea that Arturo handed me. I hadn't noticed but he and Jesus had come in the back door. "My father says that this is crazy," Jesus said. "We've got to get him away. He can stay at our house tonight."

Paul shook his head. "No, let's see where this thing takes us. But right now, I'm taking myself back to bed. Joe, will you help me undress?"

"Yes of course," as I helped him up. "Liz, will you take some water or something out to my helpers? They've done a good job and I don't even know their names. Oh, and don't talk to the reporters. Paul wants no part of them."

"Neither do I," she said as she collected some glasses.

Before dark, I saw out the window that two sheriff's cars were pulling into the drive. I went into the patio in the back where Paul and Liz were sitting and told him. He got up and went inside saying, "I don't want to talk to them. You and Liz speak with them and don't let them in the house. Be tough. I want to see what they do."

We stepped outside onto the porch. Behind the law enforcement vehicles was a big TV truck. "You can stay, but they'll have to go," Liz said to one of the officers while pointing to the truck. He reluctantly turned around and walked back to the truck and spoke to the driver. In a moment the truck began to back away. The four officers came over to where we were standing in front of the porch.

"My name is Captain West from the Pima County Sheriff's Department."

I shook his hand. "My name is Joe Peters and this is my wife Liz

Peters. We live here. Can I help you gentlemen?"

"Yes," the Captain began uncertainly, "we'd like to speak to that healing fellow. We got a problem with all these people out here and I want to see if we can't work something out."

Liz jumped in. "Captain, Paul doesn't want to speak to anyone. But if you need anything, maybe we can help you."

"Don't get tough with me, lady. We want to see him and we want to see him right now. No more bullshit."

"I'm sorry, I said. "If we can't help you then you can't be helped. Please leave."

One of the other deputies pulled West back and spoke to him out of our hearing. "All right, you win, but can we come inside."

"No, but we can sit on the porch here." I sat down on the steps. Liz sat next to me.

West shrugged his big shoulders and found a place on the steps. The others remained standing. "Here is the deal, Mr. and Mrs. Peters. Your man in there has caused us a major problem. If you thought today was a mess, wait until tomorrow. Planes full of people are coming in from all over the world to see your Mr. Paul. It is going to be even hotter than today. People might die. So, we don't know what to do."

"What would you like to see happen?" asked Liz.

"We were hoping that he either would go someplace else for awhile until we can figure things out, or quit this bullshit of healing people."

"I don't think he will do either," Liz offered. Maybe you could do something, like have more facilities out here to handle the crowds, more refreshments, more ambulances, more shade. Or you could block off Rainbow at both ends and only let so many cars through when we call you."

"Oh shit, lady. You want us to be your little servants. When you call us we send so many cars through? This is a joke. You want the county to set up tents with water and beds and see to it that ambulances are on the scene. What do you take us for, a bunch of patsies?"

I started laughing. "What else can you do?"

"We aren't getting anywhere here boys. Let's go. Maybe when

we come back we'll have arrest warrants for the whole bunch of you."

Before they left another officer came over to me and asked me if Paul worked with kids with asthma. He said that his boy had a bad case and they didn't know what to do. I told him to bring him by and maybe Paul could help. He waved and jumped into the back seat of the car.

They backed out in a hurry. We went in the house and told Paul what happened. He was delighted. "I'm doing this to see what life will do with a situation like this. Also, with your assistance, we can help them learn something about themselves."

Paul was rested so we all sat on the bed in our bedroom and watched TV. There were specials on every station about the situation. There was a long string of interviews with people who were here today. They described Paul variously as kindly, or saintly, or energetic. One even one said that Paul reminded him of the devil. Another station had a national news team set up in a Tucson hotel. They discussed it from a more philosophic viewpoint; "What would happen if a real healer came. Would science want to test him?" or, "What would it mean to humanity if someone could just come by and touch them and they'd get better?"

In between all of it were interviews with doctors who had investigated the cures. Some said they seemed on the surface to be genuine. Others said they were not valid because nature cures on a flash also on occasion. And besides more testing is needed. The best ones, at least the ones that made Paul laugh were the ministers who were asked to comment. All of them suggested the possibility of evil forces or the anti-Christ. They clearly were the most worried about their jobs.

After about an hour of this, Paul left us and went into the other room. We shut it off and joined him. "What did you think?" I asked him.

"Did you ever hear the question posed about what would happen if Christ ever came back to earth?"

"Sure," I said.

"Mostly in sermons." Liz added, "The preachers always assumed they would be on the right side of Christ during that time."

"Well, my children, now many of them think it might be happening and they are scared to death. It should be quite a show."

"Aren't you afraid they will kill you?" Liz asked.

"Don't forget I'm dying anyway."

"Yes, I forgot about that," Liz answered. "So you don't care?"

"No, Liz, I don't care at all."

Chapter 12

At six the next morning Captain West knocked on the door. I got up and came to the door. I stepped out into the sunlight. "All right," he started, "you win. We are setting up roadblocks on both ends of this road. We will station a car here and you tell us how many you want to let in and we will let that many come. Is that good with you?"

"Yes, that is very good. What about the people already here," I pointed to the cars parked along the side of the road.

"We'll move them back to the roadblocks. Oh, by the way, the board of supervisors is in emergency meeting at seven this morning to figure out what to do, so this may change after that meeting."

I stuck out my hand. "Thank you officer. Paul starts working at nine sharp."

The captain ignored my hand and went back to his car. He was not happy.

As he was pulling out, Liz came out. I told her what happened. "I just saw on TV that they expect 100,000 people to try to get in here today."

"100,000!" I exclaimed. "What is going on Liz?"

"Paul is upsetting the balance. Everything was running fine and now this. There are no rules for this sort of thing. I'm going to call my mother, she must be going crazy." She went in and plugged in the phone. We had to unplug it because it never stopped ringing. I saw her dialing.

I was watching the television when she walked back in. "Mom has got problems of her own. Big Jim had a stroke last night. He is in intensive care right now. She was on her way out the door when I called. I told her I couldn't come up right now and she understood."

"Look at this," I pointed to the TV.

The Bishop of Tucson was preparing to make a statement. "Until such time as we determine just who this Paul is and what he is up to, the Church is going to hold back official comment, but from my point of view he seems like the worst kind of charlatan preying on people's hopes. I also do not discount the possibility that he is somehow connected to the underworld. That is all I have to say at this time. Thank you."

They broke from him to a scene of the road around the area of Rainbow. It was packed with cars and every other kind of vehicle. From there the screen panned to Captain West who was talking to a group of reporters. "We decided to block the road to the property. They did not like it but I told them that's what we decided. We will let a few people through the barricade beginning around nine o'clock, and then a group when that group comes back. Paul's spokesman, a Joe Peters, actually wanted us to let the same thing happen as yesterday. I informed him that we are worried about public safety and not their minor concerns." Someone asked West for his personal opinion. "I think it is a cruel hoax and a bunch of you-know-what, if you want to know what I think."

I turned off the set. "He is lying; flat out lying."

Paul came into our room. "You should have seen it Paul. Old Captain West lying to the press big as you please."

"We'll probably see a lot of that from now on," he answered. "Life at it's lowest."

"Do you want some breakfast?" I asked.

"That would be great," he said, "I'm going to need a lot of strength today."

I jumped up and began the process of feeding Paul and us two apostles. Helicopters flew over at intervals and destroyed the impact of Mozart's 41st Symphony as we ate. Liz told him about her step-father. Paul said he would like to visit if him if he could. I assumed it would be to cure him. I hoped he could. Could he really heal people? I couldn't really believe it myself yet, even though so many people were taking it seriously. I was shaking my head in disbelief when another helicopter went over. I was having a hard time controlling my temper.

Paul called us into the living room where he had taken up his usual seat. "It is time for a little schooling. Are you ready?"

"Are you sure you want to teach today?" Liz inquired, "I mean with all that is going on?"

"I'm trying to teach all the time you are around me; if not verbally, then by example. I am very aware that first and foremost, you are my students. That is a sacred trust that I take most seriously. As long as you are with me, you both will come first over everything else, even this little silliness that is going on right now."

"Teach away teacher," I said.

He stretched his legs out in front of him and crossed his hands in front of his stomach. "I want to talk for awhile about buffers because you are going to be seeing a lot of them with all that is going on. But first you will have to notice them in yourselves before they become clear in other people."

"Buffers?" I asked.

"Buffers are the psychological apparatus that allows all our inconsistencies, contradictions and idiosyncrasies to go on without our awareness. Buffers are excuses, explanations, or just plain lies that are produced automatically by us to keep different parts of ourselves from seeing each other. We are a mass of contradictory I's that manifest without our control because they are just responding to the environment. These I's coalesce to become whole personalities. These personalities may be quite different and one personality will be ignorant of another. They are kept ignorant of each other by buffers, these shields. Many times too, buffers serve the purpose of keeping us from seeing that we do not have abilities and capacities we think we possess. For instance, someone who thinks of himself as liberal may carry on all kinds of bigoted activities without realizing it because their buffers will make excuses for each contradictory action so they can still consider themselves a liberal.

To really see your buffers, try to observe yourself at the moment you receive a criticism. A buffer will be there immediately excusing yourself—making everything all right, at least in your own mind. Even if you don't get to say the buffer out loud, your imagination will be working overtime to generate buffers; 'I didn't get much sleep last night,' 'Nobody told me!' 'John forget to tell me,' 'He doesn't know what he is talking about.'

This is interesting because on one level we know we are lying, but on another we okay it because it is important to preserve our image, even if we have to lie. The same thing happens when we receive a compliment, we will buffer it, that is keep it away by saying something like, 'I'm not this way at home, believe me,' or, 'I still have to lose another five pounds.' We try to keep ourselves in a predetermined cocoon of our imaginary picture. If you observe your imagination for a while you will notice that you will practice your buffers constantly, just in case someone questions or criticizes you. This is because we know what we are doing is questionable or wrong, but wish to do it anyway for some reason. In this way, we can still like or love ourselves no matter what we do.

Do you understand this so far?" he asked.

"Yeah, I do that," I admitted.

"Everyone does it. If you didn't you would be from another planet."

"I hate it when people pay me compliments," said Liz.

"That is because they make you feel uncomfortable even if they are true. You want people to notice that you are pretty or efficient or good at your job, but if they say it, you might have to acknowledge that you think that too. So, instead you offer a buffer to keep the complement away. Is that right, Liz"

"Yes, but I'm embarrassed to admit it."

"It would be real unusual not to be that way. So, buffers protect us from seeing ourselves, kind of like the people in Plato's Cave Allegory. It would be too unsettling to see beyond the shadows, so we close our eyes to the truth. Now when our buffers do not work for some reason, perhaps the transgression is too great, we will have a bout of conscience. At that point, we see ourselves as we are, sans excuses and lies. It is a painful experience. There is no pain quite like a true vision of how we actually are. It may be that the person experiencing the conscience will never be able to buffer it away and he will suffer for many years. Some buffers operate simply by talking about the incident enough until we are immune to its impact. The Catholic confession is an official buffer. Therapy is based on this concept also.

Another interesting part of buffers is that we will tend to buffer even before anything can be said about a problem. For example, a person might admit a mistake by saying how stupid they are or they've gained weight lately. The idea is that if you can say it first, it will take the sting out of someone else saying it. What we hate the worst is to have that someone else find fault before we can admit it. It will make it seem that we didn't know it and now have to look at it. Many, or most, arguments have buffers as the best defense mechanism.

If you want to get rid of your buffers, try not to respond when someone either compliments or criticizes you, even to agree. What happens is that your Emotional Center will go crazy because it does not like looking at itself. This is part of training the Emotional Center to be mature. Buffering is not mature. If after years of work, you have begun to control your need to buffer, you will experience conscience on a regular basis. Conscience will lead you out of the wilderness of imagination. Without buffers you can begin to 'know yourself' because you will be out there in plain view.'"

We heard a car pull up into the driveway. We looked out the window to see Captain West getting out of the car. He was talking to Jesus who was standing by the car. Paul went in the back. Liz and I went out to see what was going on. "Morning, Captain," I said.

He didn't respond to my greeting, but went into his message. "Sorry to inform you people, but the party's over. The Board of Supervisors just banned this healing business from taking place here; it is a health hazard they said."

Liz put her hands on her hips and charged down the steps to where West was standing. "What do you mean it is a health hazard? People leave here cured from all kinds of life threatening diseases. It is you stupid assholes who are the health hazards."

"Don't get wise lady, I'll run you in."

"What are those people supposed to do, anyway?" I asked. "Are you going to block the road forever? Give out tickets; what?"

"I don't know the answer to that now buddy, but I'll throw the bunch of you in jail if you start that phony healing business."

Just then there was a call for him over his radio. He went to answer it. All that I could hear was, "God damn it, I'm not going to ask them that. Shit. Shit. All right, I'll ask them. Man, I feel like an idiot." He wheeled back toward us.

"What is it?" I asked.

"You promised my lieutenant last night that Paul would see his kid today, and the Sheriff has his wife he wants him to see. She's got some kind of cancer. Anyway, shit, can they bring them down?"

"Yes, I think that would be fine, but remember Paul does not say he is a healer," I said. Liz was grinning. The captain did not fail to notice. He turned back around and called down for them to bring the patients.

I went in and told Paul. He agreed to see the sheriff's wife and the child. About the other thing he said, "The County has got a real problem now. There are no rules to follow." He reminded me that he didn't want to see or talk to any official people.

Another car pulled in behind the Captain West's. Out of it stepped the Sheriff, his wife, and the boy with his father. They came over and we are introduced ourselves. "Paul has agreed to see your wife, Sheriff, and your son, Lieutenant, but he wants to see them alone. So, you gentlemen will have to wait outside."

"No," said the lieutenant, "I'm not letting him go in there alone."

The wife of the sheriff spoke up. "He'll be with me, John. It will be okay."

"All right then, go on in." With that Liz led them into the house. I stayed outside.

They were inside for thirty minutes. When they came out Mrs. Sheriff was ebullient, and the boy was smiling. "She looked right at her husband and pointed her finger at him. "George, you better never say anything bad about that man again. He is the most wonderful person I've ever been around."

"Are you cured?" he asked.

"I don't know if I cured or not, but that doesn't matter. Don't you ever start on Paul again."

"Yes, he was neat," said the boy, "and I feel better. I can breathe."

His father picked him up. "Do you feel congested?" The boy shook his head.

I looked at this scene as if it was taking place outside of me. The sheriff was perplexed but smiling, his wife was joyful, the boy had a smile over his entire face, and his dad was wide eyed. The captain was just staring. It was strange to see this happening in front of my eyes. Everything was in slow motion.

I snapped out of it with the sheriff speaking. "Captain West, I am assigning you to these fine folks. Give then whatever they want in the way of support. If I hear you gave them any shit I'll have your ass. Do you understand?"

"Yes, sir. Don't worry, I'll take care of them." With that the sheriff's car loaded and was backing out of the driveway.

"Captain," I said, "you can pull your car over there under the shade of those trees. I'll bring you some lemonade." Liz and I went back inside.

When I brought him the lemonade, he seemed relaxed. "Say, I've got this back problem I've had for years. I may have to retire soon because of it. I wonder if Paul would come out and pray over it or whatever he does?"

I smiled warmly. "I'll ask him."

After a while, Paul went out to talk to Captain West. We watched from the window as Paul introduced himself with a little bow. He looked so thin next to the overweight captain. They remained standing for a time. Then Paul led him to a chair where he sat down. Paul pulled a chair in front of him. I could see West close his eyes, and then Paul broke into a hearty laugh. He couldn't control himself. He stood up and walked around the patio laughing. West just sat there with a silly grin. After a few minutes,

Paul calmed down and they began talking again softly. After ten minutes they both got up and shook hands and Paul walked back toward the house smiling.

"What was so funny out there," I asked.

Paul plopped in his easy chair. "We were sitting there and I was talking to him to calm him down. I had my hands on his knees when out of nowhere and in total seriousness he said, 'Say, you're not gay are you?' I never lost it like that, but it just stuck me as funny coming from this big brut of a man who was asking me to help him. I don't know what he would have done if I'd said yes. Get up and run away maybe."

He started laughing all over again. "That captain was on TV last night saying all kinds of bad things about you last night," said Liz, "He sure looked like a little lamb out in the patio."

"I know, everyone is tough until they need something," Paul said.

"I was watching TV a little bit ago and a panel of doctors from Phoenix have assembled to look over the claims of miracle cures going on down here. And they said that the Board of Supervisors are going to have you in for another emergency session they are calling tomorrow."

"Tell them no when they ask. I'm not interested in talking to them." He rose up from his chair and began walking toward his bedroom. "That laughing took too much energy."

Liz went out to work on some roses. I didn't feel like doing anything except watch TV, but I resisted that impulse and joined Arturo replacing a rose bush that hadn't survived.

The afternoon was quiet. Only a few helicopters passed over and Paul asked us not to watch TV, so we didn't know what was really going on. I brought lunch out to Captain West. "Well, how did it go?"

" I don't know. My back doesn't hurt like it did this morning. But I won't consider it a cure until I see an xray."

"Paul got a kick out of you wondering if he was gay."

"The fucking guy...wait, I take that back. He made me promise not to use profanity any more. That's going to be hard. Let me start again. He starts touching my knees and then I thought, 'Hey wait a minute here.'"

"You did good. I have never seen him laugh so hard before. I think he needed it. Everything's becoming so serious now."

In mid-afternoon the captain got a call that he relayed to us. "The Board of Supervisors says for Paul to come into Tucson tomorrow at ten in the morning for a meeting with them about this situation."

"Tell them no," Liz said. "He will not talk to anyone in any official position."

"Can I talk to Paul about this? He's got to come out sometime."

"No," Liz continued, "you are in an official capacity now. He won't see you."

"If my back didn't feel better, I'd just go in there and get him, but now he's got me spooked. I'll tell them, but they won't like it." He went back to his radio.

Liz went into tell Paul, but he was still asleep. She came back out into the patio. "He doesn't look well."

"The doctor said he had three to six months to live. It has only been a few days."

"I know what the doctor said," she answered, "but this business he's doing takes a lot out of him. I don't think he'll make it three months."

The Captain came back after being gone for about thirty minutes. "They say that they will come out here tomorrow. Will he see them?"

"No," I said, " He won't even see you. Tell them to forget it. Figure it out on their own."

"Oh, man, I wish I hadn't promised not to cuss, because this sure calls for some real low-down-dirty cussing. He is making trouble like I've never seen before. Heck, shoot and fuzz," he said smiling. "This is almost fun." He went back to his radio.

Paul woke up after taking a four-hour nap. We turned on the TV. Most of the channels were still dealing with the problem. On one channel, three lawyers were discussing what could be done to get him to meet with county officials. "They could arrest him for disturbing the peace," said one.

"What did he do to disturb it?" said another. "It was all those people who disturbed the peace. You going to arrest all of them?"

"They could get a grand jury to make him come in."

"He hasn't done anything wrong that I know of, what are they going to investigate? Healing? We'd be the laughing stock of the country. I say they should just let him rot out there. Eventually he'll come out of his hole."

Another station had a cult expert from Los Angeles. She was saying that this was a classic cult situation. When she was asked if it could still be in a cult with only two followers, she replied, "Oh, sure, a cult might only be one member. It is not how many members, it is the leader and this leader is one of the most diabolical I've ever seen."

"Have you seen him then?" the interviewer asked the cult expert.

"No, I haven't actually seen him. Nobody has. It is just his methods are all typically cult-like."

"And can you give us details about those methods?"

"Well, again, No. Nobody can determine that yet because nobody has talked to him. But from every indication, he is leading a real bad cult."

"Just what are those indications?"

"I don't know," she said, "just everything. Is this interview over?"

Paul turned the station. He had a big smile. Another station had the latest news. A man was saying, "And on another front, that situation in the desert is still up in the air. The Cardinal sent out a message to all of his churches to strongly advise all of the parishioners not to go see or have anything to do with the anti-Christ. In Tucson the FBI has weighed in with questions about Paul's activities. This is a direct quote from the district head, Pat Masterson, 'If he is dirty we'll find out. We are investigating his background now and coming up with some very interesting facts. I am not at liberty to reveal anything at this time, but as soon it is appropriate, I will.' So that's the news in a nutshell, check-in tonight at ten."

Paul turned it off. "That FBI agent just got on the case this morning. He hasn't even started the investigation and he's already lying about it."

I wondered how Paul knew that, or if he was guessing.

Before dark, another squad car came up to the house with a message from Senator Jones, our senior U. S. Senator. It said, "Please consider seeing me tomorrow, I have a rare blood disease that the doctor says cannot be cured. Please."

I went in to give the message to Paul. "Tell the Senator to come here at one o'clock tomorrow afternoon. I will see only him. Tell him to leave his people back wherever he keeps them. Also, no reporters."

I told the officer. He left.

"Wow, Paul, a Senator," I said. "You are becoming famous."

Paul smiled. "Yes, I am now a healer to the rich and powerful. Pretty soon there will be a class war over me."

After dinner I decided to ask Paul why he was doing all of this, especially in this way. "I am doing this to try to see if I can get a message across to the world about itself. What happens now is that when packs of people detect a weak person or group who cannot fight back, they will, like hounds, descend and devour the prey. Our sad history is chock full of examples of human disregard and depravity while under the protection of the majority. The witch hunts, Jewish Pogroms, the Inquisition, and the countless injustices carried out by the world's court systems are proof that humans, when in groups, are dangerous, unpredictable, and can perpetuate the most sordid of crimes under the mantle of legality. Everyone is in on the game as they invent excuses, or buffers, to satisfy the desire to watch other humans suffer. Hopefully, by not letting myself be exposed, the world's leaders, and especially the religious leaders who have the most to lose, will not be able to destroy me before they learn something about themselves."

"What will they learn?" Liz asked.

"That they are full of vanity and their motives are self-serving even though their rhetoric is the opposite. They will be protecting the world from a monster, as soon as they can figure something out about me. They will make me a monster if they can. Well, I have no doubt that they will, but the question is can they do it before I reveal too much about them?"

"When you said that there was really something big coming, did you know it was going to be this?" I asked.

"No, I didn't know, but something, some deep dread kept me awake at night. When I've had things like that happen before, it has always been something serious. Two days before Alice fell to her death, I had those feelings of dread. This time however, they paled in comparison."

"How do you know that the way you are playing this is the right way?" Liz asked.

"There is no wrong way. I don't even think there is a best way. This is the way I'm doing it. I am not identified with the outcome. I hope that you will learn something, and if you do, that is quite enough for me. Besides, the Gods are in charge of this. They have given me some things to say as soon as it is appropriate. Truly, this is not my show."

Another message arrived at eight asking me to call a number in Tucson. I did and it was a nationally known reporter on TV. "Hello," I said, "My name is Joe Peters. Can I help you?"

"Yes, my network would like me to interview Paul for a live broadcast anywhere he says."

"Well, sir, I know the answer is no. He wants no publicity."

"But don't you know, son, that by not giving an interview, he is just increasing the curiosity of the nation; of the world."

"He knows."

"Is it money he is looking for, because if it is we have a policy not to give money for news interviews."

"No, he does not want your money. Paul wants to be left alone."

"Well," he said, "we might make an exception in his case; say $100,000."

"You did not hear me. No." Just then Paul tapped me on the

shoulder. "Just a minute." Paul whispered something in my ear. "Sir, Paul would like to consider your offer. I will call you at this number in a day or two."

"Great, tell him we can work out almost anything."

We hung up. "Is it money Paul?" I asked.

"No, Joe, I don't want them to pay money. I want them to pay attention."

After Paul went to bed I took Liz out for a walk around the property. Arturo had placed a bench under our largest tree, a twelve-foot young oak. We sat down and I put my arm around her shoulders and pulled her next to me. "Liz, we've been married not much more than a month, but I have come to see you with new admiring eyes. Paul told me once that what a woman needs is to be cherished and protected, and I do cherish you more each day. I watch you around here keeping things together like neither of us could do. I see you lavish love and affection on both of us and I see the determination with which you confront life, and I think that I truly have been gifted with a jewel of a wife."

"Paul was right about wishing to be cherished. He must have learned that from his wife. I am not sure a man, any man, could come up with that on his own. I do feel valued by you, and I think that if I had received even a shred of that from husband number one or two, I would still be married to one of them. So, maybe you did hit the jackpot with me because I swear I will never let you down Joe. You are in me in a way no other man has ever been, and I intend to keep you there."

"I would like to be in you in another way right now," I said.

"Right here under this tree and on this bench? It is not even 'our' bench. That's over by the house."

"This bench has a back on it," I pointed out. "You and I can use the support, honey."

She kissed me long and long and said, "Okay, we'll adopt this supportive bench too."

Monday morning the whole Board of Supervisors showed up unannounced. Captain West led the two-car parade onto "The True Songs." Paul was still in his room and Liz was taking a shower. I went out to greet them. They had all exited their cars and were standing in front of me. Captain West remained in his car. "What can I do for you folks?"

"My name is Carlos Manes," a short one said. "We would like to speak to Paul or someone about the situation out here. It has become intolerable."

"I would be glad to talk to you, perhaps we can all go out into the big patio and chat about this. I will ask my wife if she will help me prepare some coffee. Go ahead folks and I'll be with you in about ten minutes."

They all started walking toward the patio as I went in to get coffee started. Liz came out and helped. Within fifteen minutes we were carrying two platters of coffee, orange juice, and two coffee-cakes out to the patio. "This is my wife Liz, and I think I forgot to mention that my name is Joe Peters. Please help yourselves." The five supervisors and the captain got what they wanted and sat down.

"Mighty pretty place," started Carlos. "Did you help put it together?"

"Yes, Liz and I came on board in January. Along with Paul, Arturo and his son Jesus, we have put in 430 rose bushes."

A woman supervisor asked Liz what "True Songs" meant. "It comes from Walt Whitman's last poem. The way he uses it, it means heaven or maybe some meeting place beyond death."

"Interesting," she said.

"Liz and Joe, can we get down to business?" asked Carlos.

"By all means," I answered. "I know you didn't come all the way out here to look at roses."

"Why won't this Paul fellow talk to us?" one of them asked.

"He does not want to, I guess you would say. He has that right not to be public," I said.

Carlos jumped in. "Does he know the situation out here; that thousands, many thousands of people are milling around this area waiting to come in here to get healed. And that it is causing the county no end of problems. We've had to take over fifty to the hospital with heat prostration and all kinds of other ailments. A lot of these people are deathly sick with cancer and I don't know what all. This is tying up law enforcement and our health care facilities. We've got to get this problem resolved today. Does he understand that, Joe?"

"He may not," said Liz, "but we do now. That is why he has given us the task of working this out if we can. What would you like to see happen?"

"Could he come into town to see these people? At least there we have facilities to take care of people. Here we have nothing."

"I will make that recommendation. Can you guarantee his safety and give us a place to stay and guard this place while we're gone?" I asked.

"And can you somehow regulate the flow of people that see him?" added Liz. "He is a very sick man and I don't want him besieged by people when he can't take it."

"We," he looked around at his colleagues, "will do whatever is necessary. The world is watching what we do here."

"Fine, I said, "we'll ask Paul about this. If you would just sit out here for awhile, I'll get back to you as soon as I can, but I'm not promising anything."

We went back into the house. Paul was sitting in his chair. Liz told him what went on. "Yes, I guess I'll have to do something different. All of those people are suffering and I've got to do something. Give me a minute to think."

Paul stared in contemplation for five minutes. "Okay, this is what I would like. Have them pick a place in town where we can all stay and I can see people one at a time, or in small groups. Find some way to have a lottery or something to choose no more than sixty people a day for me to see. I am not even sure I can see that many, but tell them not to pick more than one day's group at a time. I threw up a lot of blood this morning so I don't know how much longer I can last. We will start on Friday morning, so we will leave here Thursday night. Please request a helicopter to come pick us up and have the place guarded while we are gone. That is all I can think of now."

"Blood?' asked Liz.

"I don't want to talk about it Liz. Go do your job."

After we explained the situation, leaving out the blood part. They readily agreed and would use Captain West as our go-between.

As they left, Liz whispered to me, "Blood; did you hear that honey?

"He is going to die, Liz, and we have a front row seat to learn from it."

After the supervisors left it was quiet. I asked Captain West to keep everyone away. He did bring through Arturo and Jesus, who weren't able to convince the men at the roadblock to let them in. They came in and had refreshments before attending to their duties. They told about how the people in their Latino neighborhood were taking all the news. There were two sides forming up. One that were led by many priests who thought that Paul was an anti-Christ or somehow connected with evil, and the other that were in awe of Paul's new reputation and thought he might be the Second Coming, or a saint of some type. There was at least one fist-fight over the issue last night.

"Do you remember what happened when Gandhi was murdered?" Paul asked.

None of us could remember. "There was a blood bath between the two rival religions; Hindu and Moslem. It was a real carnage as the people rioted in the streets. It was brutality masquerading as religion. Well, we may see the same thing here as emotions come to a boil. But in this case, it may be fueled by men in high places in the religions because their very existence, or at least their positions and organizations, are at stake."

"Why don't you just disappear again like you did last time and get some medical help and go on living?" asked Liz.

Then I added, "Can you cure yourself?"

"I don't know if I can cure myself, but I'm not about to in any case. Providence has prepared me for my trial and I choose to endure it. I am now ripe for the test and if my mission is to stir up humanity a bit, so much the better. They certainly need it. I also need to give them a message."

'What is it?" asked Liz.

"You will know in due time."

After Arturo and Jesus went outside Paul asked us if we wanted another lesson. We retired to our assigned seats after opening a big bottle of soda and pouring ourselves a glass. He started once we were settled.

"God doesn't love these bodies of ours any more than He loves donkeys. Human bodies are tools only, or may I say more accurately, luggage to tote around the immortal soul. The soul, called sometimes the self, and at others, essence, is loved by our creator. He went through countless immense cycles of experimentation to arrive at the right vessel. He always treats our bodies with dignity, but mostly we are the ones who cause all our own problems. In the main, people everywhere, since the dawn of time, live life backwards. Evil, with its bait of pleasure, lures us into endless pain and emotional suffering. Virtue, appearing unattractive wrapped in its cloth of effort, is avoided. Examples abound everywhere that a life of negativity and sloth is death to the spirit, but still it is almost the only choice anyone picks. To the extent that a person; an individual person, makes efforts away from the mechanical seeking of instant pleasure, is the extent of their individual inner gain. Their true happiness, or peace, comes from a higher source only possible through effort. Self-remembering is the most intense effort one can make because it is the least mechanical."

He stopped for a moment to look at each of us. We said nothing. "People live their lives trying to mount pedestals. To be thought important, if not by others, at least by oneself, is paramount. Vanity leads this parade. It is not only death defying, it is death, period. And other humans fall for this trap and measure the man and the pedestal as one. However, no one can see from atop a pedestal unless one has developed his or her soul. Few do. Abe Lincoln and Marcus Aurelius are two examples. No, high places that mortals would wish to ascend are dark places of spiritual death. Jesus gave us the idea that the first is last and the last is first in heaven. That is true. So, to end this talk, I say that it is not where you are in life that counts—it is what you are internally."

There was a full minute of quiet. "Thank you," Liz said. "If that Senator is coming at one, we'd better get lunch fixed and out of the way. What do you guys want?"

Paul looked to me to make the decision. "How about some grilled ham and cheese sandwiches with pickles; and ice cream and some of that coffee cake those people didn't finish this morning. Paul need lots of calories."

"I sure married an all American guy. Too bad there is no football on."

Paul ate only a few bites of his food. Liz tried to make him eat a little more but he just wasn't interested. I went in and turned on television to see what was happening with the world. I was surprised to see Senator Jones standing in front of a car near the roadblock. He was making a statement. "So, I'm going in there to talk to this man and see if I can find out something about him for the rest of the world. I'm going in alone so as to build his trust. I think he is a good man and I'm going to find out."

Paul, who was standing in the door-way, smiled. "He hasn't told anyone about his ailment because it may be bad for the election next year, even if he gets cured."

I switched the channel. A man I didn't recognize was speaking on a news show. "There have been a series of charges leveled against this man. His real name is Paul Martin and he spent the last ten or twelve years in San Diego. What he did for a living has not been determined except that my sources say that he is suspected of drug smuggling. Also, he lived in Mexico, in a town called," the reporter stopped to look at a paper. "Bacum, in the state of Chihuahua. My sources said that he left suddenly because he and his wife were suspected of selling drugs, or smuggling drugs."

I looked at Paul for his reaction. There was none. "Someone has decided to give me a criminal record," he said.

We heard the car drive up. It was the Senator. We went out and introduced ourselves. We went back in because it was hot, around 108. "I appreciate you seeing me like this Paul. No one outside of my wife and a couple of doctors know my condition. I'd appreciate it if you wouldn't say anything if you are able to cure me. Otherwise, I don't care. They said I have a year to live."

"No one will say a thing, Senator Jones," Paul replied.

"Listen, Paul, I just wanted to say that I have been a conservative most of my life and I haven't been very nice to the poor and all, in fact I've been a bastard most of the time, but I have been a good God fearing Christian all my life. And that's the God-honest truth. I'm a God fearing man."

"I know you are Senator, I know exactly what you are. Now maybe you and I can step over here in the kitchen for a few minutes. I want to talk to you alone." As they did that Liz and I went back to television.

The only of interest was a report from a panel of doctors who said that of the twelve "cures" they had investigated only three seemed genuine, three were doubtful, and six were cured but that it could have been from natural causes. The way the head doctor spoke, this was not a big deal at all. "Did you hear him, Liz? It is no big deal that twelve people come to Paul and only nine are confirmed healed from life threatening diseases; only nine."

"Listen, I have been around physicians all my life. They are afraid of anything that might cut into their money. I'm sure that if it were all twelve they would still make it seem like nothing."

We heard the two men in the living room so we went back in. As he was leaving, the Senator was saying, "Now, I only have to do it if I'm healed, right? I mean that's only fair, Paul, otherwise I'd be giving away money for nothing. You know what I mean?" Paul waved him out the door with a slight smile on his face.

After the door closed, Paul sank down to the couch with a big smile on his face. "I asked him to give one million dollars to the Catholic Sisters of America retirement fund, and you heard him. He only wants to do it if he gets something first. One million dollars won't even leave a dent in his net worth. If the cure doesn't take he'll die anyway and he still doesn't want to help anyone."

"He doesn't know how he appears does he Paul?" Liz asked.

"No, he is oblivious to everything around him except to his giant ego, but believe it or not, many people vote for him just because of that quality, or weakness. It makes them feel okay about their own nasty opinions. He is their hero."

"If you knew this about him, why did you see him?" Liz asked again. " I would not have."

"So that you could see that he won't change the way he is even for his own life. Just a little lesson I'm showing you. Besides, he'll die soon enough of something else. Oh, by the way Joe, call that reporter up again and tell him I've decided to have a question and answer period Thursday evening at eight o'clock."

"Where?"

"Tell him I would like it at the hotel that the county is putting us in that night. Also tell him I agree to a one-hour question and answer period. Remember those exact words; question and answer period, and also I may want to make a brief statement at the start. Tell him that I want at least three different news organizations and two members of the clergy to be there for the show. Also, tell him no commercials under any circumstances. Tell him to work out the details with the county supervisors."

I did as he requested. They were overjoyed at the other end and within minutes the whole world knew. It was a flash on every TV station we looked at. Afterward Liz and I went outside to work with the roses in the back of the property.

As we were working in the heat, I was thinking Liz appeared very disturbed by the day's happenings. "How do you feel about everything?"

"How do you think I feel? Paul is dying right in front of my eyes and I cannot even grieve because he won't have it. Lousy, that's how I feel. And look how the world is taking this. It is a circus and it is bringing out all of the worst in people."

"That is what happened to Jesus," I said. "Maybe authentic goodness is hard to take when most other people are such phonies."

The next morning Paul asked Liz to call her mother and see if there was any way to get Big Jim down to "True Songs" that day. Her mother said she would find out. An hour later Liz called back to find out. Her mother said that the doctors said no, he was in too bad of shape to travel, even by helicopter. Paul then said he could help if Big Jim could talk on the phone to him. It took a couple of hours to get the connection with his room. When he came on the line, Liz talked to him for a few seconds. "Here Paul, he can barely talk," as she handed him the phone.

Paul took the phone from her. "Big Jim," he said, "I'm going to try to help you. Do you understand that?" He paused. "Okay, Jim, if you can, close your eyes and try to visualize a light right in front of your eyes." With that he waved us away. We went out in the back as far as the cord would go. I could see him sit down and close his eyes and talk into the phone."

Liz watched him intently from outside. After about ten minutes, Paul smiled and waved us in. "Your mother wants to talk to you."

"Hello, mother, how is Jim doing. Oh, my." She smiled at me. "Well, mom, I hope he gets even better. I will. I will tell him. Good-bye mother." She put down the phone and hugged Paul. "She said he's already talking clearer, and he was moving his left hand a little. She said to say thank you, and I'm saying thank you, you wonderful man."

"It is quite all right, Liz. For some reason God has given me the power to do this. It is much stronger than before. I can't explain it, but if I am to pass on shortly, all that I can say is, 'What a way to go!'"

"Oh, Paul, I wish you'd at least try to save yourself," said Liz. "It is breaking my heart."

"Liz, sweet Liz, thank God that He gave you me in the first place. You are a gift to me in these last days, but all things must go, dear. I must go soon because my mission is over. It can't be helped."

We began packing in the afternoon for a few days stay in town. Paul asked Jesus if he would stay here at night to watch over the place. I had a feeling that Paul thought he might never be back. He walked around the property alone and smelled the roses.

He signaled us to join him. He put his finger up to his lips as a signal not to say anything and pointed to a rose. Liz bent over a smelled it. She threw her head back and seemed dazed. Her eyes were closed. Then Paul pointed me to the rose. I took a deep breath of the fragrance. I don't know what happened but I was in another state immediately. I have never experienced such pleasure. Everything inside of me was beautiful and peaceful and music was playing from somewhere. It seemed like a long time before I opened my eyes. I looked at Liz and she too seemed to have had the same experience. "How long was I out?" I asked.

"Just a moment, but in that moment you were in the 'Now,' which is another word for heaven. I have lived there for a number of years off and on. The last few months it has been all of the time. Heaven is not off in the sky somewhere, but right here in the Now. I wanted you to experience it so you won't suffer as much when I do leave. I am going home."

I thought about it as we walked back in. So, that is what all the fuss is about. That is worth dying for, I decided. I asked Paul if that was what the biblical Paul experienced when he became converted.

"Something like that I am sure. It inspired him and I hope it inspires the both of you."

We didn't have to answer. He saw it in our eyes.

We had a small early dinner about five o'clock. All five of us just sat around the living room not saying a word.

When we heard the helicopter overhead, he gave Arturo and Jesus each a check. As we were leaving he went over and hugged each man and said good-bye. He was definitely not coming back I thought. We got into the helicopter and looked down at all the roses as we flew away.

Chapter 13

As soon as we were airborne a lean black man stuck out his hand and introduced himself as Charles Washburn. "I will be coordinating your stay at the Apex Hotel," he said. "You will be on the top floor with a two bedroom suite. Once we get there and away from this noisy thing I'll tell you the itinerary." He turned back around. I looked down at the roadblock in front of Rainbow Blvd.. There were about 50 people milling around the two patrol cars. I thought that the little store on the corner must be cashing in on this whole thing. Either that or the owner is going nuts with the crowds. In a few minutes we were sweeping over the city. In the distance I could see the Apex, a place where I had often parked my cab while I waited for a fare. I read a lot of Shakespeare outside of that place. I even had some pretty decent conversations about him with the bell captain.

As we were over the Apex, I could see thousands of people in the streets and two spot-lights on the roof along with police and other official looking people. We came in for a landing on the bull's eye painted on the top. Within seconds we were inundated with photographers and police. The flashing bulbs were popping and everybody seemed to be yelling all at once in order to be heard over the noise of the helicopter blades. We were led into a doorway on the roof. Once the door was closed it was quiet again. A woman shook our hands and introduced herself as from the network. Her name was Jane.

After going down a small flight of stairs we were led into our suite. Jane, who was a pretty woman in her 30's, began giving us the lowdown on the plans for the evening. "I am so glad to meet you Paul," she started. "They say that there is going to be a billion people watching the interview tonight."

"A billion?" I exclaimed. "This is not the Super Bowl."

"It is the Super Bowl for people who don't watch the Super Bowl," replied Charles.

"All the major networks are carrying this all over the world," continued Jane. "We have Bud Burton from our own network; that's the man you spoke to on the phone. Tom Dresdan and Elizabeth Arrainian from the other networks will be there. Also, per your request Paul, we have Bishop Johns and the Right Reverend Starkmaster representing their churches. It should be an interesting night. We will come for you in about an hour and a half to go down into the ballroom. So, you folks can get some rest."

"Any problems or questions," said Charles, "and I'll just be outside the door. I've put some snacks over there. If you need anything from the kitchen, please just let me know."

We were just standing there looking around. I didn't have anything to say. They both left in an official but friendly manner. After the door closed Liz said, "I don't know about you guys, but I am a little overwhelmed."

"Me too," I added. "Paul, have you talked before a huge crowd before?"

"I have never spoken in public, at least not in front of more than a few people."

"Are you nervous?" Liz asked.

"Yes, a bit. But I think I may actually enjoy this."

"I am not nervous, I'm plain scared Paul," I said.

He smiled. "You will be fine, Joe. And if you are not, it will still be fine."

Paul went into one of the bedrooms and closed the door. I followed Liz into the other one. She slipped her shoes off and got on the bed in a fetal position. I followed her example and nestled in behind her. I kissed her cheek and ear, but she did not respond. After a time I got up and went into the living room and drank a soda and sat in a chair. I resisted the impulse to turn on the television.

I was too nervous already. The TV might just make it unbearable because I figured it was going to be broadcasting all about the big event and nothing else. I don't know why I was so nervous? It was Paul who was going to be on the firing line. No one even cared about Liz and I. Still, it was Liz and myself up there too. We loved that man so much that whatever was happening to him was also happening to us.

Liz came into the living room and said, "That was some feeling I had when I smelled that rose. I think Paul arranged that as a gift don't you?"

"Yes, and as a reminder that he is going to be all right. Once he told me: 'Fear life, not death. Life is full of chains.'"

A loud knock on the door startled me. I answered it. It was Jane and Charles. "Ten minutes," announced the woman. I invited them to sit down while I went and told Paul.

I knocked on his door. "Come in."

"We're leaving in ten minutes." Paul nodded. He had been sitting in a chair by the bed. He came out dressed in a navy blue sport coat and a pink open neck sport shirt under it. He looked frail but somehow great, I thought, as he smiled his biggest smile. "Let us go my children. Fate awaits." We walked out the door and down to the elevator. It was being held open by a security guard. The door shut and we rode in silence down to the lowest floor. I noticed that Liz was holding Paul's hand. The elevator door opened to a buzz of activity and the flash of cameras. We followed Charles to the left and into a large ballroom. It was crammed with equipment of all sorts, much of it I recognized from being in TV stations when I would go visit Barbara. That seemed like a million years ago. I couldn't even recall what she looked like.

Someone led Paul toward the front of the room, while Jane, Charles, Liz, and I were shown to seats to the right of the stage. The stage was only three feet high. It had one long table with a single chair. In front of him were four gentlemen and one woman. Paul and the panelists were testing their lavaliere microphones. Someone brought a glass of water and placed it to the side of Paul, while a woman was putting some make-up on his face. "Two minutes," said a man who looked like the director.

Paul closed his eyes as he waited. I watched the director who was making eye contact with Bud Burton. He raised his hand and said, "three, two, one, action."

"Welcome to this historic broadcast from the ballroom of the Apex Hotel in Tucson, Arizona. I am Bud Burton. Tonight four men and one woman, plus myself, will be interviewing a man named Paul Martin, who is the world's perhaps first confirmed healer. Many doctors over the past few days have examined in excess of forty individuals who have been healed, apparently completely, from a variety of incurable and life-threatening ailments. Mr. Martin has agreed to a one-hour questioning period after he makes a brief statement. With me tonight to help in this task are Tom Dresdan from CBS, Elizabeth Arrainian from ABC, Bishop Matthew Johns from the diocese of Denver, and finally, the Reverend Albert Starkmaster from the Divine Light Baptist Church in Dallas, Texas. Welcome to you all." They all nodded. "Now, Mr. Martin, you have a short statement to make?"

Paul leaned forward and looked at each of the people in front of him, and then directly into the camera. "Yes, and thank you Mr. Burton. And thank-you kind people who have tuned-in to this broadcast tonight. My mission to is to give you a message from Higher Forces. It is they I represent. It is these Higher Forces who are doing the curing of bodies. I am their tool for this work. They needed your attention and that is the only way most people will pay attention, when something startling like miracles are performed.

There is to be a dark cloud that will descend upon the earth in the form of continual and dire events that will spell the end of civilization, as we know it. The Twentieth Century, with its many millions slaughtered is but a preamble to the horrors of the Twenty First Century. There will be untold torment as our savage and barbarous natures come to the front and there is nothing that can stop it now. This is payment for our misbehavior. We have lost our spiritual lives to earthy concerns and love of negativity at every level. Humans have become corrupt more than ever. We are a festering boil. In virtually every corner, life on earth is preventing souls from being harvested. Mankind was sown on earth to bring forth the sweet fruit of the soul, and yet only bitter fruit is the crop these late days.

In the times to come, the large will prey upon the small as they always do, but also, the small will prey even more on the large. Humanity will live like savages in fear and loathing. There will be a flood of anguish.

But these hard times will bring many toward the Light and produce a multitude of lofty spirits. Great monasteries will flourish and provide comfort and safety to those that wish to wake from their slumber. Others will find the means and wit to conquer heaven by doing good works and knowing themselves.

To the others, trial by woe will mark their time. Prepare what you will.

From this hardness will spring forth, in the coming centuries, a fresh age that looks upon the Light of God as a thing to be cherished. It will be a flowering time like no other."

Paul said these things in deep earnestness. I looked around. Everyone was in shock, including me. He looked straight at the camera when he gave his message so it had a hypnotic effect on the viewers I am sure. He spoke with authority and without a trace of malice or sentiment. He looked down at the panel.

Now I would like to begin the questioning with Bishop Johns. Bishop Johns, my question to you is..."

"Wait a minute, Mr. Martin," interrupted Bud Burton, "maybe you don't understand, but we are going to interview you, not the other way around." Somebody laughed on the set. Burton looked over to his left and made a face. "Do you understand that, Mr. Martin?"

"No," answered Paul, "my understanding is that you, who are the world's representatives here tonight, are going to answer my questions as to how you could allow the world to become so corrupted and vile."

I was watching the screen and the members of the panel were in clear shock. The Reverend threw up his hands in disgust. There was open laughter audible over the TV set. 'No," said Burton loudly, "that is not the way it goes, Mr. Martin. We are not going to answer for society's woes. We want to know what you are doing here and what you really want. It is all about you, Mr. Martin. God damn it." The rest of the panel looked his way in surprise. Paul had the slightest smile come over his face.

Elizabeth Arrainian broke out in a huge grin barely containing a laugh. "Wait a minute Bud, before this turns into a farce. Mr. Martin; Paul, would you consider a compromise where we each ask you a question and you asked each of us a question? That way we both get what we want."

The smile broadened on Paul's face. "Yes, I believe that is acceptable."

"Good," said Bud, "I want to apologize to the panel and to you Paul for the profanity."

"How about the one billion people, Mr. Burton, do you apologize to them also?" asked Paul.

Bud Burton looked surprised. "Yes of course, I am very sorry to all the people who were disturbed by my inadvertent comment." He gazed around the room. "Well, I guess I don't know how to restart here. Mr. Martin, would you like to ask Bishop Johns your question? Is that okay with you, Bishop?"

The Bishop straightened up. "Yes, I'd like to hear what you have to ask me, Mr. Martin."

"Thank you. You represent an organized religion that has been functioning for several thousand years and originally supposed to be on a bed-rock of love and compassion and yet it has historically been just the opposite. The church has tacitly or directly permitted the Inquisition, the Jewish Pogroms, witch-hunts, torture, and a thousand other atrocities. Bishop Johns, what happened to the love and compassion?"

The Bishop had a wry smile. "Mr. Martin, the Church has had its problems yes, but it is not for you to question the Mother Church. We will work out our problems just fine. Besides, I don't have time to list all of the good things we have done for people."

"I think it wouldn't take that much time, Bishop; a couple of minutes perhaps."

They had a shot of Elizabeth who had her head lowered

masking a grin. "Okay, Mr. Martin," the Bishop said, "now that I have answered your question, you answer this. How do we know that you are not from the devil? This is where I think you came from; the fires of hell; sent to scare us."

Paul looked at him directly. "Yes, I will answer that. The answer is that there is no such entity as the devil or Satan. If God would have wanted to create such a creature, He would have used man as a model. No, there is no need for a devil to tempt man and bring misery; man is doing quite a good job of bringing about suffering on other men. I have come to discredit what has gone on under the guise of holiness and show a way out of the maze of evil perpetrated by man himself." He paused for a few seconds holding his hands up as if he was thinking. "Bishop Johns, you have a small tumor in the lower left part of your left lung. If you get an x ray tomorrow you will have this confirmed."

The Bishop's eyes were open and unblinking. "Now, may we move on to you Mr. Burton," Paul continued.

"Yes," he replied. "Do you want to ask me something, Mr. Martin? I had nothing to do with the Inquisition, I assure you."

"I know that Mr. Burton. What I was going to ask you is concerning your charge the other day that I was involved in drug smuggling. Where did that come from?"

"It came from confidential sources which I cannot reveal."

"Which of course you cannot reveal, especially if you made them up. You said it in an editorial so an editor couldn't question you, should one care. Was your source your own wife the other morning at breakfast who just asked the question and you jumped on it as a fact?"

Burton slammed his fist down on the table. "Mr. Martin, I can sue you for this. It is not true. I'll stake my whole career on it. You are the worst kind of cult guru and you've got the whole world believing you. You are a phony and a liar. And I don't believe that end of the world crap for one minute."

"You wish with all of your might that that was true what you just said. But it is not. And the world is not ending; it is just being rearranged." He looked at the camera again. "Ladies and gentlemen, the press has been manipulating you at will for a long time. Observe what you have just seen and think about it."

"I have had enough of this farce as you call it, Elizabeth. I for one am leaving the presence of this liar." With that Bud unhooked himself and turned and left. All of the panel except Ms. Arrainian did the same. She sat looking at Paul with a smile. "Paul, there are a billion people out there who just saw that. Are you happy?"

"Happy is not the word, Ms. Arrainian."

"Please call me Libby, Paul. Everybody else does." I took a quick look at Liz, who had her mouth open in surprise. "Do you have any questions for me, or revelations?"

Paul smiled a broad loving grin. "No, Libby, you are a good person. You would actually like to see a better world, as I am positive most of our billion viewers would also, they just don't know how to go about it. The earth and its human occupants are too confused."

"Let me ask you something then," she said, "so maybe we can get something out of this interview. Do you think that there is a chance of wholesale changes to keep the disasters from happening?"

"First of all, the disasters; the coming dark-age, is a fact. Nothing can be done about that, but you and everyone else have the protection of a strong inner life. No one can change circumstances, however your attitude can change to accept what comes. It is the perfect defense. Do not be under the power of things or desires. The suffering is foreordained, but it does not have to touch anyone who develops acceptance. The great justice of God is that we create our own heaven or hell wherever and whoever we are. This will be as true in the time to come as in the time past."

He looked up at where we were sitting and smiled. "I am tired now and would like to end this. Libby, go home now and hug your daughter and tell her I said that you are a remarkable woman."

As he rose up, she said, "Paul, I will, I will tell her that. Thank you. Thank you."

We rushed down to where Paul was coming down off the stage. People around the set were just staring at him and then at Libby sitting in her chair. I thought, well now I have seen it all.

Not exactly. There was more to come I was to find out as soon as we got back to the room. Once we entered the door, Paul collapsed in our arms. Liz asked everyone who had followed us to leave us alone for a while. We helped him over to his bed and did most of the work of removing his clothes. In his shorts lying on the bed Paul didn't look anything like the giant who had killed the dragons a few minutes before. He was emaciated and limp as we put pajamas on his frame. "Go away, I'm okay now," he said after we finished.

We closed the door and went to the couch and enfolded within each other. There was nothing to say. No words could have expressed the wonder of it all. A tiny knock came from the other side of the door. I got up and answered it. It was Charles and behind him, Libby. "Come in," I said.

Charles was as subdued as I felt. "The Board of Supervisors has asked me if Paul would come to a hospital tomorrow instead of bringing people here? The hotel management doesn't think it is a good idea anymore and no one is willing to pick the people to be healed, so there are several hospitals willing to receive Paul if it is kept secret."

"I'm sure that will be all right," I answered. I looked at Libby. She stepped around Charles and sat on the couch.

"That was truly great tonight," she said, "great in a way that I can't explain."

"I know," agreed Liz.

"I am here in an official capacity from all of the networks. They would like to know if Paul would make a full speech tomorrow night? I think we can get the stadium if he'll do it."

"Do you need an answer tonight? And why does it have to be tomorrow? Can't he rest for a week or two?" Liz asked.

"I know he looked tired, but everybody wants to see him again. No one has ever seen anything like what went on tonight."

"I'll see if he is awake," Liz said as she got up.

Liz and I went to the door and opened it. Paul was awake staring at the ceiling with his arms outstretched. "Paul," Liz said, "Libby is here and would like to know if you would be willing to make a speech tomorrow on TV?"

He brightened up considerably. "Libby? Ask her to come in please." Libby, who heard him, came in. We closed the door and left. After 15 minutes she came out and announced that it was all set. She gave us both hugs and left.

We turned on the TV and watched the tumult that Paul's appearance had created. The interview was played over and over with commentators talking and giving opinions. They were about evenly divided between pro and con. A livid Bud Burton was denouncing the whole thing as a joke. We turned it off and went to bed. Neither of us slept until early morning.

The phone jerked me from sleep at 7:00 A.M. "Hello, yeah, yeah, Okay, We'll be ready to go."

"What is it Joe?"

"Somebody down stairs says that a helicopter will be here in a half an hour to pick us up. The Apex wants us out of here as soon as possible. They are going to take us to some other location where it is safer."

We bolted up and while I ran in to wake Paul, Liz jumped in the shower. Paul seemed to be better from his exhaustion from the night before. I told him what was going on and he agreed to get ready. I got in the shower and tried not to notice Liz who was still in there. At 7:30 sharp a knock came. I opened it. An older gentleman was standing in the doorway. "I'm so sorry, but my bosses are afraid of what the crowds will do if Paul stays here much longer. A chopper is here to take you folks to a hospital where you can stay for the time being. I understand that Paul will be doing some healing there anyway."

"Thank you," I said. We filed out of the room and down the hall and up the stairs. As soon as we appeared the chopper started its rotors.

After Paul was in, Liz whispered in my ear, "Paul's bathroom had blood in the sink and toilet."

We jumped in and within a few seconds were airborne. I asked the pilot where we were going and he said to Arizona General.

"That's my old hospital. Good, I'll get to see some of my friends."

I looked down and saw thousands around the hotel. I was glad we were leaving.

We landed on the roof of the hospital and scurried down into a hall. A nurse led us into a big room where we were told to wait. As she was leaving us, she did a double take and asked, "Liz Lizetti, is that you? "

"Yes Mary Ann, it is Liz Peters."

"Well, then it's true what I heard."

"What did you hear, Mary Ann?"

"Oh, never mind," and was out the door.

While we were waiting in some incredibly uncomfortable chairs, I asked a nurse who was passing by if we could go get some food. "Well, there is a cafeteria downstairs." Then he paused and said, "That's not a good idea. There is a snack machine down the hall."

Paul laughed. "It looks like I am a hot potato, kids."

"Wait a minute," Liz said, and charged out the door. I could hear her footsteps down the hall. She was walking like she meant business. In twenty minutes she returned leading two women pushing trays. Behind was a man in a suit. "Paul, I'd like you to meet Dr. Dan Driscoll, he is the head of the hospital, and Dan, this is my husband Joe." We shook hands.

"Gee, I am sorry for the mix up. We expected you at 9:00. Do you want to start your healing right after you eat?"

"Sure, the earlier the better. I'd like to go to the cancer ward first, if you don't mind. I'd also like a wheelchair. I'm not up to par today."

"Good, I'll bring a chair up here myself in about twenty minutes."

Paul again only picked at his food. He did drink two cups of coffee though. Dr. Driscoll came in with a wheelchair and another doctor. He was introduced as Dr. Smith, in charge of the cancer wing. "Well, Liz, I wondered why I haven't seen you in awhile." I must have looked at him strangely because then he said, "Liz used to donate her lunch times to come and work with the dying patients.'

As we were walking down the hall pushing Paul, she told me that was her extra task that Paul had given her. "He said it would soften me. It has."

I said that I had seen it all the night before, but healing in a hospital was an experience not to be forgotten. The five of us went down quietly to the floor where the patients who were the most severely ill were staying. We rolled Paul into the first room with two patients. Dr. Smith asked them if they wanted to see Paul and both agreed, but they both looked very close to death. Paul rolled himself over to each one and spoke to them quietly for a few minutes. He then turned around and we went into the next room. By that time the hall was full of onlookers. When asked if she wanted to see Paul, a little bit of a woman started screaming, "Get out of here Satan. I saw you on television last night. You go back to hell where you came from." We backed out of there fast. Paul was smiling. But by the time we went into the third room, the hallway was crammed with nurses, janitors and patients from other floors. While we were in room number three, Dr. Driscoll was trying to clear the hallway.

A young woman who was visiting her mother, stood in front of Paul and said, "No thank you, my mother wants to die. Besides it is against God's law." The patient next to her had already died ten minutes before and they hadn't removed her body. Paul wheeled around to leave, but Dr. Driscoll held up his hand.

"I'm sorry, Paul this is just not working. Maybe I'll take you up to the next floor and try to bring you some people."

The hall was a sight. Some people were down on their knees praying, while others were just staring. Someone in the back said, "Save me St. Paul."

Another booming voice came from the first room we had visited. "What do you mean she's better? We've already got the estate figured out. I am going to sue somebody." Paul looked at Liz and I and winked.

It was a madhouse on that floor, people were clawing at Paul as we squeezed by. When we finally got to the next floor people had come up the stairs to meet us. Dr. Driscoll pushed us back into the elevator and we rode to the basement. "I'm sorry for all the inconvenience, but would you mind going somewhere else for awhile?"

"But," Liz pointed out, "we don't have a car."

He reached in his pocket and pulled out some keys. "Here take my car. It's the caddie over in spot 101 right in front. I'm sorry Liz, but this is too crazy." With that he left us.

Paul was having a good time for some reason. "Well, it looks like they don't need any healers around here in this hospital. They wouldn't know how to bill the patients. Let's hightail it out of this place."

I checked us into a motel not far from there under an assumed name. There, while we watched TV we heard that Paul was scheduled to give a speech that night at the stadium. The reporter also said that somehow they had misplaced the healer. They asked if anyone had information to please call the police.

Paul was roaring. "They better find me or else they will have a stadium full of mad would be worshipers." He then asked me to see if I could call around and find Libby and tell her where we were, but to keep it a secret until we had to leave. He said he could use the peace and quiet."

After I finally spoke to her I went out and bought a deck of cards and we played poker for real money--pennies. We had seven hours to wait.

We played and laughed and each told stories about our lives. Even with the impending doom of Paul's death from cancer, we were able to enjoy the time together. I remember once that he said that Jesus, a carpenter by trade, had learned to build a bridge out of a cross and that he wanted to do the same thing with roses.

Another time he said, after I asked him something about how life worked, "Everyone in life is in disguise, dressing up and playing like someone important. Costume, pose, and pretense are vital to society because we would rather substitute illusion for rock solid reality. As a result, life is fed by monumental misunderstandings and mistaken identities. So, image is the most important thing in life. The idea that a person might be seen as they are is terrifying and worth sacrificing even one's life to keep the secret safe."

The whole time was filled with little jewels of wisdom. Once he said that we now would have to use life as our teacher, but that it was quite capable as long as we remembered about the present and then everything we did in our daily life would be transformed into a graceful existence.

We were soaking this all up. All that I had to do was ask about something and he would come out with ways of looking at things that were unique and inspiring. After I asked him about ecstasy as being a goal to work towards, he said, "The highest human emotions are not exhilaration or ecstasy, but the quiet feelings of appreciation and gratitude. Exhilaration and ecstasy are self-centered and a person can be manipulated to experience them, and then they will always create their opposite, misery and depression. Appreciation comes from a realization of the worth of others and other things. It is the gateway to true understanding."

Too soon the time for intimate learning came to an end as Libby knocked on the door. She came in all excited. "Oh, Paul there is this grand tussle of different forces over you. The networks and most of the people of the world want to hear and see you talk tonight, but many organizations and a vocal minority don't want you ever to be seen or heard from again. They are calling you everything from the anti-Christ to the devil and even a drug addict. Oh, and Bishop Johns would like to have a private word with you as soon as possible. I think the x rays this morning confirmed his tumor. He sounds like a changed man."

"I'll bet he is," Paul said, "There is nothing like a death sentence to make a person rethink their priorities. Tell him I'll see him tomorrow."

"Why would you see him after the way he acted like last night, Paul?" asked Libby.

"To show the world hypocrisy in its rawest form. Whether I cure the Bishop or not, he will have to face his maker in due time.

Besides, I don't begrudge him a thing for what he said or has ever said. The Gods take care of those things."

"I guess I've got a lot to learn about forgiveness," said Libby.

"I do hope you will learn, Libby. Well, are we still on tonight?" asked Paul.

"Definitely. But there are many people around the stadium who truly hate you. We have to be very careful or they will try to kill you."

Paul asked Liz and I to go out and get some food for the dinner so we could eat before we all left for the stadium. He said to buy the best bottle of red wine we could find. It was about 5:00 when we left. Liz knew a wine specialty store near where we could find some fine reds. The proprietor suggested a Bordeaux he had. We paid $150, which included four fancy plastic glasses. Afterward, we stopped by a Mid-Eastern fast food restaurant and bought a variety of foods.

We sat around the small kitchen table and ate quietly. When Libby asked Paul what he was going to say in his speech, he said, "I don't know yet, Libby, I think something will come to me by the time I step up on that stage. If not, I'll just have to open my mouth and see what comes out."

After we finished, Paul filled our glasses with the remaining wine and offered a toast. "I would like to offer a toast to the Gods who have brought me here, and to you Joe, Liz, and now Libby, who are making my remaining time sweet beyond comparison." We drank up. For me at least there was a certain finality to his words, but I decided I didn't want to think about it right then. I wanted to be in the present instead.

Sometime before we finished at the table, Paul said to Liz and I, "It may be that you will be called upon to help humanity through the initial stages of turmoil. The earth is at a critical stage of its drama. If you do your best without vanity and with as much presence as you can muster, you will be known and blessed for your holy work."

What can one say after that? I said nothing, but I did try to be present.

At 6:30 Libby announced that it was time to go. We cleaned

up our mess and then Paul asked if we would leave him alone for a few minutes in the room. We went out in the car and waited. In ten minutes he emerged and got into the back seat. He seemed especially pleased.

Libby was driving. She said, "Paul, you may be the greatest man to come along in thousands of years, but when we get close to the stadium, I'm still going to have to ask you to lay down in the seat and put that blanket over you. It is for your safety. Okay?"

"Sure Libby, anything you say."

Liz, who was in back with Paul, turned to him and asked to tell her the truth if he was experiencing pain from the cancer. "Liz, I'll answer truthfully only because you and Joe are my students. I am in a great deal of pain. The lower part of my stomach is on fire right now and has been for days. But I do not give in to this pain because it is like gold to me. To suffer in silence is golden with God and is rewarded in the most amazing ways. Remember that, Liz and Joe. To the extent that you do not complain about your problems and your sufferings is to the extent of your prizes in heaven. Now that is all I am going to say on the subject. Let me please receive my gift of pain in silence."

Liz kissed him on the cheek. "Thank you, Paul. You are indeed a dear and great man."

"All right, great man, it is time to hide," announced Libby. "Snuggle up under that cover and lay your head in Liz's lap. We are approaching the danger zone." She then made a call on her cell phone to someone up ahead. "We are coming in."

There were thousands of people around the stadium. Everywhere there were signs and placards. Some said, "Stop Satan now!" and "Paul is the anti-Christ." But there were at least as many with positive messages; "Save us Paul," or "The Second Coming is here." I saw at least three fist-fights among the people who were there. Police made a path for us through the gate into a grassed area.

"Okay, lets go folks," said Libby, and we uncovered Paul and exited the car. We were in front of the wooden stage on the twenty-yard line. The crowd of at least 50,000 let out a roar of boos mixed with cheers as they recognized Paul going up the stairs to the podium. Then fighting broke out around the arena. It was bedlam. I looked around me as we took chairs in rear of the stage. In front were six or seven TV cameras and miscellaneous equipment. In the stands and spilling out on the grass up to about thirty yards from the stage, was a mass of chanting, bouncing, and fighting, sign-carrying humanity. It looked like it could easily bust out into a full-scale riot at any moment.

Paul took a drink of water that someone handed him. It was clear that no one was going to introduce him, or dared to, so he stepped up to the podium and bowed his head and offered his palms up to the sky. He remained that way for a full minute while the crowd brought themselves under control. Then silence: absolute silence.

Paul raised his head and looked around. "My dear people. This is why I am here; to let you look at yourselves. To hold up a mirror to the evils that have confounded humanity since the beginning of time. You have fought and murdered each other over the smallest things, and many times over religion. It is not a devil that is doing this, it is you doing this to yourselves, or you are letting others lead you into crime against other humans. Atrocities have been committed and wars have been fought over religious issues. Religions are supposed to preach and teach us to love one another, not hurt one another. People, look around at the ones you were just fighting. Can you understand that they have loved ones just like you? You do not agree with their opinion, so what? Is that worth hurting someone for? I hope not. I hope not. Do not let anyone tell you it is.

I am here to tell you what you need to do to help in the coming days of trial. First, rid your selves of any dogma that allows you to consider that you are better than others. Run from those churches who do not teach and show the way to loving your neighbor.

Second, reject any violence. Reject even the violence in your hearts where you think no one sees. It is caused by your feelings of superiority. Violence and negativity are humanity's most potent drugs. You must, for the sake of your immortal soul, rid yourselves of these drugs. Leave behind the excitement of destruction. This means to love your neighbors, love your enemies, and you will love God, and He will love you.

Most important, wake-up from your deep hypnotic slumber—your daydream world that steals your very lives away.

I say to you that beyond the sensual world is a great place. It is the place called heaven. To get there you must leave your lives of excuses and blame behind. Accept your life as it comes with the highest dignity, and try to pray with presence of mind.

Finally, I say to you, forgive and show mercy to everyone no matter how they have treated you. Your reward will be paradise.

I am going to leave this earth soon, and when I am gone I know there will be endless talk about my visit here. Very official persons with degrees and titles will discuss and write books about me. Some will try to discredit me, and that is fine. Some will praise me, and that is fine also. I was given the power to heal and do miracles in order to get your attention for a brief time, to deliver a message directly to you, with no intermediary that will distort it. Just remember, I did not come for any other reason than to deliver God's message.   I bless you and thank you."

He stepped back. There was a deathly silence as it sunk in that he was finished. And then the roar started and the surge toward the stage began. Libby took Paul by the arm to lead him away. I jumped in front of him as we started down the stairs, but as I took the first step there was something slippery that made my leg shoot out in front of me. I fell on my seat. Paul stepped around me. In an instant I had a flash of Viet Nam and falling in the mud. I pulled myself up and jumped in front of Paul again. Just then I saw an Asian boy step in front of me trying to shake Paul's hand, and at the same time, I saw another man in front of him raise a pistol toward Paul. I pushed the boy out of the way and managed to pull myself to my full height as I heard two cracks. In slow motion I felt myself fall backward into Paul. We both tumbled onto the stairs. I was lying there in shock on top of him. I remember Liz over me screaming, "They've been hit, my God, they've both been hit." I saw her contorted face as she grabbed at my chest. I rolled off of Paul and saw the blood coming out of his neck and Liz's other hand over it trying to stem the blood. I looked at Paul who was looking in my eyes. He gazed down at my chest and placed his hand over it. He then looked at Liz whose face was a mask of tears. He gave the slightest smile and closed his eyes. I heard screaming.

I remember Liz saying to me in the ambulance that Paul was dead. I remember lights in the emergency room blinding me when I opened my eyes and somebody saying, "He's hardly lost any blood. Strangest bullet hole I've ever seen."

"You are lucky man," a doctor was saying as I woke up the next day. As he unhooked the monitoring devises, he said, "The bullet did very little damage. You'll able to go home today."

Liz came to my side after the doctor left. "Paul is dead."

"I know," I replied.

"Who ever did it shot him in the throat and you in the upper chest. The crowd killed and mutilated the man with the gun. He was unrecognizable."

"So much for the concept of love your neighbor," I said.

"I thought of that too," she said. "The paper also mentioned this morning that a young Vietnamese immigrant boy said that you saved his life by pushing him to the side."

I paused and thought about what she just said. "Strange."

"What's strange, Joe?"

"Nothing. I'll explain to you later."

"Paul's two sons are coming down for his body today. They are going to take him away and have him cremated."

"That's just his body," I said, "We know where he is. He's at 'True Songs.'"

"That's right; he built it and now he lives there," said Liz. Then she added, "Joe, I just took a test--I'm pregnant."

Tears welled up from within me. "Liz," I said, "let's go home. Let's go home to 'True Songs.' That's where Paul is and where we need to be."

While I was waiting to be discharged and alone in my bed, I started to think about what Paul had told me. "Life is a play," he said. Shakespeare said it too.

"Life is a play, and we are just actors in the play. The day you realize this is the day you will begin your freedom." Paul said that. I looked out the window and thought for a moment and nodded my head.

The Four Minds of Man

(AKA Centers)

	Intellectual	Emotional	Moving	Instinctive
Intellectual part	Real Thinking *Higher Math*	*Compassion Gratitude Appreciation Understanding Real love*	Inventions *Spacial relationships*	Survival thinking *health food vitamins Avoiding danger*
Emotional part	Excitement of ideas	Extreme emotions *hate anger passionate love exhilarations*	Love of movement	Five senses
Mechanical part	Memory of facts	Memory of facts about people	Memory of movement *walking driving*	Internal working of body *digestion blood clotting*